CLIO
at WAR

PEGGY GARDNER

Clio at War

ISBN: 978-1-64184-903-6

For my children, Morgan and Wade, and for my friend Laverne, who met me when we were the age of Clio—and became, in Cicero's words, a second self.

CHAPTER 1

April 10, 1942

When Mother shoved me into a train compartment reeking to high heaven with the gamy smell of olive-drab wool, I knew I was in for it. We had over 1,500 miles to travel with soldiers packed into every available space. With compound eyes like flies anticipating a feast, the soldiers were taking in a 360-degree view of my mother.

I'd just begun to cock my elbows backwards toward her diaphragm for maximum impact if we needed a quick exit when I heard the rousing strum of "Colonel Bogey's March" on a ukulele.

"Hitler has got one ball; Goring has two but they are small. Himmler . . . whoops. Ladies present. Sorry." A youthful musician tucked his flushed face against his ukulele and began plunking out "Don't Sit Under the Apple Tree."

As though on command at the word "sit," bodies on both sides of the aisle squashed themselves together as Mother smiled genially with her perfect teeth at the soldiers taking up all the seats. With a quick shimmy of her rear end as though Colonel Bogey still played in her head, she shifted two soldiers to make space for us.

"'Til I come marching home."

As we pulled out of Grand Central Station, the last words of that silly song almost brought tears to my eyes—not sad tears, but over-the-top, raging, mad, angry tears that only the displaced can understand.

At least the soldier had a home under the apple tree. I was homeless. Bereft. I wasn't one of those weird changelings that fairies sneak into a crib in exchange for a normal human child, but I was a changeling all the same.

When the battlefields of World War II tooted the clarion call of journalism to my mother, she decided to dump me at the age of eleven with my two great-aunts, the like of which you can't imagine. Just the thought of being plunked down in the hinterlands of Oklahoma made me a bit freaky and certainly cranky.

All my twitching and fidgeting and sass during the endless train ride through the Midwest didn't get me a satisfactory answer to a question I asked over and over: "Why can't you be like other mothers?"

Other mothers worried about war shortages of sugar and shoes for their children. Other mothers couldn't sleep for fear that Kawasaki and Stuka planes might drop a bomb on their offspring.

My mother wanted to be where the bombs popped like destructive firecrackers, blowing off body parts. In

New York City, Mother took me to movies just to watch the war film clips and hear the up-beat announcer as American planes soared courageously into the wild blue yonder or groups of helmeted soldiers managed to smile across K-rations at the camera.

"That's where the news is happening, Clio. It's an opportunity I can't miss. I have to be there. With the troops. They've got stories to tell," Mother said, as the notion of being a war correspondent set her eyeballs spinning like cherries in a slot machine.

Soldiers did tell stories on this train, with Mother urging them to reveal their feelings. Soon to be on a ship to Australia, these soldiers were beset by homesickness and fear of the unknown ahead. My perky mother didn't seem to sense their hidden emotions, and she was in denial about my identical feelings.

Growing more and more desperate to change her mind, I embellished my why-can't-you-be-like-other-mothers question as we rumbled through Ohio: "Do you know that a Kamikaze pilot can guillotine you with his propeller? Do you know that Nazis will slice off your hands if you write about them—and give you what they call a bragging scar across the cheek for good measure?"

To occupy myself, I dreamed up gory tortures for Mother while she ignored me. The train was packed with talkative soldiers who got first choice of seats. Civilians had to take whatever was left, if any. It would be a long train trip to a place Mother left when she was eighteen with no intention of returning—the Oklahoma home shrouded in tight-lipped mystery.

Mother rarely went back on her word. She wasn't really returning to Wolfe Flats, as she reminded me. "Just passing through, Clio, long enough to see you settled with the aunts."

In the spirit of her new venture, Mother whipped out her blue wool armband with the gold letters "U.S. War Correspondent." She slid it up her arm, smiled in her special reassuring way, and set to with the soldiers, filling line after line in her spiral notepad.

The soldiers found an extra seat so I'd have a place to sleep and fed me more chocolate bars than I'd seen in two years. I vomited twice between Chicago and Oklahoma City. I even worked up a dramatic fainting spell to convince Mother not to leave her sickly daughter, but she wasn't in the market for homespun drama.

After hours and hours that I refused to count, the train was gliding to yet another stop. Mother vibrated with something that smacked of anticipation or nervousness as she peered out the train window at a low wooden depot that was light years away from Grand Central Station and muttered: "It hasn't changed at all."

This might be her last opportunity for a change of heart. I struck right below the belt. "If Wolfe Flats hasn't changed, what made this place so bad that you never wanted to come back to see your only living relatives? Never once in fifteen years."

"This place bruises you in ways you can never forget, Clio. You know when something unseen has bumped you and leaves a splash of purple and yellow on your body. It just stays there, quietly aching. Wolfe Flats put that bruise on me."

Mother flinched. Her eyes glazed over for just a moment, as though she had just unearthed some specter she wanted to forget.

At the moment, her grip on my shoulder let me know she was in a purposeful mood. As I struggled to get my suitcase down the aisle, hoots and whistles trailed us. Unlike reclusive me, Mother made friends with disgraceful aplomb. I just scowled at the chummy soldiers.

Just as we stepped down to the platform, Mother spun me around, fixed what I liked to call her entomologist eyes on me and pinned me to a board with her next words: "Conviction. I believe in justice. My aunts settled for subterfuge. That's a kind of cowardice. I didn't make a proper sacrificial lamb. So, I left. Hopefully, you'll have better luck with them."

As the brisk spring wind yanked her bright chestnut hair out of its pins and tossed it in all directions, Mother might have been mad Cassandra, throwing out prophesies in Greek. I couldn't make heads or tails out of what she meant by places that bruise and aunts that practice deceit.

The feeling of being in a foreign place continued as the train moved away and left us stranded by a one-story wooden depot with water fountains on each end labeled "White" and "Colored." The depot had plastered itself as close to the tracks as possible without risking head-on collisions with train engines.

A few people took off at a fast clip down the old slatted platform. The only welcoming committee I could see was a wagon with two mules hitched at one end of the depot. I might as well have landed on the moon. Mother appeared to be right at home as she pasted a big, fake smile on her face.

"Finally. We're here, Clio. Where I grew up. Wolfe Flats. A haven for troglodytes and spinster aunts. Booger Allen's cab is over by the end of the depot. Only cab in town." She waved both arms, windmill fashion, as the cab moved toward us.

"Booger?" I asked.

"You don't want to know," she whispered. "Has to do with hygiene." She pushed me toward a sputtering heap with "Taxi" lettered on the door, shoved me into the backseat, and crawled in next to me.

"Choctaw Street, Booger. Fast as you can get us there. The train to Fort Worth will be here in less than an hour." Mother was talking exclusively to someone driving the cab named Booger; I knew she couldn't face the accusations riveted on my Madame Defarge face. If I could knit, I'd be encoding revenge strategies into a pair of socks against mothers who desert their children.

She rolled down the cab window and let the breeze tousle her hair. "Nothing ever changes here. I don't know why I find that a comfort now. We need to hurry. I'll try to fly out of Fort Worth and make it back to the East Coast. Then off to Europe. I'll write you. You'll write me. We won't be apart for long." She patted my hand perfunctorily, the way she'd pat a stray dog.

With the driver popping his head toward the rear-view mirror like one of those bobble-head toys they call a wobbler, he finally got Mother's attention: "Yes, Booger. It's me. Delia. Back to leave my daughter with my aunts. Then off to the war. Park in the drive. Leave the cab running. I won't be a minute. Mind the step, Clio." Her voice had exactly the same cadence as "Yankee Doodle Dandy."

CHAPTER 2

After shoving the taxi door wide with her foot, Mother had practically pulled my arms out of their sockets to get me out of the cab, across a yard, and down a brick walkway toward massive stone steps.

Two houses took up the entire block. To the left of the drive, a monstrous white heap of Victoriana looked like Miss Haversham's melting wedding cake. Layers of peeling paint decorated segments of three stories that sagged against a central core. Along the street, diseased elms thrust up rotten fingers on witches' hands.

"Manboy Muller and his mother Claire live there. The Mullers came from Germany to Indian Territory the same year as Great-Grandfather Clower came from Georgia. They built these houses side by side. Our families were always friends, but Manboy and I were . . . ."

She paused for a moment on the sidewalk and stopped as though startled. "Their house looks neglected. Something must have happened. All that paint flaking off. The house appears forlorn. Surely people don't think that they . . ." her voice trailed off.

At that very moment, a flash of white behind the crazed glass of an uppermost window caught my eye. Ghastly and bloodless. A terror-stricken face with a gaping mouth and black holes for eyes looked directly down at me. "Mother, what is that . . ."

Ignoring my question, she gripped my arm and spun me around to face a Queen Anne mansion, strangely out of place in this backwater town on the southern cusp of Oklahoma. My first impression was that a European cathedral stood before us, probably full of dead people under the aisles and corpses tucked into nooks and crannies. "This is the place where you'll be living while I'm in a foxhole with Martha Gellhorn, Mary Breckinridge, and Margaret Bourke-White, trying to bring a female point of view from the battlefields in Europe."

Mother often talked about the "three Ms," Martha, Mary and Margaret, as though she belonged to that exclusive club of women journalists. She'd never met them. In fact, she knew, and I knew, that she struggled to get a byline in a New York City tabloid.

"A successful journalist has to be in the right place at the right time. It's all about timing. This war is that place and that time." I'd heard her say that so often it had become her mantra—and it cut me to the core. Other mothers cared about where their children lived. Mine was more interested in getting close to a bunker where Hitler was up to no good with Eva Braun.

Dragging me behind her, Mother took the stone steps of her aunts' house two at a time, whacked a bronze lion's head knocker twice, hugged me painfully hard, and said: "I'm avoiding any last-minute dramatics. You'll be fine here, Clio. I grew up with my aunts and made it out with backbone to spare. I'll be in touch."

Before I could turn around to howl in anguish like the motherless child I had just become, my mother, Delia, was speeding down the street. Her arm, encircled by "U.S. War Correspondent" gold lettering, waved at me with something like a limp salute.

Not an orphan like little Oliver Twist left in a workhouse, I was a changeling. A greedy fairy, my mother, had exchanged me for her career in journalism. Like Hemingway's wife, Martha Gellhorn, Mother claimed she'd be happiest in the middle of a war.

Mother did like war. I grant her that. My earliest memories are of her screaming down the rafters of the first apartment where we lived in Brooklyn. By the time I was three, she had routed my father and all traces of him from our lives, moved us to a shabby apartment in Manhattan, and erased all but one memory of a tall, red-faced, angry man.

With a gap between my two front teeth and a fracture in my heart, I was left on a street of dying elm trees to take up residence with two strange women in the backwater town of Wolfe Flats. That day, I discovered that all the elms in town—not just the Mullers' trees—were dying of Dutch elm disease. Their limbs were cracking and splintering like our pitiful Clower family tree. The remains included: an angry eleven-year-old, Clio; a tsarina named Aunt Norma; her eccentric sister

Aunt Harriet; and, an irresponsible crusader mother, who had just gone off to war.

As Mother's cab spun around the corner, a huge door, festooned across the top with brass rosettes, swung wide. A tall, spare woman with a mouth pursed tight as a frozen zipper, looked down at me through bifocals with eyes bulged as a frog's.

"After a dozen years of no more than an occasional postcard for everyone down at the post office to read about private things, Delia didn't have the common courtesy to come inside to see her aunts."

Still blocking the doorway, she turned and with only a slightly raised voice said: "Harriet, you'd better get out here and see what's been left on our doorstep. Prepare yourself for a shock."

At that moment, I'd have settled for Mr. Bumble and Oliver Twist's life of picking oakum in the work-house. The doughy face framed with silver curls that peered around the side of the one who must be my Great-Aunt Norma reassured me instantly. Her plump, blue-veined hand reached around her sister, latched onto my arm and pulled me solidly against her in an embrace scented with lilac.

"Delia! You've come home. I never let anyone go in your room. Everything is just the way you left it, your maps all over the walls." Great-Aunt Harriet's lips trembled, and her eyes flushed with tears as she backed away from me.

"Get a grip on yourself, Harriet. This is Delia's child. I spotted Delia getting back into the cab. She blazed out of here without so much as a word. Left this foundling on our doorstep." She stooped down, picked up my scruffy suitcase, and held it away from her as though it might be hatching colonies of deadly bacteria.

"I remember now. She sent us a real letter when you were born. Little Clio. She named you for the muse of history. Delia loved her history classes, especially reading about those long-ago battles. She said it wasn't fair that girls were kept on the sidelines. Got downright prickly about it." Aunt Harriet draped her arm cautiously around my stiffening shoulders.

"A byline was all Delia ever wanted. A little scrap of fame. Traipsing off to New York City without so much as a word of thanks to us for all that nurturing." Aunt Norma huffed across the foyer, dropped my suitcase at the bottom of a big, curved staircase, and glowered in my direction. "I knew she might be coming with Clio. She called a week ago. Said one of the newspapers wanted a female correspondent immediately. The opportunity of a lifetime, she said."

"But why didn't you?"

"Tell you?" Aunt Norma's voice thumped like a battering ram. "So you could be disappointed again? Mope around for months because Delia never follows through on a promise? I decided to wait and see. And look what I got for my trouble."

She poked me between my shoulder blades and nodded toward the suitcase. "Upstairs, Clio. Take the first room on your right. Bath is down the hall. You're downright grubby—from all that travel, I guess, unless your mother ignores your hygiene. Neither cleanliness nor Godliness made any headway with Delia. Scrub yourself. Unpack and get back down here. We will have some questions."

The bedroom upstairs and to the right must have been a mistake. The ceiling was high as the Empire State Building. A giant must have done the shopping for the furniture in the room. A four-poster bed with great swaths of brocade embroidered with sickly greenish ivy fought with a massive walnut highboy that, unbelievably, had a china chamber pot atop it.

I placed my alligator cardboard suitcase in the center medallion of a thick Persian rug and trotted down the hall. Their bathroom couldn't be more oppressive than this Edgar Allen Poe chamber. A raven screeching "Nevermore" wouldn't have surprised me in the least.

The bathroom reeked of Lysol. Every brass fixture shrieked that cleanliness vied with Godliness and God was losing the battle. The enormous white porcelain bathtub weighed down its cat paws into splayed agony. A circus fat lady would fit comfortably in that chalky crater, might even drown without a hitch inside it.

An authoritative rap on the door startled me. It swung wide, and the circus fat lady filled all the space within the doorjamb. Her lovely mocha-colored face beamed with a welcome I hadn't seen since I arrived in this chamber of horrors.

"Well. If you ain't a sight for sore eyes. Purty as I reckoned. Delia done replicated herself. No wonder you give your Aunt Harriet such a fright. I do love that Delia. Alays have."

She swooped across the room, her feet simply flying over those small white octagonal tiles, and scooped me up as I pushed back against her. "Lordy, your mama surely tole you 'bout me. Closer than friends. I alays knowed where she wuz."

"Lucinda." I muttered. Mother had told me that the only person who kept her sane when she was growing up was the family housekeeper or cook or member of the household—or possibly blood kin. Nobody would say.

In those few stories Mother told me about her life before there was *us*, Lucinda was a constant character. Always wise. Always reliable. Most wonderful woman she'd ever known. Always there to catch my mother when she fell out of grace with her aunts—a daily occurrence to hear her tell it.

Maybe all children want to hear about their parents' childhoods, but because I had only one parent to remember, I was insatiably curious about my mother. She occasionally dropped a nugget or two. "The streets in Wolfe Flats are safe, as small towns go, but bigotry was as infectious as the plague."

The only time Mother looked the least bit sad about what she'd left behind was when she talked about Lucinda. "That's why you're her namesake. Clio Lucinda Clower. Nice ring to it, don't you think? Licthmann never really fit you. Or me. Mismatch. At best, your father was truculent. He thought childbirth would rejigger my brain. For a small fee, the New York City Clerk's office put you back on the Clower family tree."

She'd smile slyly at the remembrance. "I'll take you to see Lucinda one of these days. I got a kick out of sending that postcard to your aunts when I had your name changed from Licthmann to Clower—I knew the postmistress would broadcast my divorce and your name change. Aunt Norma would be really aggravated. No one divorces in the Clower family. Not many get married."

She'd get a kind of faraway look in her eyes, as though they might tear up at any moment, but they never did. "Lucinda was in that house when I was born there. Just how and why she came to be there is a mystery. Small towns are gossipy places. I heard something about my grandfather doing business over near Lawton and having to take on the Comanche to get her away from the reservation."

Mother had shaken her head in frustration. "I asked, but Lucinda zips her lips about her past. My aunts refused to discuss anything that might hint of skeletons in the family closet. Lucinda sometimes calls them 'nami.' She said that means sister in Comanche, but it doesn't have to mean kin. All I know is that the flu pandemic made it into Oklahoma the year I was born. First, my father died; then, Lucinda laid out my mother in her coffin, and took me under her wing. My aunts were my legal guardians. Lucinda was my substitute mother."

I had imagined some kind of fairy godmother, one with blondish hair like Glinda in the *Wizard of Oz* and knobs on her back that might sprout wings. I'd even fantasized that Lucinda might be one of those children like the little Parker girl captured by the Comanche, her blue eyes more fearful of her saviors than her captors.

Wedged next to that massive bathtub, I stared up at the mountainous woman towering over me as thoughts of fairy godmothers and captive children evaporated.

"Delia swung by my house on the way back to the depot. You don't think she'd leave without seein' me? She's relyin' on me. Yore mama's got a hunger that this little town couldn't fill. I doubt that big ole' Europe will fill it either."

While she was talking, I was barely aware that she had untangled my braids and was whipping them into order. "Just a wet flannel acrost your face, and we'll go down to dinner. I brung a big pot of my chicken and dumplins. You'll need to be fortified against them two."

Lucinda was right. Eight feet of polished mahogany stretched between Aunt Norma and Aunt Harriet. A third setting was equidistant from each aunt at a table that could seat a small battalion.

My great-aunts could make Torquemada quake in his boots. Aunt Norma's Inquisition technique was of the flaying variety, one layer of hide at a time so that the bleeding could be stanched and the torture continue.

"Your father's name sounds foreign. Russian or worse. You must remember something about him. Who was he? Where is he? When did he leave? Why?" Aunt Norma had mastered the four W's of journalism better than my mother. The How would come later, as in

"How can we be responsible? How could Delia be so thoughtless? She didn't leave her ration books, so how are we supposed to . . ."

That first night over the dinner table, like a shellac record with a big scratch that reproduced questions over and over, Aunt Norma probed the lives of my mother and me until I determined to lock our secrets so far inside that she couldn't get them out by sticking bamboo splinters under my nails.

Aunt Harriet sat with her head cocked like the RCA dog listening for voices that only she could hear. I wanted to hear what they would say about me after I was dismissed from the table for an early bedtime, so I ducked behind the newel post by the stairs, straining to hear Aunt Harriet protesting about something regarding Mother.

"She was justified, Norma. You know it. It happened to Delia. Not us. We were wrong."

"I'm not weighing right or wrong, but things like that need to be hidden. Forgotten. Not ever mentioned again. We agreed, Harriet, that it would be best for Delia." Aunt Norma's rat-a-tat-tat cadence had the same impact as a firing squad. Not another word came from the dining room.

CHAPTER 3

Cats have secret names. So did my aunts. In my head, Aunt Norma was Aunt Nasties, because she embodied all the bad traits I could list—infuriating, irritating, ill-tempered, ill-natured. I could probably go on, but the slate would crack with the weight of her faults.

At first, I thought of Aunt Harriet as Aunt Haywire, not to be unkind, but there was no way she could be a stable force in my new world in Oklahoma. She plants bulbs upside down, puts hot water in the goldfish bowl to warm the little creature, and can't understand why it goes belly up. There was a kind of sweetness about her, sticky around a hard core, like those safety lollipops you get from the Fuller Brush man.

After the first night in that lumpy medieval bed, I awoke to find that my suitcase had disappeared. My least favorite dress, the black and yellow striped one that made me look like a bumblebee, was folded neatly at the foot of my bed. Somebody else's black socks were tucked inside my brown oxfords. My patent leather Mary Janes had been slipped under the edge of the bed. As I stomped down the hall, I could hear voices coming from the kitchen.

"Can't you let her be herself just until she gets used to this place, Norma? They are just play clothes." Aunt Harriet stopped talking the minute I charged through the door.

"Where's my suitcase? I can't find any of my things. Just this stupid dress that Mother made me bring if I had to go to church." I had been in St. Patrick's Cathedral in Manhattan many times. Loved the place. Awed by it. All that stained glass and those massive stone columns magically holding up the ceiling. I felt as though only a monk's robe or a bishop's miter were suitable garb for St. Patrick's.

Faux steeples without a bell tower in sight seemed to be the architectural code for churches in Wolfe Flats. My bumblebee dress would be just the thing. That thought brought me back to my missing suitcase.

"Mother had trousers and khaki shirts made for me—identical to the ones she's wearing in the field. Where are they?" I glared at Aunt Harriet. A seated aunt looking ill at ease was a better target than a standing one dangling car keys.

"I took them to our church rummage sale. Early, so no one would know the source. Surely your mother didn't expect you to go to school wearing trousers. Girls do not wear trousers in Wolfe Flats unless they're doing farm work. Certainly not to school. We're going shopping, Clio. I'm pulling the Pierce Arrow out of the shed." Just as Aunt Norma pushed open the back kitchen door, Lucinda grabbed my arm.

"Pig in a blanket, Clio. Nice sausage wrapped in one of my buckwheat cakes. I don't know why Norma gets herself so het up about things like who wears what. But she does. Alays has." Lucinda gave me a tight squeeze. "Jes act grateful 'en maybe she won't make all the decisions."

Even though this burg was a far cry from Manhattan, I was stoked. Shopping with Mother meant going to Bergdorf Goodman to look in the windows or wandering through the perfumed aisles of things we could never afford—not counting a few trinkets Mother managed to sweep into her bag. "Floor samples," she'd whisper.

Even at Bergdorf, the racks were showing signs of the wartime shortages. So, we looked through a Simplicity pattern book and asked our neighbor, Mrs. Abrams, to do her best. Her best usually meant that Mother and I looked like refugees—regardless of the dress pattern we'd chosen.

Fabrics were in short supply after the government issued L-85, saying that we needed to conserve material for victory. Because Mrs. Abrams had a cousin in the garment district, she could get scraps of wool left over from mass production of uniforms. Our color choices were about what your average sparrow would be wearing.

The yellow bands on the black dirndl dress Mrs. Abrams whipped up for me brought her such pleasure that I dared not complain. Besides, against her better judgment, she made me two pairs of trousers identical to Mother's—with deep pleats along the front of the waistband and a real bone button as a fastener.

"Just like Rosie the Riveter, you'll set a new trend for girls' clothes in Wolfe Flats. For women, it's a new world," Mother had proclaimed as we strutted around the apartment in our new duds.

Obviously, Mother had forgotten that Wolfe Flats was *The Land That Time Forgot.* Edgar Rice Burroughs nailed everything but the dinosaurs. As I stepped out the back door, Aunt Norma rounded the house seated in one.

"Get in. The starter gets temperamental when I turn it off."

Mother couldn't afford a car. Didn't need a car in New York, but Mother had grown up with cars. "Your Aunt Norma had a 1920 Pierce Arrow that would seat seven people comfortably. It was a marvelous beast. She let me drive it once—just to get the feel, she said, in case of an emergency. Lucinda taught me to drive. She had an old Model T Ford pickup. If you can drive that, you can drive anything."

Just as Aunt Norma gunned the car backward into the Muller hedge, I saw a person who might be a child standing in the Muller doorway—except the head and shoulders were too large. Aunt Norma shouted toward him with preternatural gaiety: "Running errands. Clio's here, Manford. We'll visit later when your mother feels better."

Clipping the concrete edge of the drive, Aunt Norma bumped to a stop, whipped the wheel to the right, and said quietly. "Manford Muller is a dear boy. Successful lawyer. He has a nice little practice in Ardmore. He's the soul of kindness to his mother. She's been down with the flu for a week. Manford's not neglectful like a certain person I could name."

Then she named her: "Delia and Manford grew up as best friends. His little infirmity never made any difference. She should have been grateful that he found her at the lake when . . ."

"When what?" I wanted to know why Mother owed gratitude to that odd man next door.

"That was a long time ago. We shouldn't dwell in the past. Good Christians forgive. She can't. That's all there is to it." The finality in Aunt Norma's voice let me know in one fell swoop that some subjects were off-limits and that my mother was a heathen.

THE PIERCE ARROW top was a bit ragged at the edges where it capped the frame, but the glossy body flashed in the morning sun. We swept out of the driveway, making a great arc almost to the other side of the street.

"Drivers in this town give me a wide berth. The Clowers owned the first motorized vehicle in the county. Then the local doctor got a little coupe thing. We still have the right of way."

I had no doubt of that. Aunt Norma drove right down the middle of Choctaw Street, turned onto Main Street, and parked parallel through all the ninety-degree stripes lining the street—and a good four feet from the curb.

"Lewin's is the only department store in town. Not quite up to Daube's in Ardmore, but we have to be mindful of gas rationing and shop close to home."

The glass door swung wide as an eel-like man slithered toward us, waving his arms as though he might be treading water. A paper-thin part segmented his oily black hair into two equidistant coifs, plastered down like one of those old skullcaps worn under armor. He seemed unnaturally pale, with the grayish shadow of a beard longing to burst free from his chin.

"Hello, Whi . . . Lester," Aunt Norma added firmly, as though she'd almost forgotten the man's name.

"Miss Clower. It's been far, far too long since you've been in our little shop." A faint lisp marred his attempt at precise diction. "Dear Mother has missed seeing you. Your sister came in for a card of buttons last week. Mother was just beside herself. Do come and say hello."

Spotting me, he reached around Aunt Norma without stirring so much as a ruffle on the tiers of her driving coat and tweaked my cheek. "Delia's darling daughter. I heard she had brought you for a visit."

"To stay," Aunt Norma retorted firmly. "This is Lester Lewin. He and his mother own the store. My niece, Clio."

After the second cheek tweak, I fought the impulse to wipe grease off my face and dropped back behind Aunt Norma. At a fast clip, she preceded Lester down one of the narrow aisles, stacked ceiling high with dusty boxes that might have been there since World War I.

I followed Lester Lewin through the store aisles at a cautious distance, checking the old wooden floorboards for the gleam of a slime trail I knew he was leaving.

The best was yet to come. Behind a huge rolltop desk that was angled across the back corner of the store sat Alice in Wonderland's Hookah-Smoking Caterpillar. Curls of smoke wafted up from two lit cigarettes and a deep ashtray bristling with dozens of butts.

Slabs of the whitest skin I'd ever seen flopped from her chin down her neck. A tight blue knitted affair covered her lumpy torso. Her legs splayed out like sausages mashed into the ill-fitted casings of nylon. Her oiled black hair was identical to her son's, except that it hung just below her earlobes.

Struggling to her feet, she flicked at the cigarette smoke with one hand as she reached for Aunt Norma with the other. "I had almost given it up, but I think it helps my condition. Not enough melanin, my dear." She gave me stare for stare. I looked away, embarrassed that I must have seemed rude.

"We don't want to disturb you, Hedy. This is Delia's daughter, Clio. Clio, Mrs. Lewin." At her nudge, I tentatively poked out fingers that were sucked into hands that resembled Maytag ringers.

"Delia's daughter? Lester! Lester! Delia's come home." She bawled like a separated calf, although Lester was not four feet away and moving closer.

Trying to stave off a reunion while keeping family business under wraps, Aunt Norma hooked a Cuban-heeled shoe over the end of a rack of dresses and spun it between the two of us and Lester. I had to admit that it was a smooth action.

"Clio is with us. Not Delia. War work. Secret journalism assignment. Had to go so quickly that she forgot to leave a ration book for school clothes. Will that be a problem for you?" Aunt Norma had managed to provide minimum information for gossip, tuck in a minor falsehood, and slide the problem of missing ration stamps off her plate and onto Mrs. Lewin's.

"We don't need to bother about ration stamps, do we, son?" She gripped Lester's limp hand and hauled herself up. "We got an order of plaid skirts in day before yesterday. The Brown twins had their eyes on them, but our preferred customers always come first. That's what I always say. That's what Lester always says."

"Always. You rest yourself now, Mother. I'll show Miss Clower anything she wants to see. And her sweet niece. Clio, is it?"

When his arm snaked around my shoulders, I almost passed out. Something must be dead in his armpit. Maybe he was shedding his skin, and it was holding on in his nethermost parts. I didn't want to think about it. Or the too-familiar arm squeezing me like a ravenous boa.

With the panache of a brigade's lieutenant colonel, Aunt Norma seized my other arm, whipped me to the far side of her and demanded: "Skirts, if you please, Lester."

Never have I seen a more ugly assortment of plaids. Nothing cheerful enough for a Highland fling. Murky brown on urine yellow. Persimmon orange crisscrossing rust. Elephant gray crosshatched with faded black.

"You choose, Aunt Norma. I can't make up my mind." I would concede this battle to Aunt Norma. There was nothing to lose.

"The gray and the brown, I think." Lester snatched up skirts, snapping the waistbands in an intimate way against my shrinking middle.

"And blouses. White would be nice against that lovely skin of Clio's." He held up something with a banded collar that looked like an undecided cleric's shirt. "This and the one over there with that nice braid down the front."

Ghastly. That's the only word that came to mind. I eyed a stack of bibbed overalls, fingering the stiff denim.

"Don't even think about it, Clio," Aunt Norma muttered.

"Underthings, Lester," she added.

"It's amazing, Miss Clower. Such a timely visit. We just got in a shipment of the loveliest nylon slips and . . . ur . . . companion garments. Mother couldn't believe it. Nylon is rationed, impossible to get. We made this order a year ago, and it just showed up. You are in luck. Or should I say Clio is."

The fingers reached for my cheek again, but this time I feinted like a first-class boxer. Hopped to the left and knocked over a display of that orangey tinted cream that women use on their legs when they can't buy nylons.

Ignoring tubes and jars rolling around the aisle, Aunt Norma proclaimed: "Young girls wear plain cotton next to their skin. Nylon is unhealthy. An unnatural material. I wouldn't dream of putting such things on my niece. Just point me in the right direction. Come, Clio. We don't need any more assistance. Thank you, Lester."

Well. We really did. I was envisioning something silky like the panties Rita Hayworth let us imagine when she flipped across the dance floor in *You Were Never Lovelier* with Fred Astaire. Or one of those peekaboo tops with a lacy slip to match Veronica Lake's peekaboo hairstyle.

Lester Lewin tugged on one of my mousy braids. "I bet this little lady would like something nicer, Miss Clower. Clio's a big-city girl—sophisticated like her mother. Those cotton things have to be washed dozens of times to get the stiffness out."

Mrs. Lewin thumped her son's arm. "I believe that Miss Clower knows her own mind, Lester. The delivery truck is at the back. You need to help unload. I'll show Miss Clower what she needs." Unwinding herself laboriously, Mrs. Lewin made it down one aisle, pulled three stacks of white garments from a shelf, and settled her folds down on a tall stool behind a glass-fronted cabinet.

"Don't pay any mind to Lester, Norma. Business is slow with all the rationing. He's trying to practice his sales skills. Now. Here's what I think will work for you."

Mrs. Lewin spread out four identical squared-off cotton slips. No frills. No lace. Coarse and raspy to the touch. Camisoles followed. Same stiff white cotton. The bloomers would fit Aunt Harriet. Big and boxy with elastic that seemed to have lost its springiness around the waist.

Aunt Norma fingered it and frowned. "These must have been in the store for some time. The elastic has rotted."

"Not that long. The war uses all the rubber in production. Civilians get inferior products. I'll throw in a couple of cards of elastic. You can just run a new piece through the waistband if it doesn't hold," Mrs. Lewin responded dismissively.

Is that before or after I've dropped my drawers in public?

I could see Lester moving down the aisle toward us with that cheek-pinching gleam in his eye. His mother stared at me from lashless, shoe-button eyes that looked like buckeyes tucked into a snow bank.

"Clio looks so much like Delia. I remember that . . . well . . . she and Lester, same grade and all. The time the class all went out to Lake Murray on the hayrack. Lester was so . . . I thought they might have . . . If it hadn't been for that George Whittaker, Lester and Delia might have . . . then she just left without . . ."

People who leave the interesting part of sentences hanging usually get my attention. Mrs. Lewin's reminiscing was making me physically ill. My mother and Lester Lewin? No way. I looked up at Aunt Norma and saw that her mouth had become as fixed as George Washington's, holding in all those wooden teeth.

"I'd appreciate it if you'd tally the bill and put it on my account. Please have your delivery boy bring Clio's things to the house. We're in a mighty rush this morning, Hedy. So much to do getting Clio settled. I'd love to visit longer, but we simply can't." Aunt Norma was backing away quickly, as though she had outstayed her welcome.

CHAPTER 4

Within seconds, we were in the Pierce Arrow, making a big illegal swoop across Main Street and heading for home. I had to admire Aunt Norma's decisive management of the car's gears. When they screeched in agony, she simply ground them more fiercely.

"Before you feel called upon to comment on the town merchants, Clio, let me advise you of something. Mrs. Lewin has had a difficult life. Her mother had albinism. It is a genetic condition. A family thing. Two sides of the family. It's a wonder that Lester didn't . . ."

Aunt Norma pumped both hands along the bottom of the steering wheel as though she were juggling invisible balls. The car skidded sideways and headed east on a gravel road at a fast clip.

"People who grow up in Wolfe Flats assimilate its history. We develop a kind of tolerance for our neighbors that an outsider might not understand. As a Clower, you will be expected to understand. I'm telling you this for your own good." The tone of admonishment in Aunt Norma's voice was so familiar, I had to look twice to be sure Mother hadn't suddenly appeared in the driver's seat.

"We're going to swing by the far side of town so you can see the Lewin homestead. Hedy's grandfather, Gideon Lewin, got hold of a considerable parcel of land when the Choctaw and Chickasha parted company in the mid 1800's. Some say he downright stole it. I couldn't say."

As a tractor inched out from a shelterbelt of Osage orange, Aunt Norma swerved and ploughed ahead of it without missing a beat. "Hedy's grandfather, Gideon Lewin, was part Choctaw with the palest blue eyes. Startling. They say Hitler has those eyes. Mesmerizing. I wonder if he has a touch of ocular albinism in his makeup."

I glanced over at Aunt Norma. She had slowed down to about one mile an hour, literally crawling down a remote gravel road—about the same pace as her story was moving. Boredom was setting in. I liked history, but I wasn't getting the connection between albinos, Hitler's eyes, and the theft of Indian land. I rolled down my window and let out an audible sigh.

"Sit up straight, Clio. Poor posture suggests a certain laxness of character. Delia never slumped in my presence. I suggest that you model yourself after your mother in that respect at least."

Hearing one backhanded compliment of a sort about my mother from Aunt Norma got my attention. I tried to rearrange my face into the slightly-interested-I'm-listening one I use in school.

"That's better. The Lewin house is actually outside of city limits, but I'm taking the back way so we won't appear nosy. Hedy and Lester are at the store, but the housekeeper might be there. Their house started as a cabin and then became a fortress." Aunt Norma eased the car onto a patch of lawn and ducked her head.

A massive two-story, log structure perched atop a foundation of limestone blocks reared up next to the Pierce Arrow. Under a wide porch, odd, symmetrical slots sliced between the blocks.

"Those apertures in the lower level were for guns. Comanche were raiding then. Before statehood, this was one of the largest ranches in Wolfe County. Just a few acres are left with the house now. Gideon's son, the first Lester, didn't like ranching or farming, so Gideon built him the biggest department store this side of Fort Worth. Wolfe Flats could never support it," she clucked as though provoked.

A sinister chain link fence coiled around the side of the house, like one of those compounds where they keep prisoners of war. I thumbed toward it: "They keep tigers or vicious dogs here?"

"Gideon. In his dotage," Aunt Norma sniffed. "His son Lester was determined to keep his father at home, even after the incident with little Lester. They rescued him from the well before any real harm was . . ."

I wanted to shout "chronology" and "referent" just as Mother would have done if the facts and the people were getting muddled, but I was judicious and said, "I'm not following, Aunt Norma." That put the onus on me, not her.

"Most people grow old gracefully." She patted the braided crown of graying hair coiled on the top of her head like an ill-tempered snake. "Gideon Lewin was not one of those people. He had a downright aversion to his great grandson, Lester Junior, from the day he was born."

Aunt Norma tucked in her bottom lip the way she tended to do just before pronouncing something distasteful. "When he was a young child, little Lester had a bladder problem. Lost control in the most unlikely places. In church. In the store. On the living room carpet. Gideon tried to spank the boy, but Hedy and her father would not allow physical punishment."

I nodded sympathetically. Pounding on a child with a weak bladder seemed counterproductive at the least and brutish at the worst.

"Little Lester disappeared when he was five years old for several hours. Hedy and her father had half the county looking for him. One of the field hands found him in the well."

My first stupid impulse was to ask: "Alive?" but I remembered that skanky man that little Lester had become and shivered involuntarily.

"Lester had told his father never to strike little Lester, so Gideon decided to punish him for wetting his pants by putting him in the well bucket and lowering him just above the water. I don't know if that cured the problem, but it convinced Lester that his father needed to be locked away from his great-grandson."

Aunt Norma gestured toward a squatty cabin inside the fence. "Lester hired a man full time to keep an eye on Gideon. He locked off the far end of the house so his father could have the run of part of the house and a small piece of the yard. He could take meals with his family. Then he couldn't."

"Couldn't?" I asked.

"Couldn't," Aunt Norma responded firmly. "He threw the cutlery and the dishes at little Lester. Knowing that boy as I do, I suspect he taunted his grandfather, as children often do to their elders."

Slamming the car into first gear, Aunt Norma pulled forward across spikes of iris, and whipped smartly onto the road, still in first gear.

"Eastern State Hospital. Over by Vinita. Gideon's daughter-in-law, Hedy's mother, insisted that he be committed or she would take Hedy and her grandchild away and never return. To my knowledge, that was the only time Hedy's mother ever stood her ground. She was the one with albinism. A pale kind of personality." Aunt Norma struggled with second gear.

"Let's see. Where was I . . . Yes. Hedy did not inherit her mother's condition, but she grew up fearing that it lurked underneath her skin. People here tried to be nice and not notice that her mother was different. Pinkish eyes and all."

Aunt Norma's digressions were annoying, but I tried to plaster on a face that indicated interest—not the fear

I was experiencing as we were grinding along down the center of the road.

"Hedy married one of the Tollivers from Burney-ville, a few miles west of here, when Otis Tolliver got home from the Philippine War. Her parents weren't happy about the match. Then Otis signed up again when the Great War was underway. Many of our young men didn't come home." Aunt Norma stopped the car smack dab in the middle of the road and stared vacantly across a field of spring wheat, lost in thought. I had the feeling that Hedy's husband wasn't uppermost in her mind.

Two pickups pulled quietly around us. In New York City, they'd have been honking louder than a flock of geese.

"Lester was just a small child when Hedy got notice that her husband, the Tolliver boy, had been buried in France. She took back her maiden name. She'd already named her son Lester after her father. Almost as though the Tolliver boy never existed."

By now, Aunt Norma had found third gear and was cutting a wide swath through a knee-high crop of Prairie parsley along the gravel road.

"Hedy's mother and her Grandfather Gideon died within a year of each other. Then, a kind of obsession seemed to overwhelm Hedy and her father. They took little Lester to doctors in Oklahoma City and Dallas, trying to get someone to say that he had albinism. The doctors wouldn't, because Lester isn't an albino." Aunt

Norma spun past the corner filling station and accelerated down Main Street toward Choctaw.

"In spite of everything the doctors told her, Hedy was never convinced. She put salve and talcum powder on that boy's face to protect him from the sun. You can imagine the reaction of other children when he was growing up. They called him 'Whitey,' and the nickname seemed to stick although I . . . People around here are very accepting of differences. But, that's why we must be kind to him. When we can." Her last words were almost a question.

As Aunt Norma ground to a stop just inches from a two-story detached garage that backed up against the back stone wall, I thought about her affirmation of the people in Wolfe Flats: "People around here are very accepting of differences."

Cynicism swept over me like a foul odor as I thought. Yes. People in Wolfe Flats are accepting of differences. They take a morbid delight in them. That's why the cab driver is called "Booger," probably because his fingers strayed too often to his nose. Lester Lewin is called "Whitey" because his mother powdered his face. And Manboy Muller has an adult's head on his childlike torso. Accepting, my ass.

CHAPTER 5

A t 8:15 a.m., the next morning, I accepted the inevitable as my aunts marched me along to Robert E. Lee Elementary. We'd had one small skirmish that morning over my patent leather shoes. Conceding that I had nothing else to wear but the revolting skirt and blouse, I settled for my only good shoes.

Sandwiched between my purposeful aunts, I knew exactly how the condemned felt going to the gallows. Mine might even be a messier fate, all red and splashy with the whack of a guillotine for being born in a Yankee state.

After a brief whispered conference through the crack of a door at what I assumed would be my sixth grade classroom, Aunt Norma shoved me inside and beat a hasty retreat down the waxed corridor with Aunt Harriet protesting behind her. "Don't you think we should . . . wouldn't it be kinder to . . . Clio doesn't know . . ."

"Step right up on our little dais." The teacher's bright fuchsia lips puckered in and out like one of those anemones at the Battery Park aquarium. I expected to see little clown fish explode from between her lips at any moment. As I hung back, her scarlet nails dug into my shoulder and forced me onto a small, raised platform by her desk.

"I'm Mrs. Wallace." The lips made the only movement on that stony face framed by a helmet of hair blacker than Aunt Norma's jet necklace.

"Students, I want you to welcome the Misses Clowers' niece, Clio. She's from New York City. I suspect the schools there are considerably more advanced than our little country school," she said in a voice raised to travel down the hall after my aunts.

Thirty pairs of eyes looked at me the same way that the bums in New York City check out passersby—through downturned fringes of their eyelids. Except for one.

From a back-row desk, a pair of sapphire eyes set into a tanned face that looked as though a cinnamon shaker had been upended on it appraised me. He looked older than the other boys and was wearing bib overalls.

"Little Yankee girl come to show us sodbusters a thing or two, Miz Wallace?"

His rudeness affronted me instantly, but what caught my attention was the terrible bulge in his cheek, probably a goiter growing out of control.

Just as the class erupted in giggles, his slight-of-hand movement with a small tin can caught my eye. And that of Mrs. Wallace.

"Jeremiah Whittaker, get yourself up here this instant!" Before he could shuffle forward in his big, clumpy, unlaced boots, Mrs. Wallace was halfway down the aisle, dragging him forward.

Something flashed through my mind at that moment. Mrs. Lewin at the department store had said something about a "Whittaker" on a hayrack ride at Lake Murray with my mother. He might be related to this one being hauled up the aisle by Mrs. Wallace.

"Up. Up. Stand by the dais. Now. Swallow."

I made a visible effort to swallow my nervousness. It wouldn't do for these girls with their homemade dresses and self-satisfied expressions to see anything but a calm and collected me.

"Do it! Swallow that wad!" Mrs. Wallace's shriek rattled the chalk trays.

With a grin that took me in from my shoulder-length braids to my patent leather shoes, Jeremiah Whittaker drew himself up as rigid as a Grenadier, sucked in a great gulp of air, and swallowed that goiter with a mighty cry of pain.

Or pleasure. The entire classroom erupted in laughter. I let out a tiny squeak, like a mouse whose tail hadn't made it out of the trap.

When Mrs. Wallace's wooden ruler splintered against the side of her desk, the room became as hushed as a funeral. "Back to your desk, Jeremiah. If you bring tobacco into this classroom again, you'll be explaining to the principal and his paddle. Evil and nasty."

I wasn't sure whether she meant tobacco, the principal, or his paddle. Mother was never so careless with her referents.

I flinched as Jeremiah brushed by me and whispered, "Welcome to the boondocks, Miss Prissy Pants."

Just as he turned to look back at me from halfway down the aisle, I was seized by a terrible urge. Still centered on the small raised stage, I cocked out my elbows, put my black patent shoes in motion, and did a buck-and-wing that would have made Bojangles proud.

My impromptu tap dance turned Mrs. Wallace's face from pasty white to sickly pink. She seemed to have forgotten that I was still on the dais, shuffling into her worse nightmare. No one else in the room seemed to be breathing.

"Clio. Oh, my dear. What will your aunts think? Leaving you like that. We don't need to mention a thing about this. You settle right over there in the desk between the twins. Brenda and Bridget Brown. Nice girls. Methodists."

She pointed to a desk situated between two slack-jawed girls that could have been bookends. Their chins eased upward simultaneously as I moved toward them. I'd heard about the Brown twins from Mrs. Lewin. They were the girls who coveted the hideous shipment of plaid skirts. Maybe the very one draped around me like a tent. Their feet wedged into sturdy oxfords wouldn't snap a positive beat even if I whistled "Dixie."

ONE HOUR OF "improving your cursive writing" led into a second hour of geography. Mrs. Wallace sashayed around a two-foot diameter globe positioned by the side of her desk, pointing out tiny countries in Africa that only she could see, and she mispronounced their names. Mother was a stickler for geography. She had big maps pinned to our apartment walls in New York with flagged pins showing the locations of Allied and Axis Troops.

I fought back tears. Somewhere in Dallas or Fort Worth my mother might still be trying to get on a plane that would get her to a ship going to Europe, leaving me to watch an odd woman with blood red nails rubbing a globe as though she expected a genie to pop out of it.

"Recess! Out and back in your seats in thirty minutes," Mrs. Wallace announced to no one in particular and sunk into the chair behind her desk.

I had two choices: stay glued to the seat of my desk and perfect curlicues on my capitals; or, try to mingle with my classmates who had eyed me with well-deserved suspicion after my little tap dancing display.

"You too, Clio. Ups a daisy. Fresh air. Mingle." Mrs. Wallace's fake enthusiasm had just eliminated choice.

On the playground, not a tree was in sight. Swings hung from thick metal chains, dangling in the brisk spring wind, empty and winding restlessly with ghosts of children.

Several of the boys struggled to push each other off a rusty roundabout that slanted at a precarious angle. Girls huddled in small cliques, some glancing toward me, others carefully away. A Martian would have had a kinder reception.

The hand that tapped my shoulder was gentle. "You were a regular Shirley Temple up there, Clio. I thought

Miz Wallace would drop her drawers. She's that scared of making the wrong impression on your aunts." Jeremiah Whittaker leaned back against the red brick wall of the school, stuck his hand in his pocket, and pulled out a penknife.

Stiffening momentarily, I reached for it. If he had a sporting bone in his body, he'd give me a chance to defend myself. He pulled out a second penknife, flipped open the blade, and began digging out mortar between the bricks. As he scraped, I watched small anthills of powdered concrete rising around his feet.

I joined him. Such a companionable activity might merit a civil answer. "Why are we doing this?"

"By my calculations, and I'm good at calculating," —Jeremiah shot me a lopsided grin—"I figure that we have 180 days of school in a year with 30 minutes of recess, totaling 90 productive hours. Or less, if it rains."

"To do what? And why?"

"Dismantle the school. I figure that by the time we make it to junior high and get out of here, this entire wall will tumble in a good windstorm. And why? To make a statement. Keeping us here with that stupid teacher is no different than Nazis locking the Poles into a ghetto." Jeremiah wedged his penknife between bricks and dislodged a big clump of concrete.

"Miz Wallace should be showing the class where our troops are in the world. Not just twirling a globe. We're at war. My brother Luke is with the First Armored Division somewhere in Africa. Or was, the last we heard from him. That bitchy woman never mentions the war."

Jeremiah's face flushed so red that his freckles disappeared. He slashed his knife against the side of a brick as though he might be envisioning Mrs. Wallace's carotid just beneath his blade.

"My mother has gone to war," I interjected. Getting on the good side of a red-faced boy with a sharp knife seemed an expedient move.

Jeremiah raised his eyebrows and turned a blank face toward me, his knife still gripped tightly.

"Not to fight like your brother. She's a journalist. Maybe she'll interview him. She loves talking to soldiers. You should have seen her on the train from New York. Talk and write. That's all she did." I crossed my fingers in a clenched fist. On the train, Mother had gone to the club car twice with one of the soldiers. "For an in-depth interview," she had said blithely. I wouldn't want to speculate about what that meant.

"She should have hung around long enough to interview your neighbors."

The only neighbors I knew were the Abrams, a nice old Jewish couple who looked after me when Mother was working. We had left them back in New York City with only a perfunctory goodbye. My guilty expression piqued Jeremiah's interest.

"The Mullers. Germans. Next door to your aunts. Odd things go on in that house. They probably have a shortwave. Three people don't go missing in a town this size without a reason."

The gong stopped our little tête-à-tête in its tracks. It was just as well. Jeremiah's face had taken on a feverish hue. The furtiveness of his comments suggested he might be going off beam.

NO ONE WAS waiting outside for me when the dismissal bell sounded. My classmates scattered as though a fierce wind drove them somewhere more interesting than Robert E. Lee Elementary. As I struck off south toward Choctaw Street, I looked back at the square redbrick, two-story box. If Jeremiah's calculations were correct, one wall of the school would molt like a scruffy coyote by summer.

Jeremiah wasn't the only person good at calculating. I could count hours, days, and weeks with the best of them. And, I was clever enough to know that calculating had to do with reasoning as well as counting numerically.

Growing up with a mother who dumped me on our neighbors, the Abrams, with no more than a "watch Clio for me back in a day or so," had schooled me at an early age to solve puzzles about missing people. Being dumped on the Abrams was actually a joy for me. Mr. Abrams had been a teacher in the Floating University of Poland before leaving the country two years before the Germans invaded in 1939. He and Mrs. Abrams had watched this terrible war in its infancy, lost their worldly goods but kept their passion for teaching.

"Fractions are tasty, Clio," Mr. Abrams would say as he chopped Mrs. Abrams' kolaczki cookies into perfect pieces. By the time I finished the second grade, I had mastered adding, subtracting, and multiplying fractions—and always with a faintly sweet taste.

Sitting by the hour with the Abrams hunched over their little shortwave, listening in foreign languages to what might be happening to their relatives in Europe, taught me a lot about body language. Shock and grief don't need to be translated. If people were missing or if the Mullers were listening to Nazi propaganda on a shortwave in this remote village of Wolfe Flats in this nowhere state of the union, I could calculate all the criminal possibilities and get to the bottom of it.

As I neared my aunts' house, I reflected on Jeremiah's suspicions. They sounded a bit out of kilter to me. Shortwaves and three missing people didn't calibrate. Calculation had to be logical, balanced.

AT DINNER THAT night, I managed to unbalance the aunts. Intentionally, I might add. Aunt Norma had been drilling me like a Marine sergeant all during dinner.

"Well. What *did* you learn your first day in school here?" Aunt Norma's question seemed so you-must-be-in-the-first-grade perfunctory that it deserved an answer. A smart-ass answer.

"That a serial killer is at large in Wolfe Flats and the Mullers might be German spies." A direct hit is sometimes more effective than waffling.

Aunt Norma was smacked speechless. Like a clumsy catcher, Lucinda fumbled with the gravy bowl. Aunt Harriet stepped up to the plate.

"I can't believe that a child of this family would suggest anything so nonsensical. Really, Clio, where in the world did you get such ideas?" Aunt Harriet's protest did make me feel a bit abashed, until she stuck in her oar, again. "You have a disturbing tendency to leap to conclusions, my dear. I hope it's just a phase you're going through. Drawing wrong conclusions can be an unfortunate affliction," Aunt Harriet reminded me prissily.

Let her tell that to someone who has read all of Conan Doyle's masterpieces. I never leap to conclusions. I simply know by deduction or induction.

"If you hadn't polished off two helpings of Lucinda's meatloaf, I'd send you to bed with bread and water. How dare you repeat gossip! What girl told you such things?" Aunt Norma queried me brusquely.

Never mind Aunt Norma, but from the sour expression on the face of the meatloaf queen, Lucinda, I thought I'd better confess. "I didn't talk to a single girl at school today. Just a boy."

"Your mother all over again. Aren't we the lucky ones." Aunt Norma scowled at her mashed potatoes as Aunt Harriet flushed a nice pink.

"What boy tole you bad things about those poor folks, honey?"

It was Lucinda who brought me around. I sniffed a bit as though to fight off imminent tears. "Jeremiah Whittaker. He was the only person the least bit friendly to me. I felt like an outcast."

"Then you must understand exactly how Mrs. Muller and her son feel." Aunt Harriet was much quicker on the uptake than I had expected. I felt a tinge of shame. Not much. Just a tinge.

"Not surprising Jeremiah tole Clio about the women missin'. He's been a sad boy since his mother up and left last year." Lucinda's hand on my shoulder gave me courage to carry on.

"He said 'missing people,' not women," I retorted. "What women?"

"His mother, dear. Sonja Wittaker. She drove to the grocery store, went inside for a couple of things, walked out, and hasn't returned. That was right after Luke enlisted in the navy. Didn't ask. Just did it. He was only seventeen. A lovely boy. He sang in the church choir. Artistic. Not a thing like George, except for his nice voice." Aunt Harriet looked puzzled for a moment.

"Well, he wouldn't be, would he?" Aunt Norma blurted out. "George is not his father. Sonja moved here when Luke was three to work with the Cooperative Extension Service. She was a widow until George Whittaker sweet-talked her into giving up her independence."

I noticed that Aunt Harriet seemed distracted as she ladled another scoop of gravy over her untouched potatoes, but I was more interested in the person who might have been the victim of a serial kidnapper or murderer.

"Didn't the police have any clues about what happened to her?

"No, dear. Our sheriff wasn't involved. If he were, his assumptions are rarely supported by facts." Aunt Harriet said dismissively, turning away from Aunt Norma's narrowing eyes.

"Jeremiah's mother, Sonja, is a botanist. She helped the Mullers transform their backyard into the most amazing retreat. That is, whenever George would let her. Well, whenever she could. Lovely use of camellias over by that old magnolia. That's why she left." Aunt Harriet's only interesting sentence stopped when Aunt Norma's crystal knife holder thumped the table like a judge's gavel.

"Harriet! Didn't we agree?" Aunt Norma's question put an end to Aunt Harriet's discourse on gardening. That suited me fine. I wanted to get back to the serial kidnapper and missing women.

"So Jeremiah's mother is . . ." I gave Aunt Norma one of my better Hercule Poirot's grave stares.

"Jeremiah's mother is gone—not missing." Aunt Norma's response closed that door firmly, so I opened another.

"And the other missing women?" I tried to keep my voice disinterested, the way a good reporter does, just eliciting the facts.

"Only one, lately." Aunt Norma's voice was unnaturally gravelly. "The niece of Mrs. Wallace, your teacher. Late last summer. Her niece, Ellen Carson, who had been hired to teach the first grade, moved in with Mrs. Wallace until she could find her own place. She went for a walk one evening and never came back." Aunt Norma plunged her fork into her potatoes, pushed back her chair, and stared me down.

"That sort of thing just doesn't happen in this town. An occasional domestic fracas or somebody steals a cow or two. We don't usually have major crimes here. This isn't New York. Go to bed, Clio. I expect a better report on school from you tomorrow. This has not been an appropriate dinner conversation."

Actually, it was the best conversation I had experienced since walking through that front door. Lucinda was stacking plates from her wrist up her arm like a juggler and hustling them into the kitchen as though she didn't want to miss a word of the conversation either. She shot me a warning glance. It meant that I should skedaddle up the stairs without another word.

CHAPTER 6

That night, I stalked the perimeter of my bedroom like a caged animal. Kidnappers and Nazi spies might be prowling the streets while I was locked inside. All of my bedroom windows faced the street in front or to the south. The Muller house was north of ours with a seven-foot brick wall along the property line, impossible to see over from the yard.

Then, I remembered that small, round window in the bathroom. It was high on the wall, set just to the side of the old-fashioned toilet tank with a pull chain. With bare feet and the wary approach of a first-class spy, I eased open my bedroom door. The squeal of its hinge meant that I'd better find the oilcan or a wedge of butter. No. I should use oleo to be mindful of the war effort.

Nothing was stirring in the house. Not even the RCA Console radio with a "Magic Brain" that Aunt Norma told me I was never to touch. "It cost as much as a new Ford car. Do not push its buttons," Aunt Norma warned as she searched that crackling brain for Walter

Winchell's annoying sensational news reports or "Fibber McGee and Molly."

I inched down the hall, keeping my ears open for any suspicious sounds from downstairs. Lucinda always went home after the dishes were done. Aunt Norma and Aunt Harriet were usually in their bedrooms, down the hall from mine, by ten o'clock. Not a snort from Aunt Harriet's bedroom could be heard.

Aunt Harriet had put me on guard about the danger of hanging on to adenoids. "My first cousin twice removed had glandular fever, but our Papa didn't believe in removing body parts unless they were gangrenous. I hope you don't hear my little snores at night." I did and felt oddly comforted by the constant drone. Tonight, I couldn't hear a remote flutter coming from Aunt Harriet's bedroom; it put me on edge, as though the entire house held its breath, waiting for something to happen.

I trailed my fingers along the dark, paisley flocked wallpaper that helped muffle the sound as I tiptoed down the hall. Behind me, a single globe in the foyer cast weird shadows down the stairs where they danced like hollow ghosts on the twenty-foot hallway ceiling.

Easing my fingers around the bathroom door's brass knob with its little incised leaves and flowers, I turned it slightly. Cocked my ear. Turned it again and stepped into a warm cocoon of steam. When I closed the bathroom door behind me, I would have been in pitch dark except for the faint gleam of moonlight coming through that circular window just to the left of the toilet tank and high on the wall.

Pulling down the wooden toilet lid, I climbed up on it and walked my fingers along the wall until they came to the window—and an odd clasp on the frame. The noise reverberated like the screeching of a hundred owls as I shoved it outward. I froze. My toes curled themselves into the rim of the toilet lid. Then, my left foot stepped into space and settled firmly on the ledge of the sleek porcelain bathtub.

I was staring right into the second story of the Muller house. More than that, I was staring into someone's bedroom. A small, twinkling chandelier lit up part of the room. The bed covers were thrown back helter-skelter, and someone was walking back and forth.

A big, rolltop desk took up the entire corner of the room. Large bookcases stood floor to ceiling on both sides of the desk. The figure pacing around the room seemed Lilliputian compared to the furniture in the room, like one of those six-inch people in *Gulliver's Travels*.

I craned my neck to get a better look. The head of a man on the body of someone with foreshortened arms and legs might have been one of those carnival show posters, designed to lure the curious inside—or, as in my mother's case, send us scurrying in the opposite direction with a great clucking of the tongue.

Too late. The head with its neck-length shock of light hair looked back at me with eyes flashing sparks. A very long finger zoomed out of nowhere and pointed itself directly at me.

My feet slipped, and I crashed into the crevasse of the huge bathtub, smacking my head with a violent thump, and settled into a damp pool of my own blood. Or, as I realized when I caught my breath, someone's leftover bath water.

THE NEXT MORNING, Aunt Harriet greeted me warily. "Did you hear noises last night, Clio? Strange noises?"

I tucked into Lucinda's buckwheat pancakes without lifting my head two inches from my plate. "Only the wind. Who has seen the wind? Neither you nor I. But when the trees bow down their heads, the wind is passing by." I hoped to derail Aunt Harriet from noises she might have heard last night.

It worked. "Rossetti." Aunt Harriet beamed across the table at me. "I read her poems to Delia when she was a child. And here you are quoting them to me as though time had looped back on itself and restored Delia to our breakfast table."

I thought all those Pre-Raphaelites were a bit swishy around the edges, but I had spotted Aunt Harriet as a fan the minute I saw the red-winged Burne-Jones angel print on her bedroom wall. Mrs. Abrams always took me to visit her favorite Burne-Jones angel tapestry when we visited the Metropolitan Museum.

"We're helping your mother with your education," she and Mr. Abrams claimed—tactfully overlooking the fact that whenever she wasn't working Mother only took me to Coney Island for a hot dog or to a movie to watch the newsreels.

"You didn't hear something noisy in the house last night?" Aunt Harriet wasn't easily sidetracked.

"Maybe one of those rotten elm tree limbs from the Mullers' yard blew against the house." I dumped more of Lucinda's sand plum jelly on my pancakes.

"No. I checked this morning. Just after Norma disappeared," Aunt Harriet said.

Looking up hopefully with a jelly-coated chin, I was just about to spout out something about "another missing woman" when Lucinda smacked down a brown paper bag by my plate.

"Yore Aunt Norma is head of the Women's Christian Temperance Union. Left early to get things ready for the meeting. All the churchwomen go. Your Aunt Harriet had best be on her way. She never misses." Lucinda had an odd manner of dealing with my aunts. She indirectly ordered them about, but in the spirit of simply confirming what they intended to do.

Aunt Harriet pushed back her chair and stood. "I was planning to walk Clio to school, just to be sure she remembered the way."

Aunt Harriet seemed confused. I had managed to get myself home without any help yesterday. No one seemed to notice how quickly I get my bearings. Mr. Abrams had trained me better than a guide dog, mapping every street and every bus route so that I would commit them to memory and never get lost going to or from school or to the Museum or the Public Library. My "beat" Mother called it.

Mr. Abrams included Coney Island in my beat in case Mother forgot me again. She blanked me out when a tourist fell off a rotten pier where we were having a picnic; Mother managed to get aboard the ambulance and cranked out a rapping good story that she sold to one of the tabloids. A nice policeman brought me home. I didn't fault Mother. A reporter can't ignore a story that falls into her lap so to speak.

With Aunt Harriet standing and stretching out her hand across the kitchen table toward me, as she would a helpless child, a bit of showing off seemed in order. I whipped out a grid that I had drawn early this morning—based on an old map of Oklahoma that I found in a desk in my room.

I didn't map my personal world just as a directional guide or for fun. I did it to capture things before they changed, before a Luftwaffe bomber blew the places into smithereens. Mother told me that the British media screened news about direct hits to keep the Germans from assessing damage. But, we knew that entire blocks of houses and ancient monuments had disappeared forever. Only the maps and photos of what had been there would help the world remember. Important stuff. Mapping was a serious job.

Along the bottom of Oklahoma, the Red River looped like a noose into Texas; I didn't need to simplify the map of Wolfe Flats. What could be simpler than a town cut into four equal quarters by a railroad track going north and south bisected by a single main street? My stride was exactly 28 inches from left heel to right toe when I kicked into gear. Even without a measuring tape, I knew from far to near with the numbers in my head clicking like an abacus.

To reassure Aunt Harriet that I knew my way around, I held up my map. "I made a few detours on the way home from school yesterday, just to get the lay of the land," I added pleasantly. "The school is situated at the far side of the northwest quadrant where we live." I poked a little red box I'd made on the map, hoping no one would notice a blank spot where bricks should be. My idea of a little joke.

"The biggest and oldest houses are in our quadrant. Ready-made houses like the bungalows they sell in Montgomery Ward's catalogue are in the southwest quadrant. Three churches—Methodist, Baptist, and Presbyterian—are in the southeast quadrant, all on different streets, facing in different directions like they don't want to speak to each other."

A faint spume of giggles erupted from the kitchen, muted immediately by the crash of pans slammed together.

Aunt Harriet moved behind my chair and tugged on the corner of my map. "It's an interesting map you've drawn, Clio, but you should not be wandering around town alone. These are troubled times. Dangerous. The war and all."

I shot her a blank look. I couldn't imagine that the Wermacht would be jackbooting it down Main Street, even though Wolfe Flats sometimes observed blackouts at night in case a bomber got off course.

Signs of the war were in the windows of several houses—sad little red-bordered flags with blue stars showing sons off to war and an occasional gold for one who wouldn't be coming back.

War or not. Wolfe Flats had to be the safest place on the planet. Smack dab in the middle of nowhere. Not an ocean within a thousand miles—and a river that could be navigated only by a rowboat.

I didn't mention the northeast quadrant of my map. That area looked more interesting than all the rest put together. From Main Street, I could see cotton gins like tin castles stacked side by side. Small, unpainted houses bunched up together as though they had a common enemy. They did. It is called racism. It infested New York City too, though Mother and I tried to pretend it didn't.

"By my reckoning, Clio, you've got about fifteen minutes to make it acrost that little map and into yore seat in Miz Wallace's classroom. I hear tell she don't mind usin' her ruler." Lucinda's warning got my attention. I grabbed the sack lunch and hustled out the door.

Giving the Muller house a wide berth, I crossed the street and ran along a sidewalk that had heaved up its slabs of concrete. Maybe a volcano like the one under Mount Etna sizzled beneath this town. I had spotted the sign of Nebo's Blacksmith shop on one of those tall, galvanized gin plants in the northeast quadrant of Wolfe

Flats. I read somewhere that the blacksmith of the gods, Hephaestus, fires his forges under Mount Etna.

No active volcanoes exist in Oklahoma, but tornados try to blast this place to kingdom come every year or so. Aunt Harriet showed me the storm cellar behind the house if I needed to hunker down in a tornado.

Lucinda said that the packrats and scorpions down there would make a body think twice about hiding from a twister. I'd take her at her word. Places underground, like the subway in New York City, gave me the creeps. Newspapers were full of stories about people in London hiding underground from German bombers and never seeing the sun again after the tunnels collapsed in air raids.

With two minutes by the hall clock to spare, I was at my desk and giving the Brown twins a dazzling display of my front teeth gap. Aunt Norma had insisted that I needed to make friends with girls my own age— not the boys. That was my solitary effort and got no response from the gap-jawed Browns.

I turned to check out the desks at the back of the room. One was empty. I felt a wave of disappointment wash over me. Scraping out the schoolhouse mortar had cemented a kind of friendship between Jeremiah and me. With my help, we might bring down the wall sooner than he intended.

Or, I might be able to use my sleuthing skills to find out what happened to Jeremiah's mother, although he hadn't exactly told me she was one of the missing females. So, I'd need to exercise subtlety—a noun that Mother said was missing from my lexicon.

Just as the last warning bell sounded, the missing Jeremiah materialized by the side of Mrs. Wallace's desk. From behind his back, he whipped out a bedraggled bouquet of yellow flowers with black centers; a loop of greenish vine held them together. "Early blooms this year. Black-eyed Susans for my favorite teacher."

Your only teacher, I was thinking. Jeremiah had just told me yesterday that he thought Mrs. Wallace was a rotten teacher. At the moment, she looked like a confounded teacher, hesitant to take the flowers he was offering.

"Pa said an apology was due. He said a gentleman never takes his spittoon into a lady's chamber." The smile that split his face was instantly replicated on every face in the room, but no one made a sound.

Mrs. Wallace held the bouquet at arm's length; then, as though forcing herself to be polite, she touched a few petals and sniffed at it. "Brenda, dear, would you mind going down to the principal's office and asking the secretary if she can find a little jar for these. You can fill it from the water fountain." The twins rose in unison.

I had already checked to see if they were conjoined, fused in some manner so that one couldn't move without the other. They weren't physically, but they must have been mentally.

"Go on then. Both of you." As Mrs. Wallace's eyes flickered from Jeremiah to the flowers and to the classroom in which no one was breathing, decorum won the battle. "Apology accepted, Jeremiah. You need to take your seat. Open your math workbooks to page eleven. Work out the problems. You have fifteen minutes. Bring your work to my desk when you've finished." Her high-heeled shoe began whacking the side of her desk as though a metronome had settled inside her toes, somewhere between the metatarsals and phalanges.

Multiplying the fractions on the page took me all of three minutes. I timed myself on the wall clock and turned to look at Jeremiah. He was holding up two fingers. Rising to bring his workbook to Mrs. Wallace's desk, he whispered as he shuffled by: "Elementary, my dear Watson."

"If you finish early, just proceed to the story problems on the next page," Mrs. Wallace barked in annoyance as she slid something into her desk drawer. I had seen the book yesterday when she sent us out to recess. *Manhattan Nights* by Faith Baldwin. A bare-chested boxer sat inside the ring looking down at a goofy, open-mouthed woman in a satin evening gown.

The title had caught my attention. I'd lived in Manhattan for the last eight years of my life. If Mrs. Wallace was curious about New York City, maybe I should direct her to a book about New York that didn't look so sleazy. Or, maybe not. She wasn't exactly the kind of person I wanted to bond with. I waited the entire fifteen minutes before taking my math workbook up to her desk. Mrs. Wallace seemed to be bonding to the shirtless man in that book. Her jiggling foot had picked up the pace.

Catching my eye on her book cover, she shoved it under a pile of papers and barked to no one in particular: "Do the story problems on the next two pages. When you've finished, you can go one at a time to the library and choose a book for silent reading before recess."

Library? My heart lifted a bit. It couldn't be like the New York City Public Library. The entire town of Wolfe Flats could fit into the reading room of that library. Any library would be a port in the storm after reading those stupid story problems.

If you had an apple pie and wanted to share it equally with four friends, how many pieces would you cut? *Really? This in a sixth grade math book?* Depending on my state of boredom, I would cut it into 4 or 8 or 16 or 32 pieces until the apples screamed in agony.

I followed Mrs. Wallace's pointing finger and shuddered in disbelief. Mother kept more books on the kitchen table in our apartment than those I saw tidily lining a set of shelves next to the chalkboard. I settled on *The Bobbsey Twins at Indian Hollow*. It appeared to be well thumbed. I'd check out what the natives were reading.

CHAPTER 7

At recess, I joined Jeremiah at the wall. Wordlessly, he handed me his extra knife. Recalling his "Watson" comment, I ventured a criticism of the sixth grade library: "I noticed they didn't have a single Sherlock Holmes."

"Nope. Just baby stuff. Kids' books. Except for the one with the boxer on the cover that Miz Wallace hides in her desk when she pretends to be grading our papers." As he turned his lopsided grin toward me, a flash of mid-morning sun lit the side of his face. An odd purplish bruise flamed on his left cheekbone.

Catching my eye, he glowered down at me, but I couldn't resist. "If I were Sherlock, I'd say you took a right hook yesterday."

Jeremiah pushed his knife blade to the breaking point, popping a brick free. He looked around cautiously and replaced it on the wall. "We can't be anywhere near when this collapses. Miz Wallace is out for blood. My blood. She spotted Pa in town yesterday evening and told him about my wad."

Trenching away at an adjacent line of mortar, Jeremiah turned his bruised face away from me and remained silent. So did I. He didn't seem to appreciate my detection methods. I could wait him out. That's what Mother said she did when an interview seemed to be bogged down. People don't like blank spaces.

Jeremiah filled the gap. "She didn't need to bother him. I took my medicine. I swallowed the entire chew. Enough to make a goat puke. But she had to go tattling to Pa. He's already worried about Luke on some battleship—and my mother. He can't help losing his temper. It's not his fault."

I didn't agree, but kept my face expressionless. Mother wouldn't dream of raising her hand against me. "Civilized people don't hit each other," she was fond of reminding me when I'd pushed yet another child out of my swing at the public park near our apartment.

Mother explained: "I grew up with frequent tongue lashings from Aunt Norma. It just made me resentful. Extra tasks are a better method of discipline." Then, she'd pull on her "you let me down" mask to let me know I'd be paying the piper. That's why I could fry chops and whip up puffy powdered egg soufflés like a chef, cheap but good food.

Mother could put off what she called menial work with the best of excuses. "When I was growing up, Lucinda did all our cooking, and I was happy not to learn how."

Mother rarely did more than dunk dishes and swipe carelessly at the cracked linoleum countertop. "My aunts hired help for what they called 'deep cleaning.' They said the Clowers don't 'do' for themselves; they direct others."

So, while I imagined housemaids in frilly caps on their calloused knees scrubbing our floor with brushes, attacking years of accumulated filth, Mother would enlist me to push the furniture away from the wall so she could plaster up even more maps to track troop movements of civilized men shooting each other across Europe.

Turning away from the brick wall that we were quietly demolishing, I struggled to keep from asking Jeremiah the questions I wanted to ask—about a mother who seemed to have vaporized in a grocery store parking lot and a brother who couldn't wait until he was old enough to go to war.

The grim-faced boy digging out mortar was wearing the same overalls with ragged cuffs, the checkered shirt he wore yesterday, and still missing the laces for his boots. Privation seemed to go hand in glove with physical abuse in that household with no mother.

"Tell me this, Watson." He flashed that same cynical grin at me. "How do you think you hide a snake in the grass? Get even without getting caught?"

I pondered a moment. "I wouldn't give someone I couldn't stand a nice bouquet of flowers. No one could make *me* do that."

"Pa didn't make me. He just popped me one for causing trouble. I came up with my own apology."

"I didn't actually hear you apologize to Mrs. Wallace."

"No. And you won't. When she lifted up those flowers and sniffed them, I got enough satisfaction to last me for a week." If the devil had invented laughter, it would have a harsh, ripping sound like Jeremiah's snigger.

"She tried to embarrass you. She caused a problem with your father. I don't understand why you're laughing."

"That's because you're a city girl. Otherwise, you might have spotted that raggedy twine holding the flowers in a bunch was *Toxicodendrons radican*. My mother majored in botany. She really took to the victory garden thing. Pa had opinions about that." His voice trailed off on a sad note.

"Toxi . . . what . . . I don't know Latin," I responded huffily. Didn't really want to either. Or botany. Mendel and his peas. My neighbor Mr. Abrams could wind himself up like an eight-day clock about those peas.

"Neither do I. Just the names of some plants. It was the one thing that Mother . . . though I doubt that she would . . ." He paused as though considering something and blurted out: "Poison ivy. I wrapped a piece of fresh vine around the flower stems."

At that moment, the bell sounded. I handed Jeremiah's knife back to him, and we walked silently to the classroom. Poisoning your teacher seemed to be an extreme form of revenge. Still, bumpy skin was mild compared to what hemlock, belladonna, or cyanide would do to Mrs. Wallace.

For the rest of the day, I watched her rubbing her mouth and nose with those crimson nails. Something was afoot—or at hand—that Sherlock would appreciate.

I TOOK A quick shortcut home through the northeast quadrant on my little map. The cotton gins were silent until the fall. Eli Whitney invented the cotton gin, a simple machine that fits inside of buildings, but the locals call the whole kit and caboodle—these galvanized metal structures with their 22-foot drying towers—cotton gins. They actually dismiss school in September so the country kids can pick cotton bolls. That's what Lucinda told me. I thought that public schools only closed for national holidays, but Wolfe Flats has its own priorities. I liked that about it.

A few old ladies in rockers on their front porches sent cautious glances in my direction as I followed the roads in that part of town. There were no sidewalks. The flow of concrete ended where the unpainted houses began. Except for the Church of the Deliverance.

Wide slabs of concrete led up to a line of green, boxy shrubs surrounding a pristine white building that looked inviting. I like that name "Deliverance." It can mean rescue. I'd pay that church a visit one of these days.

I moved on down the street toward the Booker T. Washington School. A hand as masterful as a medieval monk's in a scriptorium had lettered the name on a large metal sign next to the building. A few students straggled out but pretended not to know I was in their neighborhood even though I waved up a storm.

Hot-footing down Main Street and up Choctaw to my aunts' house, I made it in record time. Or, I should say just in time to see something peculiar. Carrying a large basket, Aunt Harriet was disappearing into the front door of that peeling house next door; someone with a big head atop a short body ushered her inside with the panache of a trusted friend.

As I stood across the street craning my neck for a better look, the door swung shut, but I was sure Manboy Muller had seen me. What he had in mind for Aunt Harriet, I wasn't sure.

It's doubtful that she would be a key player in a Nazi spy network. Deciphering codes wouldn't be her cup of tea. She had a hard time remembering why I had replaced Mother.

Lucinda might have some answers. Before creeping up the back steps into the kitchen, I trotted alongside the brick wall between our house and the Mullers', looking for peepholes. Considering the size of both houses and the fact that land was probably a dime an acre when they were built in Wolfe Flats, they seemed unduly squashed together, as though rich people longed for a cuddle.

"Clio, are our neighbors of particular interest to you?" An upstairs window popped halfway up as Aunt Norma peered down at me.

"No ma'am. Just scouting out the neighborhood. I'm mapping Wolfe Flats by foot. I suspect no one has ever done that before." I reached into my book satchel, yanked out my notebook, and waved it at her.

"I suspect not. Nor would anyone with half a brain want to do it." The window slammed down. Aunt Norma had finished the conversation one point ahead of me.

Before I went inside and cornered Lucinda for answers, I made a quick reconnaissance around the Muller house, checking for aerials or any strange wires going to someplace suspicious. If espionage were going on inside that house, disguised as a ruin, someone would be making routine contacts with the enemy.

The brick wall appeared to encircle the entire house, except for a wide, wrought iron filigreed gate in front. So, I checked out the alley. Hanging ajar off one hinge, a wooden gate that had seen better days left a gap for taking trash to the barrel in the alley. I inched through the gap and faced a formidable hedge of evergreens, so fat and dense that the house couldn't be seen. Just over to the side, tucked back into a far corner of the yard, I spotted something peculiar in what must have been a kitchen garden.

Dried gourds hung along a short picket fence that enclosed remnants of a vegetable garden. The boards along the top were solid, but the few slats that remained hung like a dentist's worst nightmare, rotten and skewed. A large mound of earth humped up against the ragged fence for comfort—or camouflage. If a mound could be considered perfect, this one was: about six feet long, two feet wide, and rounded nicely on top.

A vegetable garden close to a house would be the last place anyone would look for a buried body. Or two? Jeremiah had warned me about the Mullers spying for the Nazis. He didn't suggest any connection to his missing mother. But, Aunt Harriet said Jeremiah's mother had designed the Mueller's backyard. If a link were there, I'd find it.

CHAPTER 8

Not a solitary student at Robert E. Lee Elementary had made a single overture to me—with the exception of Jeremiah. He had shared a few personal tidbits—like his knife and that little revenge plot with poison ivy. With an air of confidence, I eased the gate back in place, trotted across our yard, and slipped into the kitchen where Lucinda held forth.

"And jest as I was picking up your Aunt Harriet's ease medicine from the drugstore, who should be buying calamine lotion? Yore Miz Wallace. That's who. Her chin and nose wuz flamin' like a bad sunburn. She wuz tellin' the druggist that she didn't have a clue. It just come on."

Lucinda had one annoying habit that Mother never mentioned. She'd launch a conversation midstream—as though the first part of the discussion wasn't worth mentioning.

From the curious glance she sent my way, I decided that the less said about Mrs. Wallace the better. Lucinda had a way of sizing me up that put a gag in my mouth. Aunt Harriet's visit next door was fair game.

"I saw Aunt Harriet carrying something into the Muller house just as I was coming up the street." Well. That was a half-truth. I was scouting out the Muller house from the far side of the street.

"Part of the pot roast and carrots we're about to have when you get through checking out the neighbors." Lucinda turned to the huge cast iron Aga stove and stirred something in a pan on top. "The woman who does for the Mullers done quit. War makes folks fearful. Fear makes folks suspicious. Suspicious folks causes trouble where they least expect it to happen."

As if she'd put the matter to rest with a logical progression, Lucinda began beating something in a pot on the stove with fury. "*Whack, whack, whack*" went her great wooden spoon.

Then, holding the skillet at arm's length like one of those glassblowers with a molten glob on the end of a tube, she dumped a mound of steaming chocolate onto a greased marble slab on the table.

"Homemade fudge. I used yore aunts' ration books so there won't be no more sugar this month. Delia loved my fudge more than anythin'. Wonderin' about where she is and if she got there safe put me in the candy-makin' mood."

She chiseled off a hot limp piece and put it on wax paper in front of me. "When it sets up, I'll cut a piece for Jeremiah. Seems like you and he is thick as thieves. You wouldn't meet a nicer person than his mother. Or his brother Luke that's gone off to war."

I noticed that Lucinda had not mentioned Jeremiah's father. Neither did I. Best not to ask any more questions.

When Aunt Harriet returned with an empty basket, we polished off the pot roast at dinner without too much conversation. Aunt Norma filled in blank spots with an account of her Women's Temperance Union meeting and about how some principled woman named Carrie Nation took an axe to a hotel bar in Wichita, Kansas.

Prohibition was thriving in Oklahoma as well as Kansas. My aunts didn't drink. Lucinda didn't drink. I wasn't old enough to drink, so the dinner conversation was a bit of a bore. Carrie Nation got my attention. If there had been any alcoholic beverage in this house, I'd have taken a swig just to find out why it fired up Carrie to take her axe to town.

Our threats weren't coming from axe-wielding ladies. "Blackout tonight," Lucinda announced. "Sheriff McIver says so. They's rumors. We need to close all the curtains. Japanese planes been seen off the West Coast."

I knew better than to voice my opinion. We were more than 1,600 miles from the Pacific. Why would anyone want to waste a perfectly good bomb on a town that had nothing to offer the enemy but some old cotton gins?

I made an excuse about homework to go upstairs. Listening in silence to classical music turned up full blast on the RCA radio by Aunt Harriet made me miss Mother. When Dinah Shore belted out "Blues in the

Night" on our little table radio in New York, Mother and I morphed into sultry cabaret singers. When Jimmy Dorsey's band played "Tangerine," we danced around our shabby apartment as though we were at the Ritz.

Nobody danced in this house. Dinner was served at 6 p.m. Aunt Harriet flipped on the radio at 7 p.m. Conversation had a desultory air about it. No gossip or scandals to raise my spirits. Nothing that Mother had told me about Wolfe Flats made much sense to me when I was in New York where police cars and ambulances created constant background music to unfolding dramas that Mother discovered on what she considered her news beat.

As I watched Aunt Harriet's foot actually tapping out a beat to Bach's *Goldberg Variations*, a light came on in my head.

Mother was cagey about responding to my constant questions about why we never went to her home, why I'd never met any of my relatives. I'd use the Abrams as my exemplars: "They *can't* go home. The Nazis chased them out of Poland. Yet, they can't stop talking about home. They'd be killed if they went home."

"There are other ways of dying than being bludgeoned by a Jerry, Clio. The soul-crushing smallness of daily life in Wolfe Flats would have been the death of me if I'd stayed. That and my best friend's collusion with my aunts." Mother actually had tears in her eyes when she said "best friend's collusion."

She had said one other thing that I racked up to her comic timing. Her mocking comments always came into play when Mother thought I might glimpse that untouchable and rarely emotional side of her. "A man who might have been your father but wasn't liberated me. Then the National Guard arrived. That tipped the scales. I finally made up my mind to leave Wolfe Flats."

In my upstairs bedroom, scrunched under a canopy that gave me claustrophobia, I puzzled over Mother's cryptic comments until I felt as woozy as the Delphic oracle. I needed facts, tangible facts, like Lucinda's report about Mrs. Wallace buying calamine for her face.

BY MID-AFTERNOON AT school, Mrs. Wallace's itching had reached an epidemic stage; the entire class had watched in awe as her crimson nails demolished her nose and attacked her chin. Thinking that a crappy excuse for a teacher isn't better than no teacher at all, I found comfort in the thought that she would not be having a restful evening tonight.

Tiptoeing down the stairs after everyone had gone to bed, I checked the Muller house through the downstairs windows. They were abiding by the sheriff's edict. Sealed up tight for the night. It might be a good evening for me to take a closer look at what must be a grave out back by the Mullers' picket fence.

I stuck my head out of a half-opened window into that brooding night. Cats yowled. An owl hooted. The waning crescent of a moon dressed itself in that splendid Halloween orange. Even in April, spirits must be afoot. I went up to my bedroom, penciled in more details on my map, and tumbled into bed to have nightmares about German Stukas and Mother screaming amidst the flames.

THE NEXT MORNING, when I walked into the classroom, the strangest sight stopped me in my tracks. The boxer on the cover of Mrs. Wallace's paperback novel was sitting in her chair, with the same blondish cropped hair, the chiseled jaw, and the sculpted nose. This one had on clothes.

He swiveled the chair around, and I gasped. Mrs. Wallace's poison ivy plague had spread. The boxer's right cheek puckered and crinkled the way a nylon slip does when you smack it with a hot iron. He spun the desk chair another quarter of a circle, braced his hand against the desk, pushed himself up, and took a step. His right leg appeared to be an appendage that was obliged to follow against its will.

"You can take your seats now, students." His slightly accented English was crystal clear. "Mrs. Wallace will be staying home for a couple of days with a bad rash. The principal asked me to substitute. My name is Marek Nebojsa, spelled out there on the blackboard. Some of you know that my father and I run Nebo's Blacksmith shop." He eased himself down on the edge of the desk. I noticed that everything was stacked in an orderly fashion. There was no sign of Mrs. Wallace's romance novel.

"I arrived early and graded your math books. That level of math is far below what I would expect of sixth-graders. I was a teacher years ago. In another place." He looked out the window as though he might be checking for a quick escape route.

"Starting with the first aisle, I want you to say your names. I won't forget them. I already know some of you." He gave a half salute toward the back of the room. "Jeremiah, Papa has missed seeing you this week. I've started a new sculpture I want to show you."

Jeremiah beamed, tucked his feet in, and rearranged his face into that of someone avid for information.

Mr. Nebojsa repeated each student's name once. Then, he hobbled to the blackboard and began pulling down maps. "These are out of date, but the continents haven't shifted. Well, actually they have but not noticeably." He flashed a slight grin at his joke. "Move up here so you can see. Just sit on the floor for now. Jeremiah, get someone to help you move that stage thing over for the girls to sit on."

He pulled a fist-full of colored chalk out of his briefcase. "We're going to have a lesson in geography and history at the same time. One of our contemporary philosophers, George Santayana, said: 'Those who cannot remember the past are condemned to repeat it.' You should take that edict to heart." Within a flash, he had drawn the continent of Europe on the blackboard and segmented it with different colors into different countries, popping longitudes and latitudes along the edge with aplomb.

I was so impressed by his ability to map so many countries without so much as an Atlas at hand that I blushed in shame when I thought of my map of Wolfe Flats.

"We're going to remember the past by starting with the present—what's happening now in the world is of critical interest to all of us. Our relatives. Our friends . . ."

Suddenly silent, he turned back to the blackboard and began shaping the great continent of Asia. "I hope we'll have enough time to go back to the Napoleonic Wars so you'll see what Mr. Santayana means about repeating the past."

When the bell sounded for recess, not one of us moved. Mr. Nebojsa had mesmerized us. We could see cavalries and lines of foot soldiers moving across a landscape that he brought to life. I could hardly wait for Napoleon to make an appearance with his paunchy belly and bicorne hat.

"Up. Up. Stretch. Go get some fresh air. It's a lovely day outside. I'll visit with you after school, Jeremiah." Mr. Nebojsa turned to the board and began wiping out all his arrows and figures.

Animated by our substitute teacher's attention, Jeremiah was in a different kind of mood as we wandered out to the schoolyard. For once, we simply walked. No knives. No scraping of mortar. Jeremiah was full of information about the new teacher. "He's my friend. I call him by his first name, Marek. He's from Czechoslovakia. Flew with the RAF until an engine blew and they crashed near Dover. It messed up his leg real bad. He runs the blacksmith place with his pa. Makes sculptures."

Jeremiah looked into a wide blue sky and back down at me with those bluer than cornflower eyes. "Marek says when we've won the war and don't have a metal shortage, he'll start making huge sculptures. He says I have a knack for welding. Makes me wear a big dumb face shield. His pa won't wear one. Got real bad eyes now. From all the sparks."

Wordlessly, I handed over Lucinda's fudge wrapped in wax paper. "Wow! I haven't seen homemade candy since . . ." Jeremiah fondled it so longingly that I handed over my piece—and was instantly rewarded.

"Tell you what, Clio. After school, we can walk down by the blacksmith shop. I'll save your piece of fudge for Marek's father. They don't have anyone to cook for them. I swear they live on potato dumplings and sauerkraut soup. Miz Wallace sometimes had Marek and his father over for dinner after her niece, Ellen Carson, came to town. I thought that her niece and Marek . . ."

I waited impatiently for him to continue. This piece of information put a new light on things. The other missing woman had been involved with Mr. Nebojsa. And, Mrs. Wallace was in the mix. I love it when plots begin to thicken like Lucinda's hot fudge. Sweetens the puzzle.

Jeremiah pinched off a small corner of his fudge, handed it me, and crammed all the rest into his mouth. "Time to get back. Marek is a humdinger of a teacher.

I just wish I'd thought of something more permanent than poison ivy for that old bat."

Walking side by side with a would-be murderer didn't faze me in the least. I'd watched those old spy movies in which the villains pop a capsule of cyanide to keep from revealing secrets and foam a bit at the mouth before they stiffen like planks.

Mother told me that poison doesn't always work the way it does in the movies. She said that when assassins went after Archduke Ferdinand, they planned to do themselves in with cyanide after they'd done the deed, but the cyanide was stale and just made them sick.

I grinned over at Jeremiah. I suspected that fresh cyanide would be in short supply in Wolfe Flats. I thought about that missing niece of Mrs. Wallace and those dinners with Mr. Nebojsa. Tasty info seemed to be popping up everywhere.

Chapter 9

Three days later when we had just ended the Napoleonic Wars and were heading up the Alps with Hannibal and his elephants, the bravado of battle came to a halt. Mrs. Wallace appeared in the classroom with odd chalky pink patches of calamine on her face.

The blackboard was wiped clean. The dais was in its place. We were back to multiplying fractions and slogging through word problems. "I hope you treated the substitute teacher with respect." Mrs. Wallace glowered at us suspiciously. "You certainly didn't make much headway in your math workbooks. Mr. Nebojsa is a foreign person, not accustomed to modern education methods. Foreigners have their own ways," she said dismissively.

Praise the Lord I wanted to shout with those happy souls I could hear singing at night, the glorious spirituals ballooning up to heaven from that northeast quadrant of Wolfe Flats that was off limits to whites. The thought of spending the last year of elementary school with Mrs. Wallace gave me acid reflux.

And an idea. Jeremiah knew about plants. He said that his mother studied botany. Maybe we could concoct something out of a poisonous plant that would keep Mrs. Wallace under the weather—and out of our classroom.

In the meantime, I'd been to the Nebo Blacksmith shop with Jeremiah two times. Mr. Nebojsa praised Lucinda's fudge to the skies. She cooked him a molasses pecan pie as a follow-up. Compliments to Lucinda from my aunts came grudgingly, at best. They were both huffy about the rationed sugar being squandered in candy.

The day that Mrs. Wallace reclaimed her chair brought back old habits. Jeremiah pasted on his cynical face, and I rejoined him at the wall, scraping away the mortar at recess. "Even more reason to go by the blacksmith shop after school. See Marek. Sometimes Mr. Nebojsa pays me to help him. Pa says I can work if I get paid."

The blacksmith's was unlike any place I'd ever seen. The closest thing to it was underground at Grand Central Station with tracks going every which way and steam-pipe tunnels arching along the walls.

A forge glowing with red-hot coals took up the center of a huge room. Racks of horseshoes, hoes, shovels, rakes, and discs for plows lined the walls. The ceiling was as high as forever with some odd little window spaces at the top.

"This was an old gin before we rented it," Mr. Nebojsa said with obvious pride when he showed me around during my first visit. "Business is real good now because no one can buy new tools or ploughs. We fix the old ones. I'd teach Jeremiah more about welding, but my boy thinks he's too young. He's not."

HER SECOND DAY back, Mrs. Wallace dismissed us half an hour before the bell rang. "I'm still experiencing discomfort. You go straight home. Those of you riding the bus can wait by the flagpole. Don't be wandering off so no one can find you."

I thought she looked a bit forlorn. Maybe she was thinking about her niece who went for a walk and never came back. Or, perhaps the itching was insufferable. At any rate, I was unable to muster much sympathy for Mrs. Wallace.

JEREMIAH AND I headed at a fast clip down the street and angled through three back yards and up two alleys. With Jeremiah, I had learned a lot about mapping. Alleys in small towns were treasure troves. No one used their back yards for anything but gardens, stacks of trash too good to discard, and a metal barrel to burn what wouldn't burn in a fireplace. Alleys—and what could be seen from them—were the warp and woof of Wolfe Flats. Things were coming together.

Front porches were made for spying openly on neighbors and socializing. The covered porch on my aunts' house unrolled all along the front, generously rounding the corner of the house. Wicker furniture and huge potted plants gave it a kind of tropical ambiance.

"It's a semblance of the Bahamas right here in Oklahoma," Aunt Harriet claimed.

The afternoon sun turned the porch into an oven; the wind toppled the plants with regularity. The closest water was the muddy Red River, but Aunt Harriet held on to her fiction of a tropical island just outside the door.

When Aunt Norma sat on the porch, I noticed that passersby ventured a half-hearted wave but kept moving down the sidewalk. Aunt Harriet attracted neighbors like a magnet. And that brings me to something quite horrible. Not expected at all, but I guess that's what makes terrible things so horrid. They happen when you least expect them.

Jeremiah and I had popped into the blacksmith shop after Mrs. Wallace dismissed us early, hoping to see our substitute teacher, and primed to take Mrs. Wallace down a notch or two for her furtive way of criticizing Marek.

Mr. Nebojsa was struggling with a thick bar of metal in one hand and bellows in the other. "Trying to get this cross peen . . . drift is off . . . if I could . . ."

Blackened as Hephaestus in the furnace of the gods, Mr. Nebojsa squinted at us through red-rimmed eyes, swung his body forward and smacked the white-hot head of the hammer with a ringing blow.

I heard it without seeing it. Something whizzed past my head and lodged itself in the head behind me. Jeremiah's head.

Three screams went off simultaneously. Mine, Mr. Nebojsa's, and Marek's. Jeremiah dropped in silence onto the filthy, packed earth floor. Blood trickled from a tiny black spot next to a bright blue eye.

"Don't move at all, Jeremiah. No matter how much it hurts, don't move!" Marek's words were controlled, but his voice was high-pitched.

Like the big sissy I really was, I couldn't control the fat tears coursing down my cheeks.

"Papa. Go find Doctor Lontry! This is too close to his eye. It's wedged down into the socket."

Yanking off big leather gloves and dropping to the side of Jeremiah, Mr. Nebojsa blurted out: "He's not here. Delivering a baby in Addington Bend. He dropped off a bent hubcap on his way at noon."

Moving on his knees like one of those supplicants who beg on the streets of India, Mr. Nebojsa bent over Jeremiah's face and screwed his eyes into tight slits. "Damn and blast these eyes. If I could see better, I could . . ." Then, he said something in a foreign language. Marek shook his head. His father repeated it and pointed to a small rack of tools.

Even with my tears splashing like Niagara Falls, I could see that a small black metal object was wedged too deep for anyone to grab the end of it without doing further damage to Jeremiah's eyeball.

Marek said something between his teeth that sounded like an echo of "damn and blast it." Then, in the calmest voice imaginable, he said: "Clio, I want you to hand me one of those small cylinders from the bin to the left of me. Try to find a clean one."

Why I was walking on my tiptoes I had no idea. But, I circled around Jeremiah without touching him and sorted through some metal rods that seemed heavy for their size. They looked dusty. "I could wipe it off, but I don't see . . ." Every piece of cloth in sight was stiff with grease and coal dust. The big apron-like thing Mr. Nebojsa wore was filthy. Marek's clothes were covered with soot.

"We need something to wipe this rod and to put pressure on the wound if it works." Marek stared at me. "Do you have on a slip, Clio?"

Did I have on a slip? Didn't every girl wearing a dress? Unfortunately, mine was not a silky nylon thing with lace along the top that poked up beneath the low-cut blouses that the Brown twins wore.

Aunt Norma had taken all of my worldly goods, including that fake alligator suitcase, to the church rummage sale and replaced my clothes with what she described as "sensible things." My slips were squared off, coarse, cotton shifts. Jeremiah watched me with his one, good, blue eye as the other one leaked blood around the rim.

Faster than Sherman took Atlanta, I unbuttoned my dirty skirt, whipped my soiled blouse over my head, and stood in my white slip looking, I hoped, like the snow princess in the middle of hell. The forge blazed furiously. Smoke curled upward.

I yanked the slip over my head, thinking my little display might relieve some of the tension in this godforsaken sooty place. Two men carefully averted their eyes. Jeremiah didn't even blink.

Luckily, Aunt Norma's job as underwear Gestapo provided a plain, substantial camisole under my slip and big boxy bloomers. I wrestled a blousy cotton skirt back into place and whipped on the blouse.

"You'll have to help me, Clio." Marek motioned me down by his side. "I'm going to situate this little magnet just above the piece of metal. I think it's a tooth off a cast-iron gear Papa was working on. Must have fallen into the forge. Who knows why it shot up like that."

I knew. Behavior of physical objects when subjected to force. Mr. Abrams could rattle on about his field of mechanics until the cows came home.

As I opened my mouth to give a few pointers about what heat can do to metal, Marek interrupted.

"Jeremiah, you need to remain as still as possible. You'll feel a little pressure. Then Clio will wad up her slip and hold it as firmly as possible against your eye. We'll send someone down to Addington Bend to find the doctor."

I knew that Addington Bend was less than ten miles south and east. If Doctor Lontry were delivering a baby, how would that weigh against an eye? It came to me in a flash. Lucinda would know what to do. Mother told me that Lucinda helped deliver babies, sewed up cuts with special boiled thread, and put poultices on unmentionable parts of the body.

Mr. Nebojsa didn't look behind or in front of himself. His watery eyes were riveted down on Jeremiah.

"It hurts like the very devil, Mr. Nebojsa," Jeremiah struggled to sit up as Marek pressured him back. "Even seeing Clio in her skivvies didn't help the pain." He tried to chuckle at his stupid attempt at humor, but the blood welled into his eye socket so that the metal tip was no longer visible.

"Mr. Nebojsa, go find Lucinda. Try my aunts' place. Lucinda will know what to do. She always knows!" My voice sounded foreign to me, screechy and out of control, but Mr. Nebojsa was on his feet and out the door in seconds. That left Marek, me, and a bleeding, twitchy Jeremiah in this hellish place.

"We need to get this out now, Clio. There's too much blood to see what I'm doing with the magnet. Jeremiah, don't move. When you lifted your head, the sliver of metal went deeper. Clio, be ready to hold your slip against the wound."

Gingerly, Marek angled the magnet cylinder past Jeremiah's cheekbone, balancing it inches away from his eye. "I have to get it positioned just right. I don't know how strong the magnet is. I don't want to rip that sliver out too fast."

Not one of us dared to breath. Small sparks shot up from the forge beside us without making the least noise. With what must have been the tiniest click in the universe, the magnet made contact. Millimeter by millimeter, a fraction of a penny's edge for each movement, Marek drew the magnet back, anchoring his fingers across Jeremiah's freckled nose.

My gasp was louder than Marek's. An evil wedge, like a tiny, bloody shark's tooth, dangled from the end of the magnet. Marek shoved both the tooth and the magnet into his shirt pocket, eased my slip from my clenched fists, and pushed it in a wad into Jeremiah's eye.

Too much blood, I was thinking. Jeremiah struggled against Marek, moving his head back and forth frantically, as though to shake out something remaining in his eye.

There was nothing that I could do but pat Jeremiah's arm and beg him to lie still so the blood would subside, and I might be able to see that matching sapphire eye again.

Lucinda's flatbed pickup roared under the big overhead door of the blacksmith shop with Mr. Nebojsa standing behind the cab, gesturing like a Viking warrior who has just spotted land. Both of my aunts, wide-eyed and agitated, were squashed into the front seat with Lucinda.

"Doc will be on his way soon. I called Wiseman's store on the highway down by Addington Bend, and they fetched him. Miz Taylor's baby already come as expected. Doc Lontry likes to time them contractions so he don't waste good office time sittin' around." Lucinda swung out of her truck, continuing to talk as she moved close to Jeremiah. "He tole me exactly what to do until he gits here. Tole me to think about the bullet I helped him take out of Booger Allen's shoulder when he got in the argument with that Texas feller about the fare."

Marek reached into his pocket and pulled out the cylindrical magnet with the bloody tooth attached.

"Looks like part of a tractor's gear. Clean as a whistle. You shoulda seen that bullet after it smacked the head of Booger's humerus." Lucinda moved Marek's hand aside, gently lifted the skin next to Jeremiah's eye, and hummed something under her breath.

At that moment, I wanted to scream at Lucinda to pay attention to Jeremiah, to look at the blood soaking my slip, to make it stop oozing out of his eyeball. Then, I noticed that Jeremiah was relaxing, twisting his mouth into something that tried for a smile.

"You're humming that old hymn, Lucinda. Blessed Jesus, hear, O, hear us when we pray." Jeremiah squeaked in a voice not his own. "Am I that far gone?"

"You'll be fit as a fiddle soon as we git you into a clean bed and have Doc double check this eye. He'll give you somethin' to help you relax. They's coal dust everwheres in this smithy place. Might end up with eyes the color of mine," Lucinda chuckled.

I was not amused. Mr. Nebojsa seemed to be. More relaxed with Lucinda in charge, he was shifting rhythmically from one foot to the other as though a brass band were playing in the wings; he turned abruptly, pulled a slab of plywood away from the wall and began scooting it under Jeremiah.

"Good idea, Mr. Nebojsa. Keep him flat until Doc can see to him. You and Marek get the head and foot.

Clio, you and Norma each take a side. Harriet, boost yourself up onto the pickup and guide us dead center. We're goin' to the house with him."

Lucinda should have been on the ship to Europe instead of Mother. Lucinda could commandeer troops like nobody's business, not just talk to them and take photos.

Speaking of exposures, when Aunt Harriet scooted up to the bed of the pickup, her baggy cotton stockings left nothing to the imagination about how they cinched onto her bloomers. I saw Aunt Norma flinch. Then, like a comrade in arms, she flung one leg after the other. No one dared take a gander at her stockings rolled above the knee, strangling any possibility of her circulatory system sending blood upwards.

Like one of those high school floats, with Jeremiah representing the rival's fallen quarterback, we barreled down Main Street, spun around the corner down Choctaw, and eased into the space between our house and the Mullers. I might have been wrong, but I was sure that I saw a curtain moving. Then, two curtains moving.

As though in anticipation of a guest, windows in the downstairs bedroom were flung wide; the white counterpane was folded back; and, a pitcher of water with ice cubes sat on the bedside table. There was a washbowl with something that smelled like carbolic soap floating in it and piles of gauzy white cloths stacked by it.

"No one more thoughtful than Manford. He anticipates," Aunt Norma nodded at Aunt Harriet as we tried to angle Jeremiah's makeshift stretcher through the bedroom door. We had moved it effortlessly across the side porch, through the double front doors, and down the wide hall.

Manboy Muller has the run of the house? Knew what was needed before we did? Before I could crank out a question, Marek had scooped up Jeremiah and placed him gently on the bed.

"Somebody better go tell Jeremiah's pa," Lucinda said, letting everyone know who was in charge. "Mr. Nebojsa, take my truck. Keys are in it. Mr. Whittaker should be here when Doc comes. By my calculations, that'll be in about twenty minutes. This is Miz Taylor's third. She don't need no episiotomy."

"Really, Lucinda! Children are present." Aunt Norma clucked like a disgruntled hen, tucking towels around Jeremiah's head to keep him from moving as Lucinda sponged off layers of soot. I tucked that word "episiotomy" into my lookup file for later.

CHAPTER 10

"My boy needs to be under his own roof. We won't be beholden." The moment I saw Jeremiah's father burst through the front door, it was clear which side of the family was responsible for the red hair and freckles.

Jeremiah's coloring was nice, especially with those bluer than the wild blue yonder eyes. Jeremiah's father was a whole new ballgame. The hair on his head had been buzz cut like a new Marine so that his patchy scalp commanded immediate attention.

A big, burly man with bibbed overalls and the same clumpy boots as Jeremiah wore, Mr. Whittaker seemed to fill up the room—resistant to move, even when the doctor asked him.

"George. George!" Aunt Norma almost shouted his name the second time. "I know that you are worried about Jeremiah, but you are not helping by getting in Doctor Lontry's way."

Twice her weight and a head taller than Aunt Norma, George Whittaker backed out of the bedroom, down the hall, and squatted by the front door, refusing to take a chair.

"Soon as he's fixed, we're going. Doc Lontry will make him good as new, and we're out of here."

I watched Mr. Whittaker's back make contact with the wall, probably doing irreparable damage to the red-flocked wallpaper. Disheveled and agitated, he thumped his muddy boots on the tufts of the Persian hall runner, ridding his soles of clumps of manure as though the rug doubled as a boot scraper.

Aunt Norma would have a cow. Good thing she was in the room with Jeremiah. I needed to intervene.

"Could I get you a glass of water, Mr. Whittaker? Or lemonade?" I said, easing up the side of the rug into a fat curl, away from his boots.

"What? Sorry, girl. What did you say? I'm preoccupied." He turned eyes as yellowish green as a panther's toward me.

"My God. You can't be. You aren't. She wouldn't." The disbelief on Mr. Whittaker's face rivaled those photographs of Mr. Chamberlain when he realized that Hitler had duped him—a blend of astonishment and shame.

For such a heavy-set man, Jeremiah's father sprang up faster than a jack-in-the-box and grabbed my arm so hard that I could feel my ulna being permanently squashed into my radius. "Ouch! That hurts!" I couldn't control two sharp squeals that rang out involuntarily.

"Take your hands off Clio. What do you think you're doing?" A steely-eyed Aunt Norma tucked me against her girdled torso as Mr. Whittaker dropped his hands limply by his side.

"I don't know," he mumbled. "I thought I was seeing things. A ghost or something. Delia come to torment me when I need to think about my boy."

"I'll do more'n take yore mind off that boy if you ever lays a hand on my girl. You interfered onct when Delia warn't but eighteen . . ." The fury on Lucinda's face shocked me more than the angry mask settling across Aunt Norma's.

Lucinda pushed the bedroom door closed with a thump. "No need to agitate Jeremiah. Though I suspect he and Luke seen what you done to their poor mother to make her hightail it."

"That's enough, Lucinda. George has had a shock. The doctor told him there's a real chance of infection in that eye because of the rusty metal. Doctor Lontry is flushing it now." Aunt Norma continued to clutch me against her, but her voice was kinder.

"When Doc Lontry's done, me and my boy will go. I won't be beholden." Mr. Whittaker was standing erect now, wringing his hands like Pontius Pilate washing away sin, and repeating "beholden" like a buzzword.

"No, your son won't go. And, yes, you will be beholden." Doctor Lontry, who had the long, cadaverous face of Boris Karloff in *The Mummy*, eased open the door and confronted Mr. Whittaker.

"Eleven years ago, I delivered Jeremiah in the same farmhouse where you were born, George. I'm not about to let anything happen to him because you're too

bull-headed to recognize kindness when it's offered."
Doctor Lontry reached over and touched my cheek.
"This little girl helped Marek take care of your boy until
I could get here. I think her slip has seen better days,
Miss Norma." He looked at Aunt Norma and actually
winked. "It's a good thing it was cotton, not that sleazy
nylon stuff. That wouldn't have worked at all."

What had begun to look like hand-to-hand combat
between Lucinda and Jeremiah's father seemed to be
fizzling. I suspected that Doctor Lontry was a master
at defusing bad situations. This one still had a kind of
darkness about the edges, like those purplish summer
clouds that hold back a frenzy of lightning.

Doctor Lontry grabbed Mr. Whittaker's arm and
wheeled him toward the front door. "Jeremiah will be
out cold for hours. He cannot be moved under any cir-
cumstance. It's best that you go take care of your live-
stock tonight and let these women—and Clio—take
care of your son. I'll be checking on him later this evening. You go on home, George."

Wonder of wonders, that big man did just that.
Without so much as a fare-thee-well, he stomped out
the front door, leaving muddy clumps behind. And the
very sour odor of anger.

"Such a pity," Aunt Harriet's soft voice was like balm
on troubled spirits. "George has worked hard on that
farm all of his life, but things never seem to pan out for
him. One son going off to war without his permission—
and his wife gone like that. He was such a handsome
young man except for that temper. I guess that's why

Delia . . . but that was a long time ago. They wouldn't have . . ."

"That's the second time today I seen Whitey Lewin walking down t'other side of the street like he's walkin' the dog with no dog," Lucinda bumped Aunt Harriet aside and pointed out the window to an empty sidewalk.

Lucinda's quick change of subject was a thinly veiled effort to keep Aunt Harriet from saying something about my mother and Jeremiah's father that piqued my interest. So I narrowed my eyes at her and was just about to spin the topic back to what "they wouldn't have" when Aunt Norma interrupted.

"Mr. Nebojsa, why don't you and Marek join us for dinner? Lucinda was making a big chicken potpie earlier. A bit of company might do all of us good tonight. About sixish? After you've had time to change."

I watched Aunt Norma's squared-off chin nodding, noting the precise number of sooty tracks down her hall runner, as she ushered Mr. Nebojsa and Marek out the front door. Someone was in for it. In her Bible, the wages of sin required communal punishment.

"Lucinda. I really wish you wouldn't refer to Lester Lewin as 'Whitey.' You have no idea how that nickname distresses his mother. It's a childish thing to do. Not Christian."

I might have risen to Lucinda's defense, but she had pushed me out of shape by derailing Aunt Harriet, who was awfully difficult to get back on track—any track once she'd left the station.

I could have mouthed off, advised Aunt Norma that in Medieval England, names were related to locality or occupation—Mr. Godale sold good ale. Patronymics and nicknames are a very old practice.

However, I was dying to know what, if anything, happened between my mother and Jeremiah's father; I was just about to pick up where Aunt Harriet left off when Lucinda stood up for herself, as she always did.

"Didn't I hear you this very mornin' say 'Hello, Shivers, we'll take an extra bottle of milk now that Clio is with us.' Pore man got palsy but nobody raise an eyebrow 'bout that. Booger Allen been called Booger since grade school. Fatty Owens down at the fillin' station don't go by no other name. After all these years, Manboy's mama don't know what else to call him."

Lucinda whirled through the kitchen door with a single declarative sentence left standing behind her like a pennant in a stiff breeze: "It *is* childish because some of us 'member the chile inside our friends."

The door slammed. Aunt Norma's mouth twisted as though she'd bitten into a green persimmon.

"It doesn't do to chastise Lucinda, dear." Aunt Harriet patted Aunt Norma's arm. "She has a way of summing up things with such a flair. The heart of the matter so to speak."

Aunt Harriet reached for my hand. "Let's peek in on Jeremiah before we go upstairs just to be sure he's sleeping well. Then I'll run your bath water, Clio, and tell you a kind of fairy story."

CHAPTER 11

As she untangled my braids and pulled a big ivory-colored Bakelite comb through my hair, Aunt Harriet dumped a handful of lavender bath salts into the tub. "I gave those to Norma two Christmases ago. She doesn't use anything but Lifebuoy. It has the distinctive carbolic odor of coal tar. That's my sister to a T. From the Bible, dear, tittle."

"The fairy tale, Aunt Harriet." I wiggled impatiently, sure that the tale had something to do with my mother and Jeremiah's father.

"Just a short one, Clio. It has to do with a princess who didn't much like the tower where she lived, and she had become very angry for a good reason at the people who lived with her. So, after everyone was asleep, she climbed down the Wisteria vines to meet a prince. He wasn't really a prince, as she found out the hard way, but he was very handsome. He sweet-talked this princess into believing that his tower would be a better place to live than her tower."

Aunt Harriet stopped and stared up at that round window in the bathroom that opened out to a view of the Muller house. "There was a rather sweet dwarf who lived in a tower next to the princess who warned her time and again that handsome is as handsome does. She was not inclined to listen."

The steamy bathroom didn't make Aunt Harriet's story any less transparent than what it was. My mother either did or did not run off with George Whittaker. Aunt Harriet was not very skilled at dissembling.

"So. What happened?" I wanted to hear the good parts, the reason Lucinda seemed so furious with Mr. Whittaker and what made him grab my arm as though he wanted to wrench it from the socket.

"Not much. The dwarf got a dislocated jaw. The princess got a black eye and became a wiser girl. The handsome boy, who didn't have a royal bone in his body, found another punching bag and didn't live happily ever after." Aunt Harriet sent an enigmatic smile toward me as she opened the bathroom door.

"Lavender salts relieve tension, my dear. A good soak will do wonders for you."

I was left with a tub of tepid water that sent up waves of an odiferous floral scent that was doing nothing for my stress. George Whittaker had obviously mistaken me for Mother and was furious about something that she had done or might do. He used the word "torment."

Aunt Harriet's little fairy tale told me part of what I already knew. Mother always said that she knew exactly how Rapunzel felt living in a tower with no one around but the witch who kept her captive.

"Rules, Clio. I lived with more rules than the Continental Congress could devise. Aunt Norma had church rules, school rules, decorum rules, friendship rules, and rules that would cover every possible expediency." Mother would grin slyly at me. "Therefore, I became an expert rule breaker. That's why I never tell you what to do. I just tell you after you've done something I don't like. That's allowed."

No rules confused me when I was young. I had to learn things the hard way—like wearing mismatched socks or saying whatever popped into my head. Being tutored by your peers can be a cruel education. Our old neighbors, the Abrams, consoled me with maps and museums and gentle guidance.

However, after being in this house for less than a week with those two aunts of hers, I was beginning to get a feel for Mother's disregard for rules. She jaywalked. At the subway, she dropped only one coin for two of us. She lied about us being Catholic to get me into a closer school. She got better jobs by inventing a work history she wished she had.

"You know that poem we like by Robert Frost? "Two roads diverged in a yellow wood,' the one about how making a choice can make all the difference? That's what I'm doing, Clio. Just twisting the truth a bit to get me to that road." Her big brown eyes were as blank as a cow's as she looked past me, not at me, the morning she told me we were taking the train from New York City to Oklahoma.

Then she high-tailed it out of the country, pretending to be a war correspondent, and left me imprisoned in her tower. I scooted down in my bath water until my face was submerged. Just a few minutes more of aspirating large volumes of water into my lungs, and they would find my naked body reeking of lavender.

I heaved myself up with a mighty splash of water over the sides of the tub. They would find my naked, skinny body, and no one would much care. Except for Jeremiah. He might miss me helping to peel the bricks off the school. Or, with one blind eye, he might need me to steer him around obstacles.

As I toweled off and skewed my dripping hair into a knot on the top of my head, I felt a renewed sense of purpose. Jeremiah was lying helpless in a bedroom just downstairs. His bully of a father would probably force him to come home. His mother—or Mrs. Wallace's niece—might be decaying past recognition in that hump of a grave in the Mullers' backyard. I had better things to do than drown myself.

Later that evening, dinner with the Nebojsas was a stilted affair at best. Aunt Norma waxed on and on about the Methodist temperance work while Mr. Nebojsa looked like a man who could use a drink.

Marek charmed the socks off Aunt Harriet when he could get a word in edgewise. He had actually seen Pre-Raphaelite art in real museums, not just reprints like the one on her wall.

We marched through Lucinda's chicken potpie like a ragtag starving army. I was just about to tackle the last corner of a peach cobbler when Marek whispered to me: "Let's see if Jeremiah is awake. Something sweet might do him a world of good."

Whatever Doctor Lontry had used to send Jeremiah into la-la land left his mouth ajar and snores filling up all the empty spaces. So, until we heard Mr. Nebojsa call out that it was time to go home, Marek and I shared the cobbler and watched Jeremiah's big, white, eye patch to see if anything might be leaking around the edges.

CHAPTER 12

"Oh my Lord! You will not believe what someone has done!" Aunt Norma shouted down the house before I could rub the sleep out of my eyes. And, I really couldn't. Not in this small town where neighbors all knew each other, called each other by childhood nicknames, and carried pot roasts and cobblers to shut-ins.

Great, spidery swastikas dripped down the front and sides of the Muller house. That peeling Victorian house took on an even more sinister air with those symbols of hate on its walls.

Within minutes, Lucinda, armed with a scrub brush and a bucket of soapy water, was in attack mode. "Black paint. This don't touch them," she shouted loud enough to wake the entire neighborhood. "I'd like to get my hands on . . ."

The gasps of a wispy woman, who appeared to waft ghostlike through the open door of the Muller house, were soft yet so persistent that I imagined Beethoven's "Moonlight Sonata" cranked up full volume—the way that Aunt Harriet insists we hear it on that old Victrola of hers.

Then, the standing woman disappeared from my view and reappeared, as flat on the porch as that old rag rug used for wiping shoes. Lucinda dropped her scrub brush and began doing something to the person who must be Manboy's mother. Aunt Norma joined her on the other side of the body. Aunt Harriet just wailed.

"Clio, go call the hospital in Gainesville! They have an ambulance service. No. Tell our operator, Rayleen Turner. She'll know what to do! Harriet, go inside and find Manford!"

Everyone seemed to have something critical to do. Being told to call for an ambulance would normally have puffed me up with self-importance. Now, it just separated me from the interesting events, especially the opportunity to get an eyeful inside the Muller front door.

"I'll take care of it, little girl. You tell Miss Norma that I'll get the ambulance headed our way." The operator's voice was soothing as honey, but I resented being called "little girl." Rayleen seemed hard of hearing, so I gave her very specific information: "Choctaw Street. Second house on the northeast side of the street. Muller house. Elderly woman. Dropped like a stone when she saw Nazi swastikas on her house."

WITHIN THE NEXT forty-five minutes, I catalogued more things of interest than usually occur in an entire day. After the poking and cajoling over what appeared to be a corpse on the Muller porch, a frail, ghostly figure rose like Lazarus and tottered with baby steps into the arms of someone no taller than me and disappeared into the house.

While I was peering through the boxwood bushes, trying to get a better view, Aunt Norma's voice—louder than the siren in the distance—split the momentary calm. "Clio! What are you doing in your nightgown? Only small girls and deranged women are ever seen outside in nightclothes. Get dressed. Then, stay on our porch until I make some decisions."

As I summed up the situation, the only ones making decisions should be the ambulance medics and the doctors in the Gainesville hospital, if and when the ambulance ever located Choctaw Street.

Not true. The Pierce Arrow with Aunt Norma behind the wheel whipped around the side yard and blocked the street in front of the Muller house.

Just as she hopped out, leaving the motor running and the driver's door wide open, a familiar voice asked: "What in blue blazes is going on out here?"

Jeremiah dropped onto the porch swing next to me, his coppery hair standing stiffly off his forehead. Except for a faint, yellowish stain on his bandage, he looked almost as good as new. He would be quite dashing with a black eye patch, like a pirate—with one of those cursing parrots on his shoulder.

"Damn it, Jeremiah! Did Doc tell you to get out of bed? What in God's name are you doing out here shilly-shallying with Delia's girl? You able to *socialize*, then you can get home and make yourself useful." Mr. Whittaker shifted the box he was holding under one arm so that his cantaloupe bicep bulged against a short-sleeved shirt, with store creases still in it.

A faint spray of saliva hit my cheek when he hissed out "socialize," as though the very word stuck in his craw. Then something else did as an ambulance belched to a stop in front of the Muller house.

"Well look at that! The traitors have been nailed. Whoever did that paint job deserves a medal."

"Or a jail cell," I snapped, moving behind the swing, my hands gripping the top of it. If Mr. Whittaker came for either me or Jeremiah, I would slam that old wooden swing into him and scream bloody murder.

"Delia's girl. No doubt about it. Same smart mouth. Not the looker she was. Scrawny thing, aren't you? Must take after your father, whoever he might be."

"Pa, Clio's only eleven years old. Why are you being mean to her? She helped Marek take that thing out of my eye." Jeremiah had eased himself out of the swing and stood between his father and me.

"So she did, son. So she did. We don't forget our obligations." Mr. Whittaker shoved the box toward me.

A mound of brown eggs packed in straw took up half the box; fat bottles of what looked like golden milk clattered against each other. "Pure cream for making butter or ice cream or what ever your heart desires, Clio." Those panther eyes seemed to see right through my flimsy nightgown all the way into my heart—which was feeling very black at the moment.

As black as those polished shoes Mr. Whittaker had put on as replacements for his dirty boots. Squinting down at their sheen, I wondered if black paint would be visible on black leather.

"Come for Jeremiah, have you, George?" Aunt Norma rounded the porch.

"Yes, Miss Clower. The boy looks fit enough to me. We're leaving. I brought you fresh eggs and cream. We don't have a shortage of them. It's no sacrifice."

I rather admired the way that Jeremiah's father paid his debt. He was letting Aunt Norma know that the gift was meaningless to him, rather like royalty tossing coins to the peasants.

"When Doctor Lontry came by last night, he said you'd probably want to take your son today. He wants you to stop by the office, so he can change the bandage and check for infection. Nice having you with us, Jeremiah." She patted him on the arm, completely ignored his father, and whirled on me.

"Inside, Clio. Get dressed. Put the box in the kitchen. Your Aunt Harriet, Lucinda, and I will follow the ambulance to Gainesville. Manford was so caught up with fear for his mother. Bad sprain. Just hurrying too fast . . . when it rains it pours."

Aunt Norma pursed her lips and glared at Mr. Whittaker's departing back as though she suspected his complicity in those swastikas dripping off the Muller house. I looked at her blankly. Talking about sprains sounded as though she were confusing Manboy with his mother.

"Clio, I want you to call Mr. Edwards down at the hardware store. Tell him to get someone out immediately with two gallons of exterior paint. White. Tell him I don't want a trace of those vicious symbols showing through. This is a respectable neighborhood of good people."

Aunt Norma laid down the law as firmly as though *A Manual of Etiquette with Hints on Politeness and Good Breeding* provided her proverb for the day.

"Eat the oatmeal Lucinda made. Wash and dry your bowl." Shaking a brown-gloved finger toward me, she headed toward her car as two men carried a cot with a little pile of rags on it into the back of the ambulance. It might have been Mrs. Muller.

With an armlock, Mr. Whittaker marched Jeremiah down the street; or, he may have simply been helping his son into the pickup. Their voices were low, but argumentative. Jeremiah had given a half salute to Aunt Norma and shot me a lop-sided grin, but his freckles peppered a very pale face.

As I watched Lucinda climb into the back seat and Aunt Harriet settling herself into the passenger side of the Pierce Arrow, I took a couple of casual steps along the front walk. The faint scent of freedom was charging my curiosity register.

As the ambulance made a wide swing down the street and headed south, I eased a couple of more feet toward the Muller house. With no one at home and my keepers off on their little spree to a hospital across the state line, I'd have a world of time to investigate a few things.

The sound of screeching tires and the odor of burning rubber put every other thought out of my head but the realization that Aunt Norma had backed up two city blocks without looking behind her even once.

"Clio! Don't you even think about working on that map of yours! Put the cream in the Frigidaire. Call about the paint immediately, and don't you stir from that house. We'll call from the hospital. I expect you to answer."

CHAPTER 13

Just as the phone rang with Mr. Edwards telling me the earliest someone would be here to paint over the swastikas would be mid-afternoon, I considered my options. Never would I have a better opportunity to check out the Muller house and yard.

With Manboy and his mother aboard an ambulance tearing hell bent for leather across the Red River into Texas with my aunts and Lucinda riding shotgun behind them, I could hear that old Spiritual ringing in my head: "Oh, freedom, freedom over me."

First order of business was to find a shovel. The walls of Aunt Norma's garage sported every kind of rake and hoe known to the gardening world. Not a shovel was in sight, except for an old coalscuttle scoop. It would have to do.

I was feeling a bit queasy after putting away half a jar of Lucinda's peanut butter molasses cookies, instead of eating the oatmeal she left on the stove—or maybe thinking about the job ahead of me made me a bit green about the gills.

Grave digging was a morbid job. Exhuming bodies was disgusting. I had poked through old medical books at New York City's Public Library just to get a sense of what to look for at a homicide scene. Mother said the police are downright stingy about sharing information; so, reporters should be able to sort out bullet holes from stab wounds from the get-go.

If the body is in relatively good shape when it is buried—and if the soil is not acid or peaty—the corpse may reveal secrets, such as a bashed in skull or a ligature around the neck.

Two women had disappeared within the past year in Wolfe Flats. One of those women was Jeremiah's mother, last seen at the grocery store. The other was Mrs. Wallace's niece—just taking a stroll on a summer evening.

I sucked in and held my breath, waiting for something to gel. *Even if we only see one piece of the puzzle, we can imagine the rest.* Well. There it was. I liked to wait for those magical phrases that come into my head at critical moments. Mother called them my "little bromides." I don't think she intended that as a compliment.

Grabbing the coalscuttle scoop, I tested the worn, jagged front edge of it with my thumb. Sharp as a knife. *Time waits for no one.* I liked that. I think someone else may have said it first, but I dumped it in my bromide file for further use.

That big white shell of the Muller house appeared even more ominous with black spiders humped along the front of it. So no one passing by could see me, I took a shortcut from the alley, skirted a vegetable garden in sad repair, and scooted through the back gate to the picket fence where the gourds rattled in the morning breeze.

The heap of dirt mounded nicely, about six feet from stem to stern. In a warm climate, like southern Oklahoma, a buried body might hang on to soft tissue. That thought bothered me. I'd be prepared for hair, a few fingernails and a nice, clean skeleton.

Kneeling at what I thought might be the head of the grave, I began plunging in the scoop, flinging the soil behind me, and digging even faster. Too bad that I had forgotten to ask anyone about the color of Jeremiah's mother's hair or the hair of Mrs. Wallace's niece. One glimpse of hair of any color would be enough to make me hightail it down to the Sheriff's office and present myself as a sleuth to be reckoned with.

The soil was boggy with recent rains, so that it clumped into great clay masses that I had to pull up with both hands. I looked down at my hideous skirt from Lewin's store. The red clay of Oklahoma made an interesting new plaid. Sort of like the Royal Stewart gone native.

About two feet down, a distinctive shape formed beneath the clay. The arc of a skull and whitish molars in a jaw that seemed rather elongated. The hair. Oh, the hair was there in abundance, short and blondish and spread all over.

"Clio, dahling. I'm not questioning your little hobbies, but Martha deserves an eternity of rest." The soft, slightly accented voice whispering in my ear sent chills down my spine—as though the creature in the grave had moved those fierce jaws and spoken.

With all the strength I could muster, I flung myself back from the pit I had dug and landed in a sitting position against the rotten picket fence, a gourd dangling down each side of me like an exotic native dancer. But, my feet wouldn't move.

Smiling across the corpse of something clearly not human was the kindest human face I could imagine. His eyes were electric blue, the kind of blue that hides in deep crevasses in ancient glaciers, an all-knowing blue.

Soft, blondish curls framed a smooth, perfectly oval face with the kind of features that Julius Caesar would put on a marble plinth and claim as his own.

He pushed himself up awkwardly, using an old wooden crutch, and stuck out his hand. "Manford Muller. Otherwise known as Manboy."

No explanation was needed. Foreshortened arms stood out from a thick, squared-off body. His belt made a line across his body that was equidistant from the top of his head to the soles of his feet. His legs were the size of tree stumps. One ankle mushroomed feverously over the side of his house shoe.

Under normal circumstances of being caught in the act, I would have packed it in and dashed away—or, in a rush of adrenaline, flung that coal scoop hard enough to sever his carotid. By some strange magnetic force, I felt myself rising, reaching across the grave of Martha, and taking the hand of Manboy Muller.

"Martha was the dearest old thing. Arthritis crippled her before she finally went blind. Neither Mother nor I could bear to put her down. Your Aunt Harriet can be such a blessing." He continued to hold my hand as he stood on one leg and pushed clumps of soil back into the grave with his crutch.

I tried to envision my Aunt Harriet as a dog assassin. Then, I joined him with my left foot in what looked like a bizarre funeral rite.

"Harriet talked Doctor Lontry into giving us something for her evening milky drink, and Martha just didn't wake up the next morning. She always liked the compost pile by the fence where the sun shines in the afternoon, so that's where I put her."

As though finding a neighbor digging up his dead dog was not at all unusual, Manboy tamped down the soil a bit, still holding my hand, and turned me to face him. "Delia and I grew up together. When I saw you through the upstairs bathroom window the other night, I couldn't believe my eyes. It was as though time had looped around itself and gone back fifteen years. I was seeing Delia again."

He chuckled and swung my hand between us, the way that small children do to reassure themselves of companionship. "We strung tin cans on a wire from that little round window to my bedroom window and talked to each other. Mechanical vibrations. Not very effective, but we didn't have phones back then. Just one at the drugstore for emergencies."

He balanced on his good leg and shook his crutch. "That's why I hobbled out to look for you. Your Aunt Norma called from the hospital in Gainesville and was just this side of frantic. She said she had rung her house three times without an answer. I might have fibbed just a bit. I told her you were just in the back yard getting fresh air. Didn't say whose back yard," Manboy added. "By the way, Mother is much improved. She's been down with the flu for a week. Those swastikas were too much. Your aunts and Lucinda will stay a few hours with her."

Just as we rounded the massive line of evergreens that blocked any view of the house, the most enchanting panorama unfolded before us.

Like the magical road that bumped and swirled toward the Kingdom of Oz, a wide brick pathway meandered through immaculate rose gardens, around gray-green, leafy Hostas, past camellias casting their petals like flower girls at a wedding, and up to a wide, screened-in porch, gleaming with fresh, white paint.

"How could this . . . I mean, why would you?" I *couldn't seem to say what I meant. I knew why people in the northeast quadrant of Wolfe Flats didn't paint their houses. Being "uppity" might get a burning cross in your yard. But why would the Mullers present such a shabby front to passersby?*

"Same reason."

Manboy must be reading my mind. I dropped his hand and sank down on a bench under a little wooden trellis covered with jasmine. The seductive scent worked on my stress better than Aunt Harriet's lavender salts.

"Threats. They started coming right after President Roosevelt declared war. The first letter came in the mail a week after Pearl Harbor. Then, notes were shoved under the front door mat."

"But surely the police would," I sputtered.

"There are no police in Wolfe Flats, Clio. Just a county sheriff and his deputy. Sheriff McIver said the notes were probably from kids playing tricks. He said we shouldn't waste law enforcement resources on such nonsense."

Manboy's voice sunk to a monotone, as though he were reading from a bill of rights that didn't include the Mullers.

"He did say something else. Said it was off the record but that feelings were running high about the Germans now that boys in Wolfe County were in harm's way. Foreigners should pay heed."

"What does that mean? Foreigners should pay heed." I echoed indignantly.

"Mother and I think that it means we have no recourse under local law enforcement." Manboy's cheeks flushed slightly.

"But, what did the letters and notes say? How were they threatening?" Images of intimidating messages flashed before my eyes. The "black spot" on the backs of messages that pirates delivered in *Treasure Island* meant that death was on the way. Black swastikas on the house were even more ominous.

"The first letter traced our German origins back to Ham in the Bible and said we were cursed." Manboy grinned. "Got that one wrong. The writer doesn't know his Bible very well."

Manboy drew a fish in the dirt with the end of his crutch. "The next notes were even less Christian. Said we should not leave our house to mix with decent people."

"But that's like those European ghettos where Jewish people are forced to stay. Worse. Ghettos in cities have shops, places to go—just not very far." I was remembering what the Abrams had told me about their last days in Poland.

"We don't go anywhere now—not even to church. About six months ago, Mother stepped out one morning to pick up the milk and slipped in something caustic that had been tossed all over the porch and front of the house, causing the paint to peel."

He stared down at his fat, red ankle. "Unfortunately, Mother found the note in the milk bottle that day before I did. She became quite ill with fright. She insists we follow that psychopath's orders."

"Orders?" I had seen that small wisp of a woman being loaded onto a stretcher into the ambulance this very morning. What monster would threaten an old woman?

"The note showed a rather good sketch of me—if you like cartoons—hung from the elm in the front yard. I destroyed the note, but the words are etched here." He touched his forehead.

"Live like the slime you are. Do not put pure white on your dark hovel. Do not trim your rotten trees. Be a testament to all that is evil in your kind. Let that big, fancy house of yours rot with both of you inside, or next time I'll strike a match."

"Vandalism is bad enough. Terrorism is a worse crime. Why doesn't anyone . . ." I spurted out in exasperation, thinking of Aunt Norma's rebuke to me. *If Wolfe Flats is such a law-abiding community, why were the Mullers allowed to be intimidated?*

"They have. People from our church. Long-time friends. Your aunts. Lucinda. They've all paid a visit to the Sheriff. He tells them the same thing. As long as Germany is a threat to our national security, every German in this country is a potential undercover agent."

I stared into the gentle face of Manboy, searching for any sign of duplicity, and dropped my eyes in shame.

"That's the way people see things in a time of war. It's their natural right—doesn't have anything to do with someone else's legal rights. That's Sheriff McIver's opinion, so he does nothing," Manboy said.

"His opinion is utter horse ma . . . nonsense," I corrected myself, catching the briefest smirk on Manboy's face.

"It should be. It isn't. Our government has rounded up entire Japanese families in California, U.S. citizens, and put them in camps behind barbed wire. People are afraid, Clio. Fear makes people do things they normally wouldn't." He paused for a moment, staring off past the Victorian bibelots festooning the side of the house. "It's odd though. We haven't had a note for months, then this."

Manboy leaned toward me conspiratorily. "Something stirred up that psycho to make him paint swastikas all over our house. And this." He stuck his swelling foot out, hopping to maintain his equilibrium.

"Assault and battery," I asserted firmly. The criminal code and its assorted penalties were bread and butter to a reporter looking for headlines. Other mothers read bedtime stories; mine read the evening newspapers to me.

"No. I managed this on my own, Clio. After we got Mother off the porch, I rushed upstairs to get her some things for the hospital and missed the bottom step. My foot isn't broken. Lucinda checked. She's more reliable than an x-ray machine. She did tell me to keep it up."

He swung the crutch around and moved rather nimbly for a one-legged man toward a big glider at the back of the porch. "Let's sit in the swing, Clio, so you can admire this beautiful garden Jeremiah's mother Sonja designed. Then we need to figure out what to do about lunch. I told Norma I'd look after you."

CHAPTER 14

Just as I had been priming my pump, so to speak, for a visit down to the local sheriff's office to set him straight about the difference between *legal* rights and *natural* rights, Manboy had dropped a name that stopped me in my tracks. Sonja. Sonja Whittaker. Jeremiah's missing mother. This was her garden. Her Land of Oz.

"This garden. Jeremiah's mother designed it before she . . . disappeared?" I stuttered. My interest in the Muller back yard had waned considerably after I dug up the family dog. Now, it piqued.

"Yes. Sonja liked the idea of putting a victory garden into a setting where it didn't intrude—wouldn't take up arms against the kinds of flowers and bushes that Mother loves. Herbs are interspersed with flowers. Vegetables by the back fence. Sonja's so creative. Mother and I simply adore her."

It seemed a bit cruel to correct him, but shouldn't he be using the past tense for someone who'd been missing for almost a year?

"Do you like soda pop, Clio?"

Another mind-reading trick. This time, he was diverting me from my investigation of a serial kidnapper. I simply nodded at a question no one should need to ask.

Mother said that carbonated drinks would eat the enamel off my teeth. Aunt Norma said soda pop was banned from their house, along with alcohol. I thought that was taking temperance to an extreme degree.

"If you don't mind toting and fetching, you'll find every flavor in the icebox. There's ham and cheese on the lower shelf and a nice loaf of Lucinda's bread on the counter. We can have a little picnic out here."

Manboy scooted a low stool over and propped his foot on it as I opened the screen door. "I must apologize for being such a poor host. I'll make it up to you. Promise."

He already had. When I swung the Frigidaire door wide, bottle after bottle lined the shelves. Nesbitt's orange. Royal Crown and Coca-Cola. Overwhelming. I could choose a Grapette, but the bottle was so small. I went for the orange and grabbed a Royal Crown for Manboy.

Whacking off slices of ham and cheese with a dull knife (I checked the drawers for suspicious stilettos), I piled everything into a basket, snapped off the pop caps, and edged the screen door open with one foot.

"While we're out here in what I call Sonja's garden, I've been thinking about your friendship with Jeremiah."

I liked the way that Manboy got right down to the nuts and bolts of things. Sitting bolt upright, I clamped my mouth over delicious orange fizz that decided to bubble wastefully out of the bottle and forced myself to listen. Questions are my strong suit, although Mother says investigative reporters must learn to listen for nuances or they'll miss important clues.

"There's no shortage of orange sodas, Clio. That one's spewing like Mount Vesuvius. Help yourself to . . ."

"I'm more interested in what you were saying about Jeremiah and his mother." I was desperate to get Manboy back on track. My track.

"Well. Actually I wasn't. Now that you put it that way, I guess that is exactly what has been bothering me. Jeremiah and his mother. Do you have any idea why Jeremiah can't forgive her?"

The orange pop spewed noisily over my plaid skirt and dripped onto Manboy's swollen foot as my jaw dropped. *Forgive her? For being kidnapped?* "But . . . Jeremiah's mother . . . and Mrs. Wallace's niece . . . they . . ." My theory about a serial kidnapper was being sorely tested.

"Never met each other as far as I know. Miss Carson's disappearance is worrisome. Very worrisome." Manboy turned those pellucid eyes toward me, and all I could see in them was puzzlement.

"You don't think that . . . surely no one . . ." Manboy shook his head as though trying to clear it of an unpleasant thought. "People handle stressful situations differently—fight or flight is a physiological response of the sympathetic nervous system. The reality of long-term stress is different. The response is to endure or escape; those are either habitual or planned responses."

I might have rolled my eyes back just the tiniest bit. Hot on the trail of Jeremiah's missing mother, and here I was getting a watered down lecture in physiology.

"Boring you, am I, Clio? It's easy to do when your main company is the depressing evening war news and an increasingly frail mother who's frightened by what's happening on our property. I was trying to make a point of sorts, but you want to hear about Jeremiah's mother."

I nodded enthusiastically, trying not to think about my mother's sympathetic nervous system. She had that flight thing down pat.

"When Luke—he is Sonja's oldest son—joined the Navy without a word, Sonja felt guilty. What she had endured for . . . well, that's not for me to say. Sonja was allowed to landscape our backyard, because we could pay her. She spent three or four days a week for six months on our project. All that talent—landscaping as well as botany. She's as impressive as Capability Brown."

Back went my eyes again, rolling heavenward, as they tended to do when names were being dropped that didn't mean a thing to me.

"Capability Brown was a famous English landscape architect. That's one nickname that doesn't stick in the craw," Manboy said with a perfectly straight face.

"Jeremiah's mother designed this backyard as a retreat for my mother, because she is fearful of going out to the front porch until this morning when, for some reason, she stepped outside, saw those swastikas, and fainted." Manboy's bright eyes clouded over for an instant. "I intend to get to the bottom of this, as soon as . . ."

I've yet to encounter a person in Wolfe Flats who can stay on a topic of interest to me for more than two minutes. "You were telling me about Jeremiah's mother."

"Oh, yes, daughter of Delia. I'll get to the point. This garden became Sonja's retreat. Things weren't going well at home. Even after her work was done, she continued stopping by several times a week. We came to know her very well. Such a kind and gifted person. She doesn't deserve Jeremiah's anger. He needs to forgive her."

"She vanished from the grocery store parking lot! Jeremiah is obviously worried to death. He's too sad or too scared to even talk about her," I blurted out in frustration. This fixation of Manboy on Sonja Whittaker as a gardening guru seemed to be clouding the issue of her disappearance.

I was on board with Jeremiah about the fact that he didn't talk about his mother. I didn't talk about mine either. Some things are too close to the bone for idle chatter. My mother wasn't exactly missing, unless the Nazis had captured her, but I knew the kind of ache that gnawed into the very heart and soul of someone who couldn't produce a mother.

Having his mother snatched mid-afternoon in the Little Dixie Grocery parking lot by a nameless maniac was gut-wrenching. Why was Manboy blathering on about forgiveness? I glowered at Manboy and gave my orange soda pop a good shake to release its pent-up fury in his direction.

"Jeremiah is worried? Scared? We thought he was angry. Surely, his father wouldn't. No father could do that." Manboy tossed out clues faster than I could absorb them, then sat with what appeared to be an advanced case of lockjaw.

I rubbed the arm that Jeremiah's father had grabbed yesterday. Considering my initial rough encounter with Mr. Whittaker and Lucinda's outburst of anger toward him, anything was believable. I was just about to shove the first suspect's face, George Whittaker, into a mental file marked "fishy people" when Manboy interrupted.

"I'd like for you to go inside, Clio, and bring me a letter that is sitting on the small table by the front door." Manboy's voice held just a tinge of something I thought might be regret.

Walking quietly down a hall with paintings of slaughtered rabbits and piles of grapes similar to the ones that lined Aunt Norma's hallway, I remembered that the Abrams and I had carefully avoided those rooms in the Metropolitan. "Cezanne's still lives won't give us nightmares," Mr. Abrams had whispered, steering me past the open maws of wild game dangling amidst fruit and vegetables.

On a highly polished low table just to the left of one of the beveled glass panels in the front door sat an envelope neatly lettered: *Jeremiah Whittaker, Rural Route 3, Wolfe Flats, Oklahoma.* There was no return address.

I tested the flap with my thumb. Sealed tighter than Dick's hatband.

I trotted back down the hall, shoved open the screen door, and, wordlessly, handed it to Manboy, and watched him rip it open.

"Just read it. Then, we'll talk."

The handwriting on the onionskin paper swirled across the page with ovals and arches that would have made Mrs. Wallace proud. I'm not sure about the words themselves.

"My dear son,

This is the fortieth letter I've written to you since I left, and I am reluctant to tell you that I'm not sure when my next letter will arrive. Because of my special expertise, the government has asked me to go with some of my colleagues to a place some distance away.

If Luke, along with all those other brave boys, had the courage to volunteer, I can't do less. Because of security issues, I cannot tell you where we are going or how long we will be gone. Below is an A.P.O. address where you can write to me.

Jeremiah, my dear, dear boy. You cannot know how desperate I am to have just one word from you. Just one to let me know that you do not despise your mother for what she had to do. The person I was disappeared long before the person that I needed to be took charge of her life again. I don't expect you to understand that. When you're older, you may.

I have to believe that your father is taking good care of you. My friends tell me that you look well. Your father loves you as he does Luke in spite of the words between them.

It breaks my heart that you have not responded to a single letter of mine. I tried to explain in the initial letters why I had to leave without saying anything to you and why any letters sent to me had to go to a post office box in Wolfe Flats for forwarding. I won't belabor those issues. They must be as hurtful to you as they are to me.

Just a small note that says you are all right or one of your drawings that made me laugh would be all that I need to feel that the world will be sane soon, and we'll be together again.

Your mother who loves you more than you can imagine."

At the bottom of the letter was a tiny flower with five leaves.

Feeling overwhelmed by so much affection and regret on that single page of paper, I thought of my own mother who had flown the coop, skedaddled, and taken the slow boat to where ever the action might be.

I hadn't received a single letter since she dumped me with Aunt Norma and Aunt Harriet. Moreover, if she wrote it would be something like: "*You can't believe how exciting it is to be where things are really happening. I miss you. Take care of yourself. Say hello to the aunts for me.*"

The only notes I ever got from Mother were taped to the refrigerator, reminding me to pick up groceries or her dry cleaning—and not to forget to do my homework. At that moment, I simply could not restrain two big fat tears dripping down the sides of my nose.

Politely, Manboy turned away as though my emotional state was too personal to share. It was. So I turned it on its end.

"When a mother leaves, she should at least say where she's going and why. Anything else is unforgivable. And what's that stupid little flower thing at the bottom? She didn't even sign it."

"It's a Scarlet Pimpernel. You know the novel about a spy who helped people escape the guillotine during the French Revolution. Sonja told me that Jeremiah wanted her to read "that damned, elusive Pimpernel" over and over. It became their private joke. Something to do with laying low."

Actually, I hadn't read the book, but I had seen Leslie Howard and Merle Oberon in the movie. Mother loved movies about anyone risking life and limb for a cause.

At the very moment my mother's taxi pulled away the day she left me with the aunts, I imagined a giant guillotine hanging over her neck. Her chestnut hair would be tied up in a snood, something like Marie Antoinette wore so the blade could do its job cleanly. I might have shouted at the cab: "Stay out of France." But, she wouldn't have listened.

"I saw the movie," I muttered, staring at Manboy as he carefully creased the page and put it back in the envelope.

"That's nice. Mother and I haven't been to a movie in a coon's age. She's too afraid to leave the house. That makes it a kind of prison for . . ." He pushed himself awkwardly up on one leg, tucked the crutch under his arm, and thrust the letter toward me.

"I'm going to break a promise that I made to Sonja not to interfere—except for putting her letters in envelopes addressed to Jeremiah and posting them in Wolfe Flats. She did not want her husband to know that she was in Stillwater, back at her college. After what you've said, I don't think Jeremiah has seen one of her letters."

"Then, Sheriff McIver will have to arrest Jeremiah's father. It's illegal to take someone else's mail. I guess the feds will have to arrest him. It's a federal offense," I added prissily.

"Sonja does not want her husband arrested, Clio. She relies on him to look after Jeremiah. And, I doubt that the postmistress would be party to such a thing. That mysterious P.O. box number would simply disappear. It's a moot point now. Sonja has a new A.P.O. address. I doubt that George could track her down if he wanted to."

"Her letter said something about her special expertise. What is that? We might figure out where she's gone if we knew that." At the moment, my sleuthing impulse outweighed my curiosity for what George Whittaker had done to cause his wife to go on the lam.

"Fungi," Manboy responded without so much as a quiver of interest in where I might be going with this.

"Fun . . . what?" The only flora and fauna in our apartment in New York were dust bunnies that bred under beds and spores of mildew climbing up the bathroom wall.

"Mushrooms, mold, that sort of thing. She was doing her master's work in that field. I've no idea how it would fit in with the war effort, but it obviously does if she's been recruited."

Manboy glanced up at the sun that splintered that evergreen barrier with shafts of light. "I need to call the hospital to check on Mother. It's almost two o'clock. Your aunts and Lucinda said they'd call before starting home."

He looked at me with those glacier-deep eyes that seemed to hold a world of worry. "I don't want you to do something that makes you uncomfortable, Clio. I know Jeremiah has been a friend to you. I wouldn't want that to change. It's hard being the new kid in a small town. You need a good friend."

He held out the letter on a flat palm, a casual gesture. "You decide if you want to give him the letter. If not, I'll post it as I did the others. Maybe George will have a change of heart and tell Jeremiah that his mother has gone God knows where."

Restoring Jeremiah's mother to him tantalized me, rather like raising Lazarus without the drama. I dropped the letter into the pocket of my baggy skirt. The screen door closed softly behind Manboy. I picked up our plates and dumped the crumbs of bread and cheese and ham for the birds to find. It was time to get myself back to my aunts' house and do a lot of thinking.

CHAPTER 15

Half an hour later, to divert myself from the tricky decision about how to restore Jeremiah's mother when she had probably taken herself off to another continent, I drew up yet another crime board for my bedroom wall. Mrs. Wallace's niece still qualified as missing, and I struggled to find any clues.

The lion's head knocker on the front door banged with authority. Surely, Aunt Norma wouldn't have returned from the Gainesville hospital and forgotten her key.

Just as I swung one side of the heavy front door open, an arm the color of a corpse shot past me. The body that followed was Whitey Lewin's. Clutched under his other arm was one of those fancy gilt boxes that hold nice things. Or not.

"Hello again, dear little Clio, dear Delia's daughter."

"My aunts and Lucinda will be back at any minute. You'd better wait until they're here. They don't want me to . . ." I staggered back into the hall, startled at the number of "dears" he could crank out in a second and alarmed by the bright hue that flushed that pasty face of Lester Lewin.

"Liar. Liar. Pants on fire." He sniggered. "I called the nurses station at the hospital. Your aunts are waiting for the doctor to make rounds before they leave. Why they'd waste their time on traitors is beyond me. But, that's neither here nor there."

He poked the box toward me. No. Into me. Smack against my solar plexus, so hard that I almost tripped while backing farther down the hall.

"Sorry, Clio. Don't know my own strength. Unloading boxes for the store tends to keep me fit as a fiddle." He turned sideways like that boxer on the front of Mrs. Wallace's romance novel and raised one arm, flexing his muscles.

I was wrong. Whitey Lewin's arm was the color and texture of a marshmallow that has been dropped into the ashes. Hundreds of tiny, kinky, black hairs covered his arm from the wrist clear up to the armpit. His short sleeve left nothing to the imagination. I'd rather that it had. Steel wool in an armpit was off-putting to say the least.

"I'm a long-time friend of your aunts, Clio. I'd think you'd invite me to sit a spell. And open this little present I brought for you." Without another word, he spun into the front parlor, plopped himself down on Aunt Norma's green baize loveseat, and waited.

He'd wait a long time. Two exits were possibilities. The hall led straight to the kitchen and out the back door—or, if I were quick enough, I could lope along to the front door, down the sidewalk, and bang on the door of a "traitor."

Just as anger was overcoming fear, my visitor made his move. It was impossible to imagine, but that skinny, pale man unraveled himself into a formidable net of arms and legs in the archway leading out of the parlor.

Blocked from leaving the room, I eyed him uneasily.

He popped the box lid up and dangled a peach-colored nylon slip from two fingers. "Just your color, Clio. You have that nice dusky tint to your skin. Like your mother. Flushes like a ripe apple when you get excited. Soft as silk."

For a man whose skin color was something of an anomaly, Whitey Lewin appeared to be fixated on skin—perhaps he wasn't an albino, just as Aunt Norma had said, but his mother's talcum powder seemed to have become embedded in his epidermis.

The peach slip slithered from between his fingers and wound itself around the upper part of my body like something disgustingly alive and odiferous.

"I sprayed it with Night in Paris cologne. Delia loved that cologne." Like a boa scenting prey, he coiled along the backside of the loveseat, continuing to block the exit with one leg.

That was a downright lie. Mother hated artificial scents. Gave her terrible allergies. Just being in a room with someone who wore perfume could bring on spasms of sneezing and turn Mother's nose into a flaming torch.

"Mother is allergic to perfume. So am I." I might have lied at that point, but the mercury on my comfort level was dropping fast. "Aunt Norma doesn't like this kind of thing. She wouldn't let me accept it." I peeled the clinging slip off and tossed it back toward the box. It slid down into a pitiful, shiny pile.

Suddenly, I thought of Mrs. Muller on the front porch, lying so still, so helpless, so stricken by those dreadful swastikas painted on her house.

"Did you just call Mrs. Muller a traitor?" The booming voice that asked the question didn't sound like mine, but I was the only other person in the room.

"Well, maybe the old woman isn't complicit, but that strange son of hers has connections that are very suspect. You know she married her first cousin. Same name of Muller. He got into this country by the skin of his teeth to finish high school with decent people. That was before Germany started the first war," he sneered.

"My own father died fighting the Germans in that war. He is buried somewhere in France. A hero. I take pride in that. Those Mullers have no reason to be proud. Genetics tripped them up. No hiding the cousin connection with a freak like Manboy," he leered, picking up the slip, and folding it expertly back into the box.

"Second cousins aren't a problem. People in this part of the country like keeping things in the family. My second cousin Louise and I might have . . . well . . . if things had . . ." he blurted out.

Then, Whitey Lewin nodded toward me as though we were in cahoots. This genealogical twist his dialogue was taking seemed harmless, but odd. I thought he was packing up the slip to leave, so I relaxed my guard for just a moment.

"I'll never tell your aunts about this little present if you don't. A girl as pretty as you shouldn't be wearing tacky old cotton undies."

Before I could move one foot toward the hall, the boa constrictor looped itself into a breath-stultifying clutch around my body. Instead of a smooth, rubbery inner tube that would keep squeezing until I quit breathing, the boa sprouted arms and hands and dozens of prying fingers.

At his touch, those two little circles on my chest that I had imagined were trying their best to sprout into breasts sucked themselves so far into my rib cage that I was sure they'd never surface again.

That's when I became my mother's own daughter. Living two blocks from the worst slum in a metropolitan city gave her a healthy respect for the finer points of self-defense. When we weren't dancing to "Tangerine," we were practicing elbow jabs and a judo kick to the privates that will drop an average fellow to the floor.

Like lush green vines, Aunt Norma's velvet drapes hung behind my back. Grabbing a fistful of them, I launched myself off the floor, swinging like Tarzan into space. Those stiff-toed, patent leather Mary Janes of mine leveraged my kick into a double whammy.

The curtain rod crashed down about the same time that Whitey Lewin screamed. I'd have an easier time explaining the dangling drapes than he would as to why he was hobbling out the front door bent over like a croquet hoop.

BY THE TIME that Aunt Norma tooted the horn on the Pierce Arrow and clouted the side of the garage a good one with the left fender, I had restored order. A perfectly good peach nylon slip clung in black, sticky curls to the barrel in the alley. The velvet drape hunkered down on itself below the window as though the bracket on top had simply given up the ghost.

Some things are better tucked away for future use. The gift box covered with Whitey's fingerprints held pride of place under my bed. Sadly, my stunning use of karate that might have unmanned Whitey in more ways than he could imagine couldn't be shared with the aunts or Lucinda. Brawling wasn't a word in my aunts' lexicon.

Except for an occasional squeeze from Lucinda, touching rarely occurred in this house. A garment straightened. A bow on my pigtails retied. One of those distant air kisses flying past my cheek was my aunts' idea of affection. Passion might be found between the covers of pulp magazines at the local drugstore, but not in this house.

The most rousing events in this house came over the evening news in the form of "air strikes" that had been sanitized for public consumption and were safely on other continents, far away.

Sometimes, in the Methodist Church, when the choir finally got to the seventh verse of "O for a

Thousand Tongues to Sing," my aunts would get a kind of glazed look in their eyes—that was probably fatigue rather than arousal.

Placidity was the watchword in the Clower aunts' domain. I could make it work for me if I used my noggin. I helped Aunt Norma fold up her velvet drapes and sweep up shards of plaster; I was the soul of industry and helpfulness.

"I heard a noise, Aunt Norma. A loud thump. Looks like the weight was just too much for the screws." I held up the offending bracket. It wasn't exactly a lie. My weight was too much for the screws.

CHAPTER 16

L ike one of those ancient cartographers sketching the world with a few facts and considerable imagination, I needed to get on with the task at hand, deducing the fate of Mrs. Wallace's niece, now that Jeremiah's mother had been found—if not located.

Saturday's sun was dropping low in the sky. Two important places should be on my map of Wolfe Flats— the *Wolfe Flats Weekly* place of business and Sheriff McIver's office.

"I need to check out a book from the library before it closes, Aunt Norma." I lied with insouciance. Love that word. Casual indifference would be my cover-up while I was sleuthing about town. "A class project is due Monday."

"Fine time to be rememberin' that when it's gettin' on to closing." Lucinda eyed me suspiciously. Then she winked. "Fried chicken and gravy will be on the table at six o'clock. I figure you'll get your errands done by then."

JUDGING BY THE noise, The *Wolfe Flats Weekly* was a hive of activity. Great, slamming presses somewhere below cranked out the next edition. I pushed open the glass-fronted "Newsroom" door into a small area with a couple of desks. The stout body of a woman with a brassy, blondish hank of hair rolled into perfect submission sat with her back toward me.

"Just a sec, honey. Got to get this finished before Harold shuts down his Linotype for the day." Behind the desk, poking at a Royal typewriter with inch-long nails, sat the antithesis of Mother, who typed faster than a machine gun could fire and thought that long painted nails were a plot to handicap women.

Ripping a sheet of paper out of the black rubber roller, the woman made a few pencil marks on the page and shouted: "Jake! Come get this for Harold. If you think I'm going back there again, you've got bats in your belfry!"

She grinned at me. "Sally Tolliver. Business manager. Ace reporter. General gofer. Jake!" Her bellow was a sound to be reckoned with. "Dammit! If you're back there smoking by the press again, you'll wish you . . ."

"I wish it every time I hear your sweet voice, Sally."

A gangly teenager, with a porkpie hat and too many rolls of his droopy white socks surrounding skinny shanks, eased into the room with the panache of Mickey Rooney, deciding on a tall tale for his father, the judge.

"Get this to Harold. Front page if he can squeeze it in."

"Baptist fish fry down at the River tonight. Harold went out the back door fifteen minutes ago. I'm working the press. He said that I could crank up his Linotype as long as he doesn't know it. Union stuff. Leave it to me, Sally, my love. Don't get your . . ."

Jake glanced over at me dismissively, snatched the paper from Sally's hand, and shouted back from the doorway "Your whatever pulls your chain in a wringer."

"If Jake could set type as fast as he runs his mouth, we'd all be out of here before the stroke of midnight. Sorry, dear." She smiled at me. "What is it you want?"

"I'd like to see past issues from last August or clippings if you keep them in the morgue, any unsolved cases of disappearing people. A school project," I added. I was sure this Sally person would be impressed with me calling the file cabinets "the morgue." Newspaper vernacular rolled right off my tongue, thanks to Mother.

"You're Delia's daughter!" Her screech could have stopped the presses. "Oh my God. You look just like her. I heard she'd left you with her aunts. Lord help us! Delia Number Two come back to keep us on our toes!" Sally flushed a bright pink that took issue with that crimped roll of bleached hair blocking one eye with a cantilevered set of bangs.

Clasped against a prickly wool twin set and being jiggled past all endurance, I tried in the most polite manner to disengage myself from Sally Tolliver, who was now clinging to me like a limpet.

"I went to school with Delia—elementary through high school. There wasn't anything she couldn't dream up to do. What a hoot! I just loved her to death!" She squealed, patting my cheek as though it were a percussion instrument.

This woman's love for my mother was about to dislodge my lower mandible. I pried her hands away and gripped them in my own as though I might be overcome with emotion—in fact, I was wishing I had a pair of handcuffs.

"Sorry, sorry. Too many memories. Just caught me off guard. You're Clio. Your aunts told me when you were born. That naughty Delia didn't so much as send me an announcement. And me one of her best friends." She sank back down in her chair and stared blankly out the window. Turning toward me, wide-eyed, with mascara streaming below her eyes like a French mime, she asked: "You're looking for disappearing people in Wolfe Flats? Delia's girl wants to find the missing?"

She smacked her thigh with the flat of her hand and whooped loudly enough to bring Jake back from the pressroom. He stood quizzically in the doorway, his hands dangling.

"Go away, Jake. Go break Harold's Linotype. We're busy here." Sally's booming voice let everyone on Main Street know that we were busy.

I ducked my head and took a few shuffling steps toward the door. Obviously, for some odd reason related to my mother, I was the source of pent-up amusement for Sally. "I guess I can come back when you're not so . . ."

"So what? Busy? Never too busy for Delia's daughter. You just took me aback, Clio. I remember when Delia went missing that time. We were seniors. Her Aunt Norma called out the National Guard. She drove to Ardmore and demanded that they find Delia."

Sally flipped that Veronica Lake flap of hair back from her left cheek and eyed me with a degree of skepticism. "She was exactly where I knew she'd be. Where she shouldn't be. Delia always decided. No one could tell her what to do or when to do it. Delia's daughter wouldn't be looking for missing people in general. What missing person specifically?"

I'd better just come right out with it, although the information about my mother being missing was more interesting than Mrs. Wallace's niece. "I'm doing a report for class; I heard about my teacher's niece disappearing last August. I'm feeling really bad for Mrs. Wallace . . . and, of course, any other disappearances." I patched on something that would make my inquiry less nosy. A report, I'd said, to cover my tracks.

"That old bat might have done it herself for all I know. I met Ellen Carson. Nice girl. She wasn't too keen on staying with her aunt."

The clock on the wall above Sally Tolliver's desk chugged through the seconds. I needed to get to the newspaper archives. "If I could just see some of the newspaper files. Get an objective account from a news story." I shot Sally one of my most disarming smiles.

"Hoo, girl. You are your mother incarnate." Sally's hoot rang out gleefully. "Can't pull the wool over my eyes."

Sticking out a leg tinted an orangey hue meant to disguise the fact that nylons were in short supply, Sally hooked the toe of her black pump around a stool and pulled it over. "Sit, Clio. I'm the journalist. Rarely objective, but I've covered the stories of those missing girls. No need to rat through those old newspapers in the back. You might not be here if that first girl hadn't disappeared."

I lowered myself gingerly on the stool and stared up into the face of my mother's childhood friend who had just dropped a bombshell on me.

"That last year of high school, Delia got accepted to Columbia in New York, but her aunts said Southern Methodist in Dallas or Oklahoma University in Norman were her only options. Wouldn't hear of her going to New York. They dug in and Delia acted out. When she was . . . at Lake Murray. Never mind that. Bad incident. Delia finally came back. Yelled the house down. Might of stayed longer . . . with George . . . but that's neither here nor there."

I inched closer to her. *It was. It was. She knew something about Jeremiah's father and my mother.* "I met George Whittaker. He seems very . . . impulsive." I thought that might open the floodgates.

Sally's big brown eyes narrowed to slits. "I've said too much. Delia wouldn't like that. We always swore.

See." She held up a wrist with an odd little hook-shaped scar. "Blood sisters never tell."

I could feel my face falling. I'd never had a sister, much less one sealed in sisterhood by blood. Staring at the dirty tiled floor, I muttered: "If I could just take a look at the story in the newspaper."

Fingers light as feathers danced across my neck, alongside my chin, and lifted my face. "I didn't mean to be rude, Clio. I just promised Delia something . . . a long time ago. I can tell you about the missing girls. That was a careless thing I said about you not being here if that girl hadn't disappeared. Stupid really." Sally rolled her chair next to my stool so that our knees touched.

"Delia and I both wanted to be reporters. We dreamed of being Brenda Starr before she became a comic strip character. We didn't want to be teachers or nurses or get married. That's about all women could aim for back then. Delia was determined to go to New York. Her aunts wanted her within driving distance." She shifted uncomfortably.

"As oldest in a family of six children, I wasn't going anyplace but the workplace. I was a good speller and didn't dangle modifiers, so the *Weekly* took me on when I graduated. Been here ever since."

"But I don't see how a girl disappearing had anything . . ."

"Just in a roundabout way, Clio. Let me remember." She paused, wrinkled her forehead like a piece of corrugated cardboard, and said: "It was August, 1927, two months after we graduated. Hottest damn summer on record. The girl's name was Eula Harrison, a year behind us in school. She sang like an angel."

Sally stared into space as the Linotype clinked rhythmically, casting slugs of hot metal type. "Odd that the memory comes back so clearly. Eula and George Whittaker sang a duet that Sunday. 'Whispering Hope.' Out of the *Cokesbury Hymnal*. In D-flat major."

I shifted my stool backwards as Sally took in a considerable gulp of air. Surely she wouldn't. She did.

"Whispering hope . . . whispering hope . . . angel's sweet song." Sally scooted her chair closer. "George sang harmony until the chorus—then he sang that line just behind Eula's fine soprano voice. The whole congregation was struck dumb. I think that's when Delia. Or maybe not."

Sally shifted to a matter-of-fact tone: "That's the last time I saw Eula. George and other choir members would have seen her at choir practice on the following Wednesday. She left the Methodist Church around 8 p.m. after practice and simply vanished. That beautiful voice gone forever."

"Did any suspects pop up?" I asked casually, trying to get Sally back on track and avoid another songfest.

"George Whittaker was hauled in for questioning. His nice baritone voice made him a suspect. My off-key alto kept me out of the choir," Sally added with that plaintive edge that asked for an affirmation that her "Whispering Hope" wasn't half bad.

It was. So, I tried to move the investigation back onto Jeremiah's father. "Why was he a suspect?"

"Blood in the bed of his pickup truck. It's hard to believe, Clio, but our sheriff back then would have flunked an IQ test. He claimed hogs weren't butchered until September, so George's story about butchering wouldn't hold water."

"Did he put Mr. Whittaker in jail?" Images of Jeremiah's father yelling in a cell appealed to me. I needed to check out the local jail. The sheriff lived in the upper story; the prisoners were jailed below. A flash of envy struck me. I could hone my interrogation skills if I lived above a jail.

"No. Amos Larson, a nice colored man who helps George with his farm, came forward. George had taken the hog's forequarter and chitlins over to Amos. Unfortunate in a way that Amos got involved. That turned the sheriff's attention to the colored part of town."

Sally's voice dropped to almost a whisper. "Since I knew Eula and her family from church, I was told to help cover the story. I watched them drag farm ponds, bring in coonhounds to sniff around, and search the houses of those poor folks—simply because they needed someone to blame. Eula's home was over by that gin closest to town. Wrong side of town."

Sally reached for my hand as though she needed comfort. I inched my stool closer. She had a nice sandalwood scent.

"Delia's aunts were terrified to let her out of their sight. At night, Wolfe Flats was a ghost town. Two crosses were burned on yards as a warning. For what I still can't imagine," added, shaking her head. "That's when Delia's aunts bought her a train ticket to New York. They told her Columbia would probably be safer than this place. So she left. Met your father. Had you. I just wish that she . . ."

"You said three girls." Interviewing a reporter should be easier. I knew about my mother meeting my father, having me, and not much liking the idea of the three of us. I didn't want to relive that part of Mother's history. Not now. Not with a stranger.

"Yes. The second girl's disappearance was on Bloody Saturday. That was August 14, 1937, when the Japanese bombed Shanghai. Sorry, Clio. Your mother and I think alike when we try to relate events in history. Does she still put up maps all over the walls?"

I nodded, grim-lipped, trying to understand what the Japanese had to do with girls disappearing in Wolfe Flats.

"The second girl was Louise Lewin, a distant cousin of the woman who owns the local department store. You know that store?"

I twitched uncomfortably. The big cotton bloomers hanging almost to my knees were a testament to Lewin fashion. I wondered if Whitey Lewin was holding ice packs between his knees at this very moment.

"As I recall, Louise moved in with the Lewins early that summer. Her father had some kind of import business in Ft. Worth and was in Asia when the war broke out over there. She had no other relatives, so Mrs. Lewin offered her a home. Louise designed lovely window exhibits. People would go by the store just to look in the windows. After the Dustbowl and the Depression, seeing something pretty was an upper."

"She's Whitey Lewin's cousin?" All his blather about cousins this afternoon was trying to make a connection somewhere in my brain.

"Distant. Maybe a second cousin of his mother's. Something like that. Nice girl. We met at the soda fountain a couple of times. Louise was only eighteen but had already done a stint in some kind of design program in Texas. She loved that kind of work."

Sally seemed more caught up in what career Louise Lewin was carving out for herself than her vanishing act.

"So what happened on August 14?" I interrupted.

"Besides the Japs taking out two hotels in Shanghai?"

Sally seemed a bit miffed. I patted her knee to reassure her that I was entranced by her account, whatever account she might be tallying at the moment.

"Louise worked late, filling the windows with vases full of sunflowers and draping yards of bright yellow fabric, as though the sun's rays were paying a visit. A lovely work of art."

I waited breathlessly, trying to imagine Lewin's dusty store, piled with boxes, being anything but tacky.

"She locked the front door just at sunset, walked by the drugstore, waved to the pharmacist, turned the corner, and was never seen again." Tears flushed Sally's eyes.

Mine too as I imagined Louise locking the door on her sunflowers, waving and vanishing—never to see a flower again.

Sally dragged both thumbs under my eyes, wiped them on her skirt, forced a smile, and said: "Whenever the sunflowers bloom, I always think of Louise. That's our three girls, Clio: Eula with an enchanting voice; Louise who could create a beautiful display; and, Ellen, who was going to teach our first graders. Talented young women. Gone. No trace. No answers."

The banging on the outside window of the *Weekly* provided an answer of sorts. Lucinda, her face dark with irritation, mouthed something that I knew was not what I wanted to hear.

"Lucinda!" Sally shoved back her chair and hurried over to unlock the front door. "Come in. Clio and I have been visiting about Delia and . . . other things."

"It's them other thin's thet's gonna git that girl in a world of hurt. I had to make an excuse that I was outa milk for the gravy and come look for you, Clio." Lucinda glowered at me then beamed at Sally.

"How you, Sally?" Lucinda gave her a big hug. "Anythin' happenin' in town?"

"Besides swastikas being painted on the Muller house? And giving poor Mrs. Muller a heart attack?"

"Anxiety. Thet's what the doc in Gainesville tole us. He said stress kin make a body sick. Particularly an ole woman who ain't too well to begin with." Lucinda settled her ample bottom on the corner of Sally's desk. "If this paper has any influence on Sheriff McIver, Sally, we'd be obliged if someone would make him pay attention to folks that cain't take up for theirselves."

"Sheriff McIver is a cretin, Lucinda. The unease that this war causes is right up his alley. He fans rumors into flames, trying to make his life more interesting than hogs getting out on the highway or old Deke pissing in the water trough."

Sally looped her arm around my neck and squeezed me until I wanted to scream uncle. "I can't believe Delia's little girl is here. It's like having Delia back. I just can't quit hugging this sweet child."

Lucinda, arching one eyebrow like an inverted "V" about to blast off her face, made a noise like "Huummph," and grabbed my arm. "This sweet chile will have some explainin' to do to her Aunt Norma if we don't git home."

Sally reached over to give Lucinda a calming pat. "Tell Miss Norma that Clio was simply doing some historical research for a school project."

Just as we were pushing open the heavy glass door leading outside, Sally shouted loud enough for half of Wolfe Flats to hear her: "Thanks for reminding me, Lucinda. I'll be visiting Sheriff McIver. He needs to explain what he's doing to investigate the harassment of the Mullers. Manboy is a nice person. He and Delia were good friends. She'd expect me to do my best for him and his mother."

CHAPTER 17

Try as I might, I couldn't come up with another good excuse to miss church the next day. Belly-aches, headaches, a toothache, and an onset of melancholia due to no word from Mother had served me well for last Sunday.

Even Lucinda had joined the Easter Parade, with jet beads bobbing alongside some dead bird's wing, dangling lifelessly off her hat.

Looking as though I had merged with the spirit of the occasion in my bumblebee dress, I pulled on the white gloves Aunt Harriet handed me and slunk along behind them for a six-block stroll to the Methodist Church.

Like a parade with something at the end to attract the masses, men, women, and children, polished and crimped and smelling of camphor, joined us along the way. Aunt Norma smiled and nodded and gestured toward me like Victoria showing off her German prince. "My niece. Delia's child. Living with us now that Delia's off to war. Serving her country, as we all must. Pitching in where we can."

Good show, I thought. First, she casts Mother as dutiful. Then, she conveniently forgets the little fit she had when she scraped an empty sugar bowl this morning.

"Get another ration book, Lucinda! Find any excuse. I will not use molasses in my morning coffee. War or no war!"

Except for a sham steeple with a bell that hung precariously at an awkward angle, the church looked like a rectangular box. Inside wasn't much of an improvement. No sad plaster face of the Virgin Mary. No gilt angels with outstretched wings. Wolfe Flats Methodist Church couldn't hold a candle to Saint Peter's on Barclay in Manhattan.

The four of us moved lead-footed past rows of pews to one just two rows from the front. "The Clower pew, Clio. Your great-great-grandfather worshipped here."

Examining the aisle pew for a nice little bronze marker, I couldn't see anything that suggested ownership. "There's no name on it. On any of them."

"No need. We don't have graven images in our church. Don't need them. People just know." Aunt Norma handed me a buckram-bound hymnal and pointed to a wooden sign on the wall to the right. "Hymns 22 and 231. Study them so you'll sing on key. And, quit staring at people. Act like you've been in church before."

I had. When no service was in session, I sometimes wandered into those beautiful, lavish churches in Manhattan where small votive candles flickered in red glass. A cassocked priest might amble by without a second glance at a faceless girl making something she thought might be the shape of a cross, touching head, chest, left and right. I'm attracted to those little signs of religious belonging—the prayer rugs of Muslims, the Catholic and Episcopal hopscotch of a cross on the chest.

The morning sun lit up this place so brightly that dust motes swarmed above the head of the woman pounding on a slightly out of tune, upright piano just to the left of the podium.

The congregation stood as if on signal as a plump man, with a fringe of darkish hair circling his head like a monk's tonsure, popped out from behind a maroon panel of curtains and stood blinking in surprise at the sight of so many in his church.

"Love divine all love excelling" burst forth as the curtains parted. A scraggly choir, a dozen men and women wearing robes faded to an anemic puce, marched to their seats behind the podium, and bowed their heads.

I stood and bowed and sat and bowed and stood again, trying to get the hang of this ritual. The prayer before the sermon just about polished me off. I timed the preacher, counting one thousand and one until I had ticked off eight minutes. He prayed for the minerals, starting with adamite and going all the way through zinc.

"Pastor Wyndom was a geologist in his former life," Aunt Harriet whispered as he took a breath before "manganese" and worked on down to "melanite."

She pushed the hymnal toward me. "Read," she hissed.

Flipping to the back, I found "Whispering Hope" on page 245. I hope the tune was more interesting than the words. I couldn't imagine Jeremiah's father singing about angels with a soprano named Eula. I checked the key signature of "Whispering Hope." It had five flats. Singing it could be a challenge. Eula might have slipped off key. Considering the temper of Jeremiah's father— a man who'd smack his son in the face for chewing tobacco and make his wife so miserable that she went on the lam—he might react like a madman over a missed flat note.

I thumbed through the hymnal. Some of the song titles were curious—not fully formed notions. *What if I added a prepositional phrase to them? Something a bit provocative? Under the bed.*

That worked like gangbusters. "His Way with Thee *under the bed.*" I peeked up, but Aunt Norma's eyes were closed and her face frozen, probably trying to fathom how pyrite made its way into the prayer.

So I tried another one: "O Love That Wilt Not Let Me Go *under the bed.*" And then another: "Yield Not to Temptation *under the bed.*" The giggle that erupted could not possibly have come from me. The only stratagem left to me as I reddened and choked might be a lung-cracking cough; or, perhaps, I could pretend to swallow my tongue.

The blue-in-the-face trick did it. Lucinda shoved two gummy peppermints, coated with pocket fuzz, into my hand, and I, dutifully, sucked just as "Amen" resounded from the pulpit.

Communion was the oddest affair. Methodists don't believe in sharing saliva with a common cup. A fake silver salver covered with stingy vials full of something a bit too purple to pass for wine came down the aisles. Just as I reached for one, Aunt Norma smacked my hand. "Not until you're baptized," she hissed.

Just as well. An appetizer that followed with "This is my body" was nothing more than a saltine cracker broken into tiny bits. I had begun to regret not finishing my oatmeal, even without the missing rationed sugar.

EXCEPT FOR LUCINDA'S oven stew of big hunks of beef that she got from a local farmer to avoid using her ration book, the rest of Sunday was a waste of my time. Stores were shuttered. The library was closed, along with the *Weekly* newspaper office. As for working on my map, with a few well-planned strolls down new alleys, it wasn't going to happen.

"You will stay with your Aunt Harriet while Lucinda and I drive with Manford to pick up his mother at the Gainesville Hospital." Aunt Norma pulled off white church gloves and tugged on her leather driving gloves. "I'm taking my car because of his sprained foot."

She handed me a Bible with slivers of paper sticking out of it. "I've marked various psalms for you to read. Ignorance of Christianity is no excuse not to appreciate biblical literature."

"But, I want to go. Manboy would like my company. I've never been to Gainesville," I whined like a chained dog.

"Not today, Clio. Mrs. Muller will need to stretch out in the back seat. You can see Gainesville with us on Memorial Day." Aunt Norma picked up a heavy ring of keys, like a chatelaine might have dangling from her belt to lock the portcullis by the moat.

"We decorate with little flags that day. Remembering our boys in gray," Aunt Norma added like a rabid poet; then, she waltzed out of the house, leaving me puzzled.

"What boys in gray?" I demanded of Aunt Harriet.

"Why, our Confederate boys. Lots of them are buried in the cemetery in Gainesville. It was very pro-South during the war. The other war. Before the other one and this one." Aunt Harriet seemed bent on confusing me. Then she clarified everything.

"The Bonnie Blue flag or the stars and stripes Confederate flag. We put miniature flags on the graves of those soldiers. To let them know we haven't forgotten."

Fat tears pooled in her eyes as she sniffed into her dimity handkerchief. Then, with a broad smile, she added: "We have a fine potluck meal in the park, and the local brass band plays rousing songs. Songs from that period."

I could hardly wait. "Eating Goober Peas" or "Hooray for Southern rights" weren't exactly my kind of music. "Potluck" sounded dreadful—like something left over in the pot with botulism lurking to attack the unlucky.

"Manboy and his mother often go with us. For the music and the visiting. Lots of Wolfe Flats people are there. It's a very festive occasion."

Just at that moment, I remembered one of those little history lessons that Mother tucked away for those special moments when she was a bit nostalgic for home and wanted to "put things into perspective." That's why Gainesville had been ringing a bell ever since the ambulance had whisked Mrs. Muller away to the hospital twenty-five miles south of Wolfe Flats.

Mother had told me a terrible story: "They hung civilians in Gainesville during the Civil War. Forty of them. Called them Unionists. There was a trial, then, a mob took over and hung some that had been released. Then, they retried the ones who weren't hung again. I've always hated that flag ceremony. I stopped going when I was old enough to put my foot down. We're Yankee girls now, Clio." Mother had tried to laugh reassuringly, but I had the sense that she didn't think something was funny.

I had been conceived in New York, born in New York, and grew up to age eleven in New York. If that didn't qualify me as a Yankee, my refusal to plant Rebel flags on graves certainly would. I could hardly wait to take a stand—even though the stand was three quarters of a century too late.

CHAPTER 18

I t was almost five o'clock when the Pierce Arrow
bumped over the curb and ground to a stop, blocking
the front sidewalk. The noise of Aunt Harriet practicing
Scarlatti sonatas all afternoon had driven me to a post
upstairs, with a bird's eye view of the Muller front yard.

Galloping down the stairs, through the kitchen, out
the back door, and along the narrow space between the
houses, I made it to the car before Lucinda and Manboy,
balancing on one leg, could get the back car door open.

"I can help. Let me help." I reached around Lucinda's girth as she struggled to get something that must be
Mrs. Muller on her feet. With swathes of white flying
behind her like a mummy emerging from a crypt, Mrs.
Muller stared at me with eyes so spooky that I jumped
back. Her eyes might have been blue if a couple of
clouds hadn't dropped over the irises. As in a summer
storm, little flashes of what must be lightning flickered
for an instant, and then disappeared.

"I know this child. I've been away, but intergalac-
tic exchanges are still possible." Mrs. Muller's chill-
ing greeting implicated both of us as some strange

extra-terrestrials. She ignored Manboy's offer to help, draped one thin arm across my shoulders, and turned me gently toward the front of her house.

"Wonderfully white again. Someone has smothered the spiders with a very good paint job while I was away. On Uranus, I think." She smiled benignly down at me while I ticked off the planets and wondered why Mrs. Muller thought she'd been on the ice giant Uranus.

"Mother, I don't know why you are saying such things. People will think you've had a stroke. The doctor said you didn't." Manboy frowned at his mother.

"The bed was hard as a rock. The fan kept me chilled to the bone. Some of those nurses in their stiff white hats treated me as though I were some kind of alien presence and that I couldn't hear a thing they said about me—and other patients," she retorted. "Ice and rock and gusty winds. Must have been Uranus."

"You were in Gainesville, Texas, Mother," Manboy struggled with his crutch to mount the steps and open the front door.

"Just as I said. On another planet."

Those cloudy blue eyes searched my face, as though looking for a response. So, I winked. Seemed as though we were on the same page about Gainesville.

Mrs. Muller's sharp, bright laugh brought reluctant smiles from Aunt Norma and Manboy and a huge responsive grin from Lucinda.

"Being here with Clio is like going back in time. You can call me Aunt Claire. That's what Delia called me. Now, let's get inside. I'm feeling just a bit off center."

Aunt Claire's arm never left my shoulder, but she was leaning heavily into Lucinda and panting softly.

Dropping onto a spindly settee, its legs gleaming with brass fittings in the shape of leaves, she patted the seat next to her. "Clio, sit by me for a moment. Tell me what you've been doing all afternoon. Something interesting?"

"Reading Psalms." I raised my voice a bit so Aunt Norma could pick up on the fact that I felt put upon by all her little slips of paper marking her recommended Psalms.

"Oh, Norma. That's downright punishment for a child like Clio. Reminds me of Lester Lewin's birthday present. We thought we were punishing Delia and Manford, but they turned the tables on us." She giggled like a young girl.

His mother's memory wiped away the frown Manboy had been wearing since getting out of the car.

"Punished for what?" I tugged on the sleeve of Aunt Claire's robe.

"I'll tell! I'll tell. I love that story—at least the last part of it. Not the first." Aunt Harriet's voice rang out from the kitchen. "I brought some of Lucinda's stew for your dinner and just popped cornbread in your oven, Claire. Wait for me to tell."

Aunt Harriet bounced along the hall, chattering so rapidly that I could hardly sort out the chronology of the events she was recounting. "It rained so hard the night before that a little nest of birds had washed out of the old Sycamore at the corner of Main and Osage

Street. That's where Lester found them on his way home from school. I told his mother he was too young for a pocketknife. But, no, she had to . . ."

"The story, Harriet. You're getting off track." Aunt Claire's voice was soft but forceful.

"Yes. I tend to postpone the unpleasant. Delia and Manford were riding their bicycles home when they spotted Lester. They always rode their bicycles to school. Isn't Delia's bike out in the shed, Norma? Clio would probably love to ride it."

"The story, Harriet," Aunt Claire repeated.

"Lester was doing something terrible to those baby birds with that knife of his . . . taking their little heads . . . that's when Manford and Delia caught him. So they just took matters into their own hands."

"How?" I squeaked out, envisioning them doing something very interesting to Whitey Lewin with his own knife.

"They both took out their shoelaces and Lester's shoelaces and made enough cord to tie him to the tree. Then, they took turns charging the tree with their bicycles and swerving just as Lester screamed." She smiled with a hint of regret. "They left him tied to the tree, buried the baby birds, and pedaled on home, looking innocent as lambs."

"That's where I come into the story." Aunt Norma, for once, seemed to be getting into the spirit of something interesting. "I was trimming roses in the side yard and heard the sheriff standing on the Muller front porch, making all kinds of threatening statements. I told him that people had complained about Lester torturing animals before and asked him why he wasn't dealing with the real problem—not that Delia and you, Manford, weren't problems as well."

There was a brief, uncomfortable silence. I felt compelled to push the story back into gear. "What happened next?"

Aunt Claire smiled sweetly. "That's where retribution rears its difficult head. Lester's twelfth birthday was two days away. His mother always planned elaborate birthdays for her son. Sent stamped invitations through the mail to all the children in his class at school. She provided food galore. Bakery cake. Hot dogs. She strung crepe paper streamers from one end of their property to the other. Excessive décor, I thought."

I shifted on the wobbly sofa and made a guttural noise. My aunts, Lucinda, and now Aunt Claire couldn't seem to move ahead with the chronology of anything. Aunt Claire had just digressed to food and decorations.

"Clio is very much like Delia, Mother." Manboy flashed me a quick grin. "Reporters work from the most important to the least important elements of the story—so the editor can chop off lines at the bottom to fit available space without losing the gist. Delia always wanted to get to the point."

"Well," Aunt Claire drawled softly. "Ladies in this part of the world circumnavigate around the point. Keeps us out of trouble if we never say anything directly."

"I ken be direct," Lucinda joined the storytellers. "Them two kids absolutely refused to go to Lester's birthday party. So, the aunts of one and the mother of the other come up with a way to teach them not to 'take the law into their own hands' as Norma put it." Lucinda stopped and stared with a stern expression, as though she wanted to take issue with Aunt Norma's judgment. "Not only did they have to go to Lester's party, but they had to buy him a nice present with all the money they'd been saving in their piggy banks."

"But I don't see how that turned the tables on Lester—they had to eat crow by going to his party and buying him a present with their own money." I was miffed at the way this story was going. I knew about piggy banks. Mother dipped into mine regularly when she was short of cash.

Aunt Harriet let out a peal of laughter. "That's just it. The present. It was nicely gift-wrapped from the stationary store—that store closed a year ago. I guess it . . ."

I grunted again and mouthed my "Focus, Aunt Harriet, focus" mantra silently.

"All the children clustered around Lester when he opened that gift. Most of the children had brought simple little things, whistles, comic books, a pencil set, things like that. But Delia and Manford had given him what appeared to be an expensive store-wrapped gift. Lester could hardly wait to rip it open. He ignored all the other gifts and snatched it up first."

"I was not amused at all by that gift. The very idea that they would give a . . ."

Aunt Norma was sticking her oar in again, just as the gift was to be revealed. I could feel what Mother called my "rufous" face turning dark red with annoyance.

"Bible," said Manboy softly. "Delia and I bought Whitey Lewin a nice, big Bible. A white one. It took every cent we'd saved, but we never begrudged the gift. Whitey's mother made him write both of us thank-you notes. He never said a word at his party."

I GIGGLED ALL the way home, thinking of my mother and Manboy getting their revenge in such a subtle way. They would have been my age when they came upon Whitey torturing those baby birds. I'd have just charged into Whitey with my bicycle and splattered him all over the tree trunk. No swerving for me.

Except I couldn't ride a bicycle. "Too dangerous on city streets," Mother had claimed. "No place to store it" was her backup reason.

After leaving the Muller house, I had made a detour into the garage out back where Aunt Norma parked the Pierce Arrow. There, propped against the far side of the garage, was a dusty bicycle with flat tires. I hauled it out and turned the hose on it. Except for years of cobwebs, doodle bugs, and deflated tires, it was a magnificent piece of machinery.

Glancing over at the draped windows of the Muller house, I hoped that Manboy might be peeking out at me. He'd know where to get tires aired; more importantly, he could teach me how to ride.

CHAPTER 19

Every morning for the next three days, I put the letter from Jeremiah's mother in the pocket of one of those hideous skirts and trotted off to school—anticipating his surprise over a resurrected mother. His deceitful father would pose another problem for him. Or me, as the bearer of the letter.

By the end of the third day, Jeremiah's empty back row seat sent me on a mission to the blacksmith shop. Clearing up the mystery of one missing woman didn't throw a light on disappearances of the girl named Eula, who sang like an angel, Whitey Lewin's decorator cousin Louise, or the woman named Ellen, who had been hired to teach first graders.

With benevolence speeding me along, I considered enlisting Jeremiah in my investigation now that we had an important connection. Both of our mothers had taken themselves off to the war. I knew that mine would be getting as close to the action as possible for a frontline story.

Jeremiah's mother, the fungus expert, might be going after jungle rot, a fungus that caused toes to fall off soldiers. I'd keep this little tidbit of information to myself, not lord it over Jeremiah that my mother's job was more glamorous.

The minute I popped into the blacksmith shop, Marek lifted up his face shield and backed away from a flurry of sparks flying from his father's hammer.

"Clio, stay back. We don't want another accident here. Don't be careless, Papa."

Squinting across the forge with no protective shield, Mr. Nebojsa beckoned me over, but Marek grabbed my arm. "Papa thinks he's Hephaestus. Invincible. I'm the one with the bum leg," Marek grinned at me.

My smile back was hesitant. I knew the mythology about the god of fire, the Mount Olympus metalworker who intervened in a parental spat with his parents, Zeus and Hera, and was crippled for his trouble. My friend Jeremiah was a victim of parental issues—I could only imagine what his ill-tempered father might have done to him.

"Jeremiah hasn't been in school all week. I wondered if you had seen him?"

"From a distance in the front seat of his father's pickup. George paid us a visit yesterday. He made threats about a lawsuit. Said he might put us out of business."

"Is Jeremiah's eye . . ." I blurted out fearfully just as two strong arms lifted me off my feet and swung me in a wide arc. The odors of garlic and coal dust and sweat were as comforting as the tight squeeze of genuine affection.

"Clio. We've been missing you—and Lucinda's cooking. You don't think she'd . . ."

"Papa, we're not reduced to begging for food," Marek pried his father's arms from around me. "You're getting coal dust all over Clio. Jeremiah's eye is just fine. Doctor Lontry picked up his hubcap yesterday and told us there is no sign of infection. His father decided to keep Jeremiah out of school for a few days to help him on the farm."

Mr. Nebojsa scowled: "His father should let the boy rest. He had him working on the side of the barn that blew down last week. Missed his appointment. Doc drove out to check and found Jeremiah lifting heavy boards. He was that furious with George, because he said no lifting. They had words. Then George came here, and we had more words." Mr. Nebojsa dusted his hands together as though ridding them of residue more distasteful than coal dust.

"It doesn't do any good to argue with an unhappy man like George Whittaker, Papa. He's bluffing. He needs his plows and tools repaired like every other farmer in the county. There won't be any new farm equipment while the war is . . ." Marek's voice trailed off.

"Clio's worried about Jeremiah—not what his father's doing, Marek. Why don't we take a break? I put soda pop in the ice chest. Would you like orange or strawberry, Clio?"

If the enamel on my teeth dissolved, it did so bliss-fully as I drank one of each flavor and listened to Marek describe how the Desert Fox Rommel had gotten crosswise with Hitler for being pessimistic about the war. Marek was optimistic. "His generals must know they're working for a madman. They'll turn on him on him one of these days. Soon, I hope."

HOPEFULNESS WASN'T AT the top of my agenda as I traipsed through the back alleys of Wolfe Flats toward my aunts' house—not in the least bit hungry after a pint of fizzy soda.

Mother might be trying to get a story out of Rommel. I wouldn't put it past her to sneak into the enemy's camp, even if she had to go to Libya. "It's all about the angle, Clio. That's what makes headlines. A unique approach."

Taking her advice to heart, about a different kind of approach, I started down Main Street, walked by the drugstore, and turned the corner into the alley where Louise Lewin had last been seen. Poking through barrels of trash, I looked for clues, anything that an unsuspecting villain might have tossed away. I scanned old envelopes sticky with garbage for information, even though the trail of crime had been cold for years.

"I should have known Delia's daughter would entertain herself in a rubbish bin. The apple doesn't fall far from the tree."

Tucked into the back entry of his store, Whitey Lewin caught me off guard. Dropping a handful of discarded mail, I backed away, embarrassed.

"Your mother hasn't written for . . . let me see now . . . how many weeks? Two? Three? Not at all? If the Germans haven't grabbed her, a bullet from our troops has probably hit her for being in the way . . . what do they call it? Friendly fire. That's it. Friendly fire," he sneered.

"You should know, Whitey, after what happened when you paid me a so-called friendly visit," I burst out, pleased with myself for such a clever retort.

Rather than count how many seconds elapsed before the flush on Whitey's ashy neck reached his eyeballs, I turned and sped down the alley—and didn't stop running until I reached the safety of Aunt Norma's front porch.

CHAPTER 20

J ust after the last bell rang the next morning, Jeremiah
sauntered into Mrs. Wallace's classroom, cut directly
across to her desk, and smacked down a piece of paper.
"Been by the office. I know the rules. There's the note
from Pa. Wounded in the line of duty." He pointed to a
yellowish circle around his eye. "Blind for days."

Mrs. Wallace's beady eyes locked onto the note as
she ignored Jeremiah, while pointing one bony finger
toward the back of the room. As Jeremiah clomped
in his unlaced boots to the back of the classroom, he
ignored me. Not a glance. Not a wink. Not any kind of
acknowledgement that I might have been worried about
his absence.

At recess, he joined a cluster of boys humped over in
a football huddle at the side of the building. Suspicious
wisps of smoke wafted up from the gaggle of boys, noisy
as geese.

If he could be a jerk, so could I. Sashaying over to
where Brenda and Bridget were holding court, their legs
dangling from the buckling retaining wall that skirted

the open front door of the school, I eased up next to them, laughed loudly, and pointed toward the boys.

"They don't have a clue. Mrs. Wallace stuck her head out the window and headed toward the principal's office. Better scout out the territory before you sin." I smiled at the Brown twins, hoping for a response to my cleverness, but they maintained blank expressions, confirming that I was an outsider in this school.

We watched as the principal collared two of the boys and held up a red and white Dial cigarette package labeled "Turn to a real smoke" as evidence of their crime. Half a dozen boys shuffled nervously and cast hostile glances at me. Jeremiah said something I couldn't hear; his expression was unreadable.

That did it! I had exposed myself in ill-fitting underwear to mop up his blood with my slip. My aunts and Lucinda had rushed to help him. Marek and I watched his bloody eye patch while he snored in the guest bedroom. His bully of a father had mistreated all of us.

So, I took the only reasonable action in the most public way possible. I walked into that pack of oafish boys, pulled out the letter addressed to: Jeremiah Whittaker, Rural Route Three, Wolfe Flats, Oklahoma, and handed it over to a blue-eyed boy who refused to look into my eyes.

JEREMIAH DISAPPEARED AND didn't return to class for the rest of the day. When I took the short cut home that he had shown me across back yards and down crooked alleys, he was standing by the back shed, examining the bicycle.

"Chain needs oiling. Don't know if the tires will hold air. They may need patches. Manford loaned me his pump." Jeremiah's concern about the state of my mother's bicycle filled the space for words that I knew he couldn't speak.

"Manford told me that you've never ridden a bike. I'm here to show you how."

For the next hour, Jeremiah stabilized a wobbly bike and shrieked with laughter as I missed a head-on with the iceman's truck and half a dozen diseased elms.

Just as I was getting the hang of pushing pedals while balanced atop two wheels, Lucinda shouted: "Hot gingerbread! Clio has been bruised enough for one day."

So had Jeremiah, judging from his swollen eyes as he worked his way through two hunks of gingerbread that Lucinda set out by the front porch swing for both of us.

"Pa's been giving me a ration of . . . well. To be polite. A hard time. He acted like I got that spike in my eyeball on purpose. And went over to the 'enemy camp.' That's what he calls your aunts and the Mullers. They were Mom's friends. Never his. Something in the past. Something about your mother pissed him off years ago. He still blames Manford. He won't say why."

Jeremiah sat, staring down at his dirty boots, until I was downright uncomfortable, almost ready to fill in the gap with questions. Then, I recalled Mother's reminder that a good interviewer knows when to wait. So I waited. It came like an explosion. "I hate him! I hate him! I hate him for making Mom leave. For telling me she had run away and forgotten about us."

He pulled the crumpled envelope from his pocket. "This says she wrote me every week. It says she told me why she went. She never forgot me for a day."

He lifted a plaintive face to me. "Why would somebody's pa do that to his son? Make him sick with worry? I really hate him. I can't ever go home again."

"You can and you must." Aunt Harriet's soft voice surprised both of us as she eased to a sitting position off the hammock strung up just around the curve of the front porch.

Flushing so red that his freckles disappeared, Jeremiah jumped up. "I didn't know you were . . ." he stammered.

"Eavesdropping is what I do best," Aunt Harriet offered glibly, but I could see that she was visibly shaken by Jeremiah's distress.

She walked over to him, trailed her fingers along his cheek and said: "Your eye is healing nicely. We are lucky to have caretakers like Lucinda and the good doctor."

The flush left Jeremiah's cheeks; his freckles stood out like stipples on a guinea's egg. When Aunt Harriet wasn't into her mode of digressing, she could be very calming—though she had just digressed to Jeremiah's week-old injury.

"Now that you know your mother is safe and thinking of you all the time, I believe that you should give your father an opportunity to explain himself," Aunt Harriet said primly, as I stared at her wide-eyed.

"But she's just gone off to . . ." I blurted out, thinking of my own mother somewhere near a battlefield.

"We know, dear." Aunt Harriet interrupted and patted my arm. More forcefully than I thought she should have. "She's a botanist, doing something important for the war effort. Surely not where the fighting is . . ."

For an instant, I thought Aunt Harriet wouldn't breathe again. Something in her eyes, something so deep that I couldn't see what she might be thinking, leached all the color out of her hazel irises, making them eerily blank with pain.

"That's the difference, you see. Sonja is happy helping people like the Mullers by making their backyard into a tranquil retreat. Our Delia doesn't know the meaning of tranquility. Your mothers are not exactly alike, but they both love their children."

I eased away from this conversation by planting myself next to Aunt Norma's huge calla lilies. Jeremiah's mother might have left without a word, but her letters to him must have been full of love if this letter in his hand was an example. My mother had shouted goodbye, but never said a word about regret or love.

Aunt Harriet patted Jeremiah on the back. "You run on home now and ask your father to please give you all the letters your mother has sent you since she left. I suspect he has them."

From the expression on Jeremiah's face as he strode off the porch, I hoped his father would quietly hand over the letters and offer some kind of explanation for keeping them from his son. I wanted to remind Jeremiah that stealing mail is a federal crime, but this didn't seem the time to talk about sending his father to prison.

JOE PETE SAUNDERS wheeled up to our front door on his rusty bicycle just as we watched Jeremiah stalking north on Choctaw Street for a confrontation that might not go as Aunt Harriet suggested.

"Telegram for Clio Clower. From overseas. Don't get too many of these in Wolfe Flats. Some from the military that I'd just as soon not deliver."

Although my name and address appeared behind the little see-through window in a sealed envelope, I suspected that Joe Pete knew exactly what was inside.

It wasn't much. Little strips of glued on paper with all the letters oversized as though the recipient was expected to be half-blind or teary eyed.

"Arrived Scotland. Cannot reveal next post. Safe. Busy. Miss you."

"Miss you" would be the closest my mother would get to the topic of love. Telegrams seemed to be urgent communications but so impersonal; they were read by the transmitter and the receiver before they reached their destination. Two steps removed from the sender. Even so, I beamed with pleasure as I held out the telegram to Aunt Harriet. "She's listening to bagpipes, wearing a kilt, and eating haggis."

"Knowing Delia, I suspect she's doing all three at the same time. It's a lovely message, Clio. Delia is safe. I'll go tell Norma and Lucinda. They'll be so happy."

It was amazing that Mother could make people happy with so few words. That's probably because she managed to make herself scarce. Still, we had those words. "Safe" meant for that brief moment in time. It was enough. I slept a dreamless night for the first time since she'd left.

CHAPTER 21

The next day at school, Jeremiah hustled up to me at recess and handed me a knife. We scraped mortar companionably. "He had them. Hidden in a box under his bed. My letters with my name on them. He handed them over without a word. A brick fell from the wall. Quick as a flash, Jeremiah scooped it up and placed it back. "Shit happens when I'm ready. Not until. I've got nothing to say to him."

With a mischievous twinkle in those blue eyes, Jeremiah said. "We can go noodling Saturday. Manford said he'd take us."

The sudden jab of my knife dislodged another brick. Whatever "noodling" meant in this part of the world, it most certainly had something to do with sex. The idea of Manboy being along disconcerted me. I thought of Manboy as a sort of uncle—my friend because he was Mother's friend. Noodling with Manboy close by smacked of incest.

"You can wear old clothes—something that you don't mind getting wet. The river's down. Noodling for the first time can be exciting." Jeremiah picked up my brick and placed it carefully back in its slot. "Holes don't scare me. I like the idea of poking around in dangerous places. With a girl like you, it should really be fun. Your mother did it when other girls wouldn't." Jeremiah's smile was actually sunny.

What a perverse boy he had turned out to be. I narrowed my eyes and prepared myself to lose the best friend I'd made in Wolfe Flats. I geared up to deliver my mother's "I have too much respect for myself to" speech, when the words burst out like steam from a pressure cooker.

"That is so rude! It's bad enough that you think I'm that kind of girl. I can't believe you'd say such hateful things about my mother."

The screech that Jeremiah let out resounded over the clanging of the bell, announcing that recess was over. He gasped, turned red, then purplish, and gripped his sides as though his tortured lungs were about to explode.

"You think . . . you think . . . you don't know what I'm talking about, do you?" He sputtered between howls of laughter.

"I've never heard it called that in New York, but, yes, I think I do," I retorted stiffly. The ice princess mantle settled nicely around me as I folded his knife and smacked it into his open palm.

"Wait up, Clio." His voice was low and insistent as he hurried after me.

I kept up a lively pace, hoping to put Jeremiah and his vile suggestions behind me. Maybe I would join the Brown twins on the retaining wall during lunch. Their icy stares might be less upsetting than Jeremiah's nasty mouth.

"Fishing, Clio. For catfish. That's what noodling is. You don't use a pole. Just your hands to wrestle them onto the bank. Big as hogs sometimes. Best sport imaginable."

With my imagination now firmly in check, I struggled to rein in the flush that was turning my face the same color as my hair, as Jeremiah, politely, turned on his heels and left me to sort out the linguistics of southern Oklahoma.

ODDLY ENOUGH, MY aunts and Lucinda were more than willing to send me off noodling to Red River with Jeremiah, so long as Manboy came along as a chaperone.

Lucinda dragged an old-fashioned wicker picnic hamper out of the pantry and packed it with buttermilk battered fried chicken, potato salad, baked beans, and oatmeal cookies. "Just bring me some catfish to fry up. That's all I ask for my trouble."

Manboy heaved a galvanized tub with a giant block of ice into the back of his pickup. "For our catch."

The minute that Aunt Norma disappeared back into the house, Manboy flipped up the lid on the picnic basket and pointed to the leather straps. "That would have been for wine. We're in the company of teetotalers around here. We'll have to make do and hope our tooth enamel holds." He grinned as he positioned bottle after bottle of every flavor of soda pop imaginable around the ice block.

In the distance, I could see Jeremiah peddling at record speed down the street. Gasping for breath, he threw something in a pillowcase towards me. "My Mom's. She called them playsuits. It's a kind of short coverall she'd wear to the river in summer. She's small. I think it will fit. You don't want to wear that big skirt to noodle." He glanced back at the house. "You can change in the woods by the river. Keep your Aunt Norma in the dark."

SITTING ON THE front seat of the pickup between my two best friends in Wolfe Flats—not counting Lucinda who was more than a friend—I felt as though spending more time in this place might not be so bad.

"Why are you helping the bad guys? Those Germans over at Camp Houze? Pa says you go talk to them. He says they get three square meals a day and play soccer when they're not working for farmers. He thinks they should be shot." Jeremiah's voice quavered a bit, but his eyes drilled directly across me at Manboy.

"Your father probably thinks I should be shot, Jeremiah. Name like Muller." Manboy's voice sounded resigned, fatalistic.

"Well, I don't. You're my friend. I just wondered about those German prisoners living right across the river." Jeremiah ducked his head and sighed. "I don't agree with lots of things Pa says. He has a bad temper and a long memory. Clio, Pa said your mother tried to play him for a fool. Pa said she sicced the National Guard on him."

Speechless, I glowered at Jeremiah. He was being particularly contentious today. First Manboy, then my mother. I was just getting ready to tell Manboy to turn his pickup around when a peal of laughter exploded in the pickup cab.

"Delia never *tried* to do things. She just did them. I don't think she had any particular designs on your father, Jeremiah. He and I had a little set to about Delia's decisions that summer she left." An uncomfortable pause followed as he shifted gears and pulled across a cattle guard. "Delia and George had a few dates before she left for New York. She always made it clear to everyone that she was going to be a famous reporter—that meant leaving Wolfe Flats," Manboy's voice tapered off to almost a whisper.

"She didn't leave exactly the way . . . something unfortunate . . . a disagreement with her aunts sent her into a tailspin. Delia didn't call the National Guard. Norma did. They came. Sent a search team. The Clower name has considerable power in this part of the world."

I sat, dumbfounded, as the pickup chugged down a deeply rutted road. Sally, at the newspaper, told me the same story about the National Guard searching for Mother. Nobody said why she left home. Whenever I asked, they'd just clam up or change the subject. Maybe I'd use that old journalism trick of the oblique question before I sprung the real one.

"What Germans are you talking about?"

"POWs. Over at Camp Houze outside of Gainesville. I've been asked to help interrogate them. I speak German. I'm a lawyer. Couldn't qualify for military service. I'm 4F. Heart murmur." Manboy slammed on the brakes and turned an exaggerated perfect smile toward us.

"I could have made it in the Civil War. I have four front teeth."

"What are you talking about?" Jeremiah asked testily. "What does four front teeth have to do with anything?"

"If they were missing, you couldn't rip open gun powder cartridges with your teeth, so you were 4F for Civil War service. The label stayed. The requirement didn't. Better dentists now. Different ammo." Manboy flipped the pickup into gear and eased it out of deep ruts so that one wheel rode the high, grassy center.

Just as the conversation between Manboy and Jeremiah seemed to be veering in the direction of gunpowder, I headed it back to the POWs and the kinds of questions that would interest Mother if I ever got to talk with her again. "What kind of interrogation? What are you learning from those Germans?"

"That most of them are young and frightened. They simply did what they were told to do. Followed military orders. We don't get any high-level prisoners here. These are farm boys. But, I question them, just to be sure there isn't a rotten apple in the bunch. Now the prisoners work for local farmers. We don't want them escaping. There are lots of places to hide along this river. Right,

Jeremiah?" Manboy reached across me and clapped Jeremiah on the shoulder—one of those male-bonding smacks.

"That's why noodling is such a gas. Those lazy old catfish snuggle down out of sight and then look out!" Jeremiah's hand whacked my knee. "They just explode, Clio. You wouldn't think a sleepy fish had that kind of power."

Jeremiah probably didn't realize his own strength. My knee would be black and blue tomorrow, but I didn't flinch. All signs of civilization were far behind as we turned through great groves of pecan trees into the forest primeval. I was in this thing for the long haul.

As we bumped along beside curls of rich, dark soil in newly ploughed fields, Jeremiah explained the sport of noodling. "They'll lie back in those shallows under the bank just as quiet as a mouse. I like a real smooth stick for poking around. Might be moccasin somewhere. Slide it back and forth until you know you're right on the back of one. Then, wham! Grab 'em, ram 'em down the throat, and the wrestling match begins."

"The river can be treacherous, Clio. What appears to be a solid sandbar can drop you right down into a deep hole. This time of year, the river's low so you don't have to worry about currents. You can just swim out easily if you step in something over your head," Manboy assured me.

"Or not," I muttered.

"Or what?" Jeremiah asked.

"Can't swim. Never learned. Mother said she'd teach me, but she never did. I'm sure I could have learned quickly."

With only a brief telegram from my mother since she'd dumped me on the doorstep of her aunts' house, I wasn't above an implied criticism as long as it didn't make me look inept.

Manboy eased the floor gear forward and said: "Delia was a fearless swimmer. She'd take on this river in flood stage. She'd do a broad jump from sand bar to sand bar in the most treacherous conditions."

Manboy patted my arm sympathetically. "This isn't the place for you to learn how to swim, Clio. I'll take you to Lake Murray when it warms up in late June. It's safer."

I nodded, trying to look relaxed. Even on the beach at Coney Island, I never got into the water past my knees. That muddy, churning river ahead of us did not look inviting.

The playsuit of Jeremiah's mother did. The navy twill wide-legged shorts hit me mid-thigh. The clever little bib and straps kept the entire affair from dropping off my skinny body. Still, it was infinitely more fashionable than that baggy skirt Aunt Norma had bought me.

Knowing that I looked like one of those awkward shore birds with long, pale, knock-kneed legs, I sauntered out from behind a thick stand of willows where I'd changed into the skimpy playsuit. As the shrill wolf whistles of Jeremiah and Manboy rang out, forcing me to blush uncontrollably, I had to retaliate. Show them that I was Delia's daughter.

The "hell-broth boil and bubble" of the witches' pot in *Macbeth* couldn't hold a candle to a roiling river the color of old blood. I stood on the edge of the river, just above a deep slash in the bank and shouted: "Eye of newt, and toe of frog, wool of bat, and tongue of dog" as I tensed my body into the mightiest coiled spring I could muster and sailed at least six and a half feet to land squarely on a thick sand bar in the middle of the river.

"Shakespeare is alive and well in Wolfe County," Manboy hooted. "Not sure how he's going to help a non-swimmer get back to the bank. You're a long way from the food, Clio."

"We'll take the mountain to Mohammed." Jeremiah rummaged around in the back of the pickup, pulled out a coil of rope, and flung it in my direction. "Tie that end around the roots of the old driftwood tree. We can slide the picnic basket down. I'll float the tub with the soda pop over."

BY THE TIME the sun was at mid-day, Jeremiah and Manboy were almost dry, and my legs were a bright pink. We had eaten an entire chicken, mounds of potato salad and beans, and drunk three soda pops each.

Rolling up his pants to above his knees, Jeremiah said: "I'm gonna poke around on the south side where the sand is banked in those willow breaks. You two can stay here. I'll call when I get one. If I can't land it by myself."

Sated by too much food and sun as hot as it can get in April, I stretched out on the warm sand, trying to relax. I watched the river swoop and foam against the far bank, teasing out the skeleton of what must have been a dead cow.

The thought of those three missing girls popped into my head. Their bones must be hidden somewhere. According to the reporter Sally Tolliver, searches had been conducted, primarily in the houses of the poorest, the darkest, and, probably, the most innocent people in Wolfe Flats. Nothing was found. Only the misery of friends and relatives kept their memories alive.

"About those three missing girls . . ."

"Yes. What about them? Eula Harrison and Louise Lewin disappeared years ago. It's been almost a year since Ellen Carson . . ." Manboy paused. "You can't be worrying about something that's over, Clio. You seem fixated on them."

Fixated was probably the mildest description Manboy could muster for the girl who had dug up his dead dog Martha, but I guess I was fixated. I would try to explain.

"It's like this, Manboy. Next to our apartment in New York City was this little antique store, mostly junk and second-hand stuff. Mother bought used jigsaw puzzles there because they were cheap. She liked doing jigsaws better than I did," I added to let Manboy know I wasn't addicted to that kind of mindless activity.

"Invariably, when we'd get the puzzle together, critical pieces were nowhere to be found. Can you imagine London's Big Ben with the face of the clock missing? Or the Giza Pyramids looking like volcanoes with blown out tops? Those missing pieces, those gaps bothered me so much that Mother quit bringing puzzles home."

Sitting up, I stared wordlessly down the river where Jeremiah had just disappeared around the bend. Only the bright flash of blue from an irritated dragonfly interrupted the silence.

Manboy broke the stillness. "Jigsaw puzzles make all kinds of connections to create an image. Those young women just seemed to evaporate. No one could find any connection to anything or anyone. They didn't know each other. Eula Harrison, the first to disappear, was two grades behind Delia and me. Her father worked in the cotton gins. Her parents weren't very social, but Eula sang in the church choir."

He paused for a moment. "Eula had a remarkable soprano voice. Vanished after a Wednesday choir practice. Just vanished." Manboy flipped open the picnic basket and began tossing in empty pop bottles.

"Louise Lewin was a distant cousin of Hedy's. I don't recall the details, but her father was in the import business. Didn't make it out of China. I talked briefly with her about her father after church one Sunday."

A sad expression formed just behind his pale, blue eyes. "The bombing of Shanghai was in the news. Louise had come from Fort Worth to stay with Hedy and work in the store. She worked late one evening—not that late. The pharmacist waved to her when she walked by the drugstore. It was almost as though she vaporized when she turned the corner. That's been about five years now."

Like an angler feeling just the tickle of a nibble, I reeled in the line slowly. "To say that someone vaporized is eerie, Manboy. Did Mrs. Wallace's niece vaporize too?"

"No. That was a crass description. I think our town is still in a state of shock, even more so when Ellen Carson disappeared not quite a year ago. She had been hired as the first-grade teacher. She was a good pianist. She had offered to take over the music at church while Pastor Wyndom's wife was off for their third child."

Manboy's eyes turned slate blue with the coldness of his next words. "Ellen went for a walk one fine summer evening last August and never returned. Wolfe Flats doesn't appear to be a very safe place."

The jigsaw of my brain was fitting pieces together faster than I could find a pattern. Manboy's words "a safe place" caused me to remember our neighbor Mr. Abrams back in his tiny apartment. He was safe from the Nazis in Poland but cramped in body and spirit by the loss of his country, his place on this planet.

A wash of late sunlight jogged my memory as I recalled how the light would come on in Mr. Abrams' sunken eyes as he said over and over: "The world works by geometry." Then, he taught me planes and angles and spheres in what he called the perfect language of geometry. He said: "The flawless order of geometry in this world is a mirror of God's works."

"Where do the Nazis fit in with God's works?" I remember retorting snidely when triangles were getting the best of me.

"Temporal, Clio. Messy. Not part of the immutable laws."

Around the sandbar where I sat beside Manboy, the river throbbed with all the takings from the land—willow leaves, dead wood, a rusty can, and the desiccated carcass of a sparrow. The rains sweeping leavings from the land into the river made sense. Logical. Cleansing.

"His eye is on the sparrow and I know he watches me." Why on earth was that odd hymn they sang in church last Sunday rattling around in my head?

All at once, a kind of perverse rapture struck me. Who, what, why and how of mother's journalistic method took a back seat to *where*. That was the connection. Every one of those missing girls had been involved in the Wolfe Flats Methodist Church.

CHAPTER 22

I simply marveled at the process of my brain, how a part of my mind could whittle away at a problem while the rest of it was some other place, worrying about where Jeremiah might have gone around the river's bend.

Squelching both bare feet in and out of the sandbar to make small pools of quicksand, I studied Manboy's tranquil face in the sunlight. What could be described as chiseled features, a mop of blond hair, and blue eyes made him a perfect candidate for one of those Nazi propaganda posters. His foreshortened arms and legs might have condemned him to the Action T-4 euthanasia program.

I pulled both feet out of the sandbar with a great sucking sound to disturb Manboy. He needed to stay alert for questioning. "Don't you have any idea about who painted swastikas on your house and who sends you those hateful notes?"

"I might, but I don't have proof. Lawyers must be very careful about slander. Two of the notes were written on our church's stationery. It's in the church office—open to members most of the time. Or anyone for that matter."

"How many members?" The words popped out of my mouth with entirely too much enthusiasm. I needed to keep my conjecture about the link between the church and the missing girls to myself.

"Around 300 the last time I served on the Council. Why are you so interested in the church?" The cool blue of Manboy's eyes could bore right through a lie.

"I'm not. The hymns are OK. The preacher is a bore. The whole place smells of camphor and mothballs. Aunt Norma harps about something called MYF. Sounds contagious." I snickered at my wry sense of humor.

"Methodist Youth Fellowship. Delia and I were active in the group when we were teenagers. It's something to do in a small town. All the churches have their own youth groups. They plan outings. Come to think of it, the MYF sponsored that wiener roast at Lake Murray our senior year when . . ."

"When what?" People kept zipping their lips every time the subject of some kind of outing at Lake Murray was mentioned. "Sally Tolliver started to tell me something about my mother at a senior party at the Lake. Then she clammed up just like you did."

"It was a long time ago. Best forgotten. Some of us probably can't, because . . ." Manboy stopped speaking and stared at the cow bones tucked into the far bank or, maybe, something much farther away.

"You'd make your aunts very happy if you would show an interest in the Methodist young people's group,

Clio. They want you to fit in here by being part of the community. Our ancestors built this town. Your aunts and my mother are pillars of the Methodist Church." Manboy flashed a disarming smile at me, as he segued from something interesting involving my mother to church pillars.

I wanted to take Manboy down a notch or two by advising him that real pillars were not elderly ladies. Pillars are giant columns like those on the Forum in ancient Rome, over 55 feet tall. That thought saddened me as I thought about that smug face of Mussolini, planning to build a new Roman empire at the expense of Italy's neighboring countries.

"Many of our neighbors are Methodists; early settlers of the same faith tended to build close together." Manboy's comments disjointed me. He had an unsettling habit of using words as though he'd just snatched them out of the glossary in the frontal lobe of my brain.

I was one step ahead of him, remembering last Sunday when Aunt Norma whispered to me as the collection plate was passed: "Only a hundred or so members support the church," she had said in a soft undertone, as she dropped in the carefully sealed envelope with her name facing down in the collection plate.

The pillars of a church could surely get their hands on a membership list. I could begin the process of elimination by crossing off the names of women and children. Snatching women had to be a man's offense. With only a hundred active members, I'd be looking at a reasonable number of possibilities.

Basking in the warm sun while digging my bare heels into wet sand sent my brain into overdrive. I could never relate to those frozen yoga poses for meditation to stimulate the neocortex. The stark clarity of it hit me. Suspects were cropping up in my brain faster than I could sort them.

George Whittaker had taken my mother to her senior class Methodist party at Lake Murray when something bad had happened to her. But George hadn't stayed around after he and Mother had words that night, according to Sally Tolliver. When my mother disappeared from the party, it was Manboy who found her on the top of a rock structure called Devil's Kitchen. Sally said that he drove Mother to the Ardmore hospital.

I cast a sharp glance over at Manboy, digging his bare feet into the sandbank. How could he have known where to find my mother at night and on top of Devil's Kitchen? What part could Jeremiah's father have played in what happened?

Limiting my suspects to male Methodists of a certain age might be a promising but disquieting strategy. Much as I was beginning to like Manboy, as a Methodist, he had to stay on the suspect list. Even though Jeremiah was the only friend my age in Wolfe Flats, his father had to remain in the lineup. My Sherlockian brain couldn't be swayed by personal feelings. I was onto more than one suspicious character.

"It's possible that Jeremiah is onto one." My head snapped around at Manboy's comment, as though he had been reading my mind again.

"He disappeared quite a while ago." Manboy squinted down the river in the direction that Jeremiah had gone. "I guess I'll have to get my feet wet again. Go see if Jeremiah has caught anything."

As if on command, loud and persistent squeals ricocheted through a stand of willows just where the river changed its course. "Big as a damn hog! I need help!"

Like an unlikely target popping out of the river, a shock of red hair flashed in a ray of sun, filtering through pecan trees that drooped over the south bank. Then, it sank under heaving water.

Emerging seconds later, Jeremiah stood no more than fifty feet away, chest deep in the river with his arms around something that looked like a giant, gray shark. He flung himself forward toward the far end of our sandbar and rolled frantically about while Moby Dick devoured him.

The howl of laughter from Manboy stopped me in my tracks. I had snatched up a log of driftwood and was on my way to club a very big fish.

"He's got it, Clio. Landed. Let's get the tub over to him." Manboy swooped up river water and dumped it in with the remains of the block of ice.

"It's at least a thirty or forty pounder. Skint me something fierce." Jeremiah thrust out one freckled forearm with bramble-like scratches. "You think Lucinda would fry up some for Pa and me if I give her the lion's share of it?"

With a darkish wet mane of hair lopping to one side of his tawny face, Jeremiah reminded me of a young lion, fearless as he dared that river and that monstrous fish's den.

Not wanting to think about how Lucinda would go about extracting bloodless fish fillets from that heaving monster in the galvanized tub, I muttered: "Knowing Lucinda, she'll will whip up something good from that whiskered thing when we get home."

As I glanced over at the wide swath of river blocking me from the high bank, a sinking feeling planted itself firmly in my gut. Red River must teem with catfish even larger than this one. Only a swimmer could make it off this sandbar. I dropped to my knees, prepared to wait until someone could find a rowboat and save me.

"If you will carry the basket, Clio, Manboy and I can manage the tub. It's shallow down at the far end of the bar. Ankle deep across to the bank. You'll be perfectly safe," Jeremiah said casually, pretending not to see the fear of hesitation on my face.

"We'll make sure to keep you safe," Manboy added.

I had the feeling that he wasn't talking about ravenous fish or muddy water.

AFTER WE PULLED into Wolfe Flats, Manboy swung the pickup down the alley behind his house. "We'll gut the catfish back here and hose down the truck. Lucinda likes to cut the hunks a certain size. You might want your aunts to know that we brought you home safe and sound."

I looked down at that cute bib on the playsuit. My hideous skirt hid the bottom half, but I had lost my blouse when I changed in the woods. I might be sound, but I wouldn't be safe if Aunt Norma spotted me before I could manage a quick switch of clothes.

Sneaking around the house to the side porch door, I was just about take a step up when I heard the sharp punctuation of the front porch swing as Aunt Norma said: "Thank God, Delia didn't take up flying as a profession. When she went up without permission in that little Interstate Airway Company plane the month before, I knew it did not bode well for the future. Two dollars and fifty cents to risk life and limb."

I squatted down among the cannas and listened with bat ears.

"I know the date is a month away, but every year on the anniversary of Lindberg's flight to Paris, we relive that day in May fifteen years ago. You'd think we could put it behind us. While people were celebrating Lindberg as a hero, we were in that hospital room in Ardmore afraid that Delia would never wake up," Aunt Norma said.

"If she had taken up flying, she would have been safer than she was at that party at Lake Murray. It's etched in my memory forever—I just wish that doctor had not told her she'd been . . ."

"Hush! Hush! Harriet. We agreed never to say those words. At least the doctor didn't tell anyone else. I told him he'd be practicing medicine in another state if he dared to breach confidentiality. You need to repress that memory. I shouldn't have brought it up. Things better forgotten have been wearing on me lately."

I scrunched down lower, peering through one ragged leaf. I was looking through a pinhole at my mother's life. What should have been as familiar to me as my own past had been shuttered by silence. Now, I understood that "through a glass darkly" business that Pastor Wyndom nattered on about in his Sunday sermon.

My mother had been taken to a hospital by Manboy after he found her in a coma on top of something called Devil's Kitchen. Now, I was learning that my aunts were afraid that she would never wake up. No one ever told me about that terrible time, but Mother hightailed it out of this place, never to return until she had to unload me.

Aunt Harriet lowered her voice. "You know I suffer from tinnitus, Norma. It started that night. Echoes vibrate in my head. *Find him. Find him. Find the one.* That's what I hear, over and over."

"Delia didn't say find him. She said: 'Nail the bastard.' We didn't even try. We were too fearful of gossip, I guess. That's probably why she went to see if George Whittaker would . . ."

An ear-splitting sneeze erupted right out of the middle of the bed of cannas. Aunt Norma squinted one eye as though she were sighting down the barrel of gun at a condemned spy. I needed to back paddle fast.

"I was just coming to tell you that Jeremiah caught a really big catfish. He's staying for dinner—Manboy and his mother are coming too."

"Did you eavesdrop on our conversation, Clio?" Aunt Norma wasn't buying into my little social gathering for dinner diversion.

"I heard you mention Mother's name and something about Lindberg. She told me she'd never forget the day he flew to Paris. May 21st. She said it was a dark day for her, because she needed to believe in heroes. She told me that he had clay feet like the rest of them. Lindberg wanted us to sign a neutrality pact with Germany. He didn't care for Jews like our neighbors, the Abrams. That's what Mother said."

Standing amidst the chest-high cannas, I was hoping Aunt Norma would be more alarmed by what I was doing to her flowerbed than by my bib top—or my next question. "Why was May 21st, 1927, a dark day for Mother? Why did she say that?"

"Why did Delia ever say anything that wasn't intended to get a rise out of someone? I've always believed that Lindberg was a good citizen. He was misled for a while. Just like that poor Neville Chamberlain in England. Who are these Abrams you keep mentioning, Clio?"

Aunt Norma had mastered diversionary tactics while I was still Ned in the first reader. The words came out with the staccato of gunfire, but I noticed that her face was flushed and her hands clenched.

"If we're to have guests for dinner, you'll feel better if you get that Red River sand off with a nice bath." If guilt had an expression, it was plastered all over Aunt Harriet's face. She hadn't forgotten that dark day. She extended her hand to tug me out of the flowerbed. "Freckles popped out on your nose today, just like Delia after she'd spent a day in the sun. You go on upstairs. I'll help Lucinda with dinner."

FROM THE UPSTAIRS hall window, I could see Lucinda heading out back with what she called her skinning pliers and a sharp knife. While I soaked in the great claw-footed bathtub, I knew that Lucinda, the culinary magician, would be working miracles on a monster from the deep.

Turning on the faucets full force to drown out screams of a dying fish, I scooted down in the tub and practiced holding my breath under water. When the time came for my swimming lessons in Lake Murray, I intended to be ahead of the game.

Jeremiah made excuses that he had to go home, but Lucinda put an end to his protests. "Manboy kin take you and your bike in the pickup. I'll fix your pa a nice plate to take home. Someone who wrestled a forty pounder has to be the guest of honor."

Jeremiah ducked his head and colored with embarrassment. I had the sense that compliments were few and far between at his house—as well as pleasant conversation. He told me that his father was tired and tight-lipped in the evening. I needed to loosen those lips, to prime Jeremiah with questions for his father. George Whittaker might hold the key to that odd discussion between my aunts that I had just overheard in the flowerbed.

Something very bad had happened to Mother while Lindberg was crossing the Atlantic in 1927. She was eighteen that year and had just graduated from high school. Mother's friend, the newspaper reporter Sally, had dropped a dark hint about something that happened at a senior party at Lake Murray.

Because of my skill at eavesdropping, I now knew that Mother had ended up in the hospital with some kind of injury that caused Aunt Norma to threaten her doctor if he talked.

None of the pieces fit. Mother never told me about being in a hospital, except when I was born. She always said that she was disgustingly healthy. It was questionable that my aunts would tell me anything of interest about a time that so troubled them.

I cornered Jeremiah in the kitchen so that the noise of Lucinda in the throes of dropping battered fish into hot grease would give us privacy. "Just ask your father about a picnic the Methodists had at Lake Murray fifteen years ago. Ask him why the National Guard came to his house that summer."

"I told you that Pa doesn't like being questioned," Jeremiah's hiss was as loud as the pop of grease in Lucinda's skillet. "He gets riled up when I ask him about things in the past. Even about Mom. He gets red in the face and clams up."

I tried another tactic: flattery and bribery—the twisted twins of Oklahoma hospitality. "Anyone who could wrestle a fish the size of a whale all by himself could surely get a few little answers from his father. I'm certain that Lucinda will send him a nice plate of food tonight."

"You two get outa my kitchen afore you get scalded. Tell everbody to get to the table. Fried fish has to be et hot." Lucinda swung one arm like a train conductor, pointing toward Aunt Norma's winged Griffin dining room table.

Mounds of golden catfish graced each end of the table that Aunt Norma said came from her grandfather's house in Atlanta. A fried concoction of cornmeal, salt and boiling water that Lucinda called "real-hush-puppies-not-Yankee-hush-puppies" took pride of place next to a giant peach cobbler.

Frankly, I was gratified not to have Mother at the table asking: "Where is the green food?" For someone who never cooked, Mother had an obsession with the B vitamins. Lucinda's table usually groaned with carbohydrates, gravy, and sugar. Heaven-sent food.

CHAPTER 23

The invitation that arrived by afternoon post the next day might just as well have come from the Netherworld.

"It's an invitation to Lester Lewin's thirty-fourth birthday party tomorrow evening. Can you imagine, Norma? The last time Hedy threw a birthday party for Lester, he was twelve." Aunt Harriet waved a blue-scalloped piece of paper. "It says no presents. Of course, we'll have to go." Her voice had sunk into a mournful range.

"We certainly will." Aunt Norma's affirmation sounded a bit forced. "Not a particularly select group. Seems that Hedy has invited half the church. Pastor Wyndom got his invitation two days ago. So did Claire and Manford. For some reason, the postman put ours in the wrong box. The Carstairs got it in error. Jehovah Witnesses. They wouldn't be invited."

Me neither. Nothing to do with me. I wasn't about to celebrate sleazy Lester's birth. I picked up the Bible from the entryway table and pretended to be memorizing verses. That was the best way to get into Aunt Norma's good graces.

"Hedy put a little postscript at the bottom here. It says that she and Lester particularly want Clio to come. It's mostly for grownups, but she says Delia's daughter is special," Aunt Harriet said, beaming over at me.

I could think of several ways to take that smile off her face. The lingerie box with Whitey's fingerprints on it was still under my bed. The drapery that I'd swung on when I kicked him in the scrotum had been re-hung, but the new plaster around the screws spoke of repairs. If Lucinda knew how he'd groped my chest, she'd tear out his fingernails with those fish-skinning pliers of hers.

"Sounds like a thing for grownups. I'd just as soon stay home and work on memorizing Psalms. I'm really getting into it. 'Blessed is the man who walks not in the counsel of the ungodly, nor stands . . .'"

"'According unto the multitude of thy tender mercies blot out my transgressions.' Psalm 51. You have a way to go before you get on the pulpit, Clio. You can wear that nice black and yellow dress of yours." Aunt Norma's voice carried the authority of the crash of cymbals on judgment day.

I would probably be the only person there under thirty—and looking like a giant bumblebee. Comforting myself with the notion that I could probably pry around a bit while the hosts entertained, I nodded glumly in Aunt Norma's direction. I was particularly interested in that fenced-in area with the little shed that had served as a prison of sorts for Whitey's great-grandfather.

The fact that old Gideon Lewin had dropped five-year-old Lester down in a well for peeing in public places might strike someone else as maniacal. I wondered if the old man had seen something else in that child. Someone who would chop the heads off baby birds? The kind of sinner that caused Mother and Manboy to empty their piggy banks to gift him with a Bible on his twelfth birthday?

As though answering my question with a bang, Lucinda was making an unholy racket in the kitchen. I poked my head around the door. Her wide, usually serene face was puckered in anger. "I'm part of this family. That's my church too. My name should have been on that invite. Not that I give a hoot about them Lewins."

"If it's any consolation, Lucinda, I don't give a hoot about them either. Aunt Norma is making me go. I have no rights around here," I added, huffily. "I understand why Mother got out of this place the minute she could."

"You don't understand a thing, Clio. You're just flappin' your jaws because you don't like bein' bossed around by your Aunt Norma. That's what grownups do. They boss. Get over it. Delia never did, and it's hurtful for everbody."

My jaw dropped just an inch or so. I'd never heard Lucinda say a single critical thing about my mother before. I needed to defend her. "Mother always gave me choices. I understand her frustration with being bossed around all the time. That's clearly why she had to leave this house."

"It isn't. Had nothin' to do with your Aunt Norma's disposition. Had to do with a decision. Somethin' Delia couldn't tolerate no more. I've said too much, Clio. I said it all them years ago, and we ain't never gonna agree about it. Go take the trash out to the barrel. How's that for bossin'?" A sly expression lurked about Lucinda's eyes as she turned away from me.

What Lucinda hadn't said intrigued me much more than what she had said.

NOTHING WAS SAID the next evening as Aunt Norma, Aunt Harriet, and I climbed into the backseat of the Muller's big, boxy Buick Roadmaster. Nobody seemed to be in a party mood, especially not the weather.

A mist of gray rain doused the paper lanterns dripping along the edge of the Lewin's front porch. A dozen cars were parked along a wide swath of the gravel driveway. Manboy swung the Buick right up beside the front steps with a kind of panache that I admired. "I'll move it later if it's in the way," he said dismissively.

Having sloughed off that blue knitted caterpillar tube I'd seen her wearing in the store, Hedy Lewin had decked herself out in something even stranger. Billows of red and yellow voile streamed damply behind her as though she'd emerged from her pupa, sprouted wings, and been out in the rain.

"It's Delia's daughter!" She squealed. "Little Clio. What a treat to have her in our house. Look, Lester. Clio came with her aunts. You said she probably wouldn't come to a grownups' party."

Mrs. Lewin hastily touched the hands of my aunts but barely nodded to Manboy and his mother. I couldn't imagine why I was getting so much attention. Then, I could.

Whitey oozed carefully into the space between us like a slug fearful of being salted. Wide comb marks separated the strands of his oily black hair into shiny rivulets. "Clio. Darling Clio. You honor us with your presence. Let me be sure that you know everyone here."

Just as a smarmy hand gripped my arm, a firmer one grabbed the other one. "Clio! Imagine seeing you here. Just like old times, huh, Lester. We were just about Clio's age at your last birthday party. When you opened that beautifully wrapped box from Delia and Manboy and found a Bible, I laughed my head off."

Gratefully, I hung onto the arm of Sally, as she inched between Lester and me. "I'll show Clio where the food is, Lester. You've got lots of other guests to see to."

Sally hissed: "I'd be careful around Lester, Clio. He's been weird all his life. Probably before his granddaddy dropped him in a well. You have to feel sorry for someone with a mother like Hedy. She was always after Delia to partner up with Lester. Had a fit when Delia turned down Lester to the prom and showed up with George Whittaker."

Just the faintest worried expression crossed Sally's face. "Seniors weren't supposed to bring anyone older to the prom. Delia said she didn't give a rat's ass what anyone thought. George was the best-looking man in town."

"So she liked Jeremiah's father?" An answer to that question would nail down something that had been troubling me ever since George Whittaker had been so rude to me after Jeremiah's accident—when he mistook me for my mother.

"I don't know if 'like' is the operative term here." Sally's wide, pleasant mouth made a series of short, explosive sounds. "Dated. Flirted with. Escaped to. Used when she needed help. That was our Delia. She had no intention of being tied down to anyone. I told you before—when you visited the newspaper office—Delia and I were going to be famous reporters. I guess she made it."

I squeezed Sally's arm as comfort. I didn't think Mother was getting famous very fast. She was probably somewhere in a foxhole doing in-depth interviews with soldiers, who were counting themselves lucky that a beautiful redhead was drilling them—and not a German.

"Where's the well?" I whispered. "The one Lester's grandfather . . ."

"Sally, why haven't you taken Clio to get goodies?" Trailing her wilting swaths of red and yellow, like the wings of a damaged Monarch butterfly, Mrs. Lewin tugged Sally and me into a dining room that was more startling than the one in my aunts' house.

Hanging from a twenty-foot ceiling on a thin cord over our heads like the sword of Damocles was a giant cluster of deer horns with twinkling lights threaded onto the tips. A massive burled slab of wood formed a table that reached from one end of the room to the other.

A silver coffee service sat perched uneasily at one end next to several pitchers of lemonade and tea. Marching down the center of the table were assortments of odd little star-shaped sandwiches. A lop-sided, three-tiered cake, that looked like something left over from a wedding that didn't come off, graced the other end of the table. Around the bottom rung, bilious green edible letters spelled out: "Happy Birthday Lester."

"We'll manage, Hedy. You can get back to your guests. I think Pastor and Mrs. Wyndom just arrived. With all of their children." Sally turned toward the front door, one arm flapping like a windmill, as Mrs. Lewin hurried off with a grim expression towards a huddle of dripping children.

"You were asking about the well, Clio. I'll take you down the back hallway and point to where Hedy's grandfather was caged before they shipped him off to the asylum. I've done three feature articles about this house. Sold one to the *Daily Oklahoman*. Much of the house predates statehood. Hedy never let me see the fenced part, but we reporters have our ways," she giggled softly.

Deer heads, bear heads, and stuffed bass on plaques lined the hall. I was getting the willies from all the animal corpses over my head when Pastor Wyndom's melodic voice projected down the hall—just as it did from the pulpit.

"Sally. If you have just a minute, I need to talk to you about a church notice for this week's paper if it's not too late. The missus and I have to take the kids on home. We just stopped by for a minute to give our regards to Lester."

"Three kids out in the rain. I don't think so. He thought they'd be welcome. Hedy must have set him straight. I'll be just a minute, Clio. Don't wander off."

As I watched Sally pacing down the dark, creepy hallway, I chose the better path. Twisting the doorknob on a door thick enough to withstand a siege, I pushed it open and stepped down onto a small covered porch.

Through a faint drizzle, I could see the sickle-shaped moon centered right above a fenced enclosure. From there, I could see a well-worn lane, circling just inside the fence. It was the kind of track those African wild dogs make at the zoo, a desperate want-to-escape path with no way out.

A thick pad of buffalo grass spread out toward a chest-high circle of stones next to a shed. Without a thought for the reprimand I'd get from Aunt Norma about my soggy patent leather shoes, I squashed through wet grass toward what appeared to be a well.

Flat, rectangular pieces of iron attached a thick slab of wood to cover the top of the well. A substantial padlock chained the hinge holding the top down. I hoisted myself up and plastered one eye against a gap in the wooden cover. As far as the eye could see below lay only darkness. In the faint rays of moonlight, the padlock looked unnaturally bright. I gingerly swiped one finger against it. Well-oiled. An old rusty bucket with part of a chain attached lay sideways on the ground.

A noxious odor settled around me. Like clams gone bad.

"Curiosity killed the cat. And maybe its kittens. Deep wells can hold lots of secrets." Lester's voice purred just below my left ear.

Shuffling around to the other side of the well as fast as my too-tight shoes would carry me, I pointed toward the chain-link fence. I didn't want to mention the well to someone who'd been so traumatized by it. "Sally told me that your great-grandfather built this place and was famous in these parts."

"He was a nutter, if that's what you mean by famous. I used to poke sticks at him through the fence. After he . . . after . . . My Grandpa Lester built this fence to corral that old fool. Less said about him the better."

Lester sidestepped around the well. "You look more like Delia every time I see you. She wouldn't be caught dead in that black and yellow thing you're wearing. I still remember exactly how she looked in that white wool bathing suit at that last MYF party at the Lake. Sexiest girl imaginable. Legs up to here." He pointed toward his naval.

"She didn't . . . she never . . . I don't think . . . Delia would . . ." Lester sputtered like a faucet clogged with air. "I hope our little misunderstanding the other day won't affect our friendship, because I really have this . . ." He took a giant step toward me.

An old bucket hanging from the end of a chain was the closest thing I could find to a medieval mace, but it worked. The noise of it clattering against the metal flanges on the well rent the air with a scream.

Lester scooted back toward the house as though the Hound of the Baskervilles had just been unleashed.

CHAPTER 24

I wasn't about to go back into that house of horrors. Sprinting over to the chain-link fence, I planted the toes of my shoes in impossibly small places and scaled it like a monkey. The rough edges along the top shredded the bumblebee wool of the dress Mrs. Abrams had been so proud of making me. I'd send her a nice letter tomorrow, telling her I'd simply outgrown it.

Ducking down among the parked cars, I found Manboy's Buick on the far side of the graveled lot where he had moved it. Opening the back door quietly, I snatched up the blanket that he had thoughtfully tucked in for his mother. I smacked down the locks on all four doors, wrapped the blanket around me, and sat as rigid as a cigar store Indian until Manboy came looking for me.

"What are you doing out here?" he asked as I cracked the window just a few inches.

"Thinking. About Whitey Lewin and my mother," I replied sullenly and flipped up the chrome door cylinder lock.

Manboy eased the door open and slid into the back seat beside me, snapping on the oblong, dim, overhead lights. "Delia had no interest in Lester. Quite the contrary, in spite of what his mother was always hoping. In fact, when she was a junior in high school, Delia clouted him in an unmentionable place, after he got familiar with her in the gym." Manboy's chuckle went on and on, as though he couldn't quit enjoying the moment.

It annoyed me. Not funny. "So did I."

"So did you what?"

"Clout Whitey Lewin in the you-know-what."

"What!" Manboy shouted. "When?"

We might have been playing Mother's verbal hopscotch, having mastered two of the four "Ws."

"I wasn't going to say anything. I told Aunt Norma that her drape just fell off the wall. It didn't. I swung on it. Mother might not have taught me to swim, but she did show me how to clobber a man so he won't forget." I sniffed self-righteously at the memory of Whitey gripping his crotch.

"You're not making any sense, Clio. What drape?"

I hadn't intended to say a word, but remembering Lester Lewin snaking around the side of that old well toward me unleashed a few words and a torrent of sobs.

"When Aunt Claire. Your mom went to the hospital at Gainesville. Aunt Harriet, Aunt Norma, Lucinda. They all went. That day when you and I had lunch in your back yard. After I went home, Lester came to the house. He had a dumb pink slip." I could feel Manboy's awkward pats against my humped back, as I gulped between convulsive words.

"A pink slip? A piece of paper?"

That really riled me. "No, dummy. Underwear. A slip with lace on the top. I burned it. First, I kicked him. Hard. I swung from Aunt Norma's drape. Like Johnny Weissmuller in a Tarzan movie."

My tears dried up just as quickly as they started, because the expression on Manboy's face was priceless. I couldn't restrain the spurt of laughter. "You look like a doubting Thomas. You don't think I can swing like Tarzan? Kick that hard? Maybe you're related to Johnny. Weissmuller. You just chopped off the intro." I giggled.

"Nothing you are saying is the least bit amusing, Clio. You are as mercurial as your mother. I find emotional swings difficult. Now, tell me. Did Lester Lewin do anything . . . uh . . . bad . . . to you?" Manboy's low voice sounded gravelly and stressed.

I flashed him a snarky grin. His mother must have taught him never to use certain words in front of girls. So, I'd use a couple.

"Rape. No. Molest. Yes. If an unwanted quick feel qualifies. Threaten. Yes. If a blocked door qualifies. I don't want my aunts and Lucinda to know. I didn't intend to tell anybody. I figured I'd taught him a lesson until . . ." I stopped, remembering our little encounter by the well.

"He got close to me out by that old well tonight. Sounded weird. Kept talking about Mother's legs. I threw the bucket at him and climbed the fence. Wild horses couldn't drag me back into that creepy house. Tell Aunt Norma I didn't feel good and came out to the car. That's all she needs to know."

"No it isn't. Why would Lester come into your aunts' house when they were gone? A gift you say? Personal? He touched you inappropriately? It just doesn't sound like Lester. I don't think he's ever been on a date. He doesn't . . . Delia thought that he was, but I . . ." Manboy's face had gone from white to purple under the dim light as though something festering for a long time had exploded.

An instant later, the hand that gripped my arm as though Manboy might be strapping on a life-saving tourniquet dropped away.

"We're discussing a man who is a pillar in this community. He's a member of the choir. He belongs to the Masonic Lodge. Knights of the Pithias. You won't find an elderly woman in the Methodist Church who doesn't think he hung the moon. It seems so out of character. When he was young, he was . . . but now he takes food baskets to shut-ins, drives widows to church and doctors' appointments. I could file a restraining order, but I think the judge would toss it and me out of court." Manboy sighed as though contemplating something disagreeable.

"Young girls sometimes . . . Are you sure his touch was . . . inappropriate?"

That calm, reasoned lawyerly voice of Manboy niggled my frayed nerves. Then that mention of the Methodist Church unearthed a memory of Mother. She said "I'm more Taoist than Methodist." Her favorite Lao Tzu quote was: "If you do not change directions, you may end up where you are heading."

If Manboy doubted my statements about Whitey Lewin, how could I convince any local authority that an eleven-year-old from New York City wasn't a fanciful taleteller? *By changing directions.*

"No restraining order. Whitey won't come near me again, and I won't go near him. I was talking to Sally tonight and got curious about that fenced area where the old grandfather was kept. It was dark out there. Whitey surprised me. That's all. I don't want my aunts and Lucinda to worry. Don't say anything to them about what I said." *That wasn't all, but I wasn't about to say any more about that pillar of local society, Whitey Lewin, to my former friend, Manboy.*

"On one condition." Manboy now sounded more like a judge than a lawyer. "You do not go anywhere by yourself. When you ride the bike, you ride with Jeremiah. When you go downtown, you go in broad daylight when lots of people are around. In the evening, you stay home. If your aunts are out, you stay with Mother and me. Understood?"

Manboy could see my nod. What he couldn't see were two sets of crossed fingers. My little fracas with Freaky Whitey was nothing compared to the importance of solving the disappearance of three young women, two of them just girls.

As we drove back home from the Lewin's house that night, I pressed my face against the car window so that the tears streaming from my eyes were at one with the cloudburst pounding the Buick. I could no longer confide in Manboy. A lawyer, who probably also belonged to the Masonic Lodge with Whitey, had stepped into Manboy's shoes.

I was on a mission. That hadn't changed. I needed to be more prudent about the direction I took and the Doctor Watsons in whom I could confide. If I could find out what happened to those girls in this backwater place that Mother said was so much safer than New York City, I might discover what happened on that dark day when she was just eighteen and why she left Wolfe Flats, never intending to return.

Chapter 25

The night after Whitey's thirty-fourth birthday party, I dreamed about our old neighbor, Mr. Abrams. He kept saying "common notions" over and over as he faded away into the bright sun and metallic chirp of a male cardinal in the giant sycamore outside my open bedroom window.

"Jus cause our opinions don't alays coincide don't mean I ain't in perfect agreement with yore Aunt Norma that you will get up in time for a good breakfast afore school." Lucinda's shout traveled up the stairs and drowned out the cardinal's song, as well as final traces of my dream.

"Coincide." That word was in my dream and in the archive of my foggy brain. Right out of Euclid's common notions. "Things that coincide with one another are also equal to one another."

I hopped out of bed, pulled on the cleanest of three, ugly skirts, and rummaged through piles of blouses for something dark enough to hide the residue of a week's use. Detectives in fiction were always seedy looking. I'd fit right into the genre.

I was looking for a man who fit the profile of a serial killer. Unlike Jeremiah's mother, who had run away from her husband, these missing girls would never come back. They and their killer had some kind of connection to the Wolfe Flats Methodist Church. That was my only clue—the point where their lives and their deaths crossed paths. To coincide, they had to happen in the same time period, but the dream about Euclid had triggered the notion of equal or similar. I had to make the most of that one fact with only forty-five minutes before I left for school.

If an urge to kidnap or kill women started with male puberty and lasted for fifty years or more, I needed information about church members from fifteen years earlier to last August when Ellen Carson vanished.

While wolfing down a plate-sized griddlecake, I cornered Aunt Harriet who pointed toward the telephone stand.

"Don't talk with your mouth full, Clio. The church membership directory is where we always keep it."

A directory of purplish names copied off a jelly graph plate was on the stand under the big black phone with the dangling earpiece. I needed to have a little help digging up the dirt on all the males between the ages of sixteen and sixty in the critical timeframe so that I could narrow my list of suspects.

Aunt Harriet was a sucker for believing that I had developed a sudden yen for learning about everyone who was a member of the local Methodist Church. "I declare, Clio. You are so like your mother. Delia loved history.

Roman. Greek. Modern. She never gave a fig for local history. I know all these people. I've known them most of their lives. You seem to be getting into the spirit of this place. That makes me happy." Her halo of soft white curls gave Aunt Harriet's face an angelic frame.

I felt absolutely devilish prompting her to go through that list of church members to find any clues that might reveal a killer lurking among the membership.

"Yes. Theo Jones has had four wives. All were members. Two died in childbirth, one of pneumonia, one of old age, I guess. Theo is in his nineties. Still drives to church in a Model T. Why do you keep asking about dead wives? Those women are in heaven now, past the pain of this world." Aunt Harriet cocked one ear up as though listening for celestial screams.

I was looking for a man who might have sent some women off to heaven. Like a good hunting dog, I was on point for a certain type of villain—not like William Burke and William Hare who offed people to sell fresh bodies to a medical school. Mother let that one slip when I asked her about Jack the Ripper. She told me that bodies were needed for Dr. Knox's popular anatomy course, so the two Williams provided them.

"Dr. Knox claimed he didn't know the source of such fresh corpses. Hare testified against Burke; the seats to Burke's hanging went for a pound," Mother had explained. Instead of expounding on what appeared to be a deliciously gruesome story to a person fascinated by the science of autopsy, she added: "An Edinburgh newspaper reporter got interested in a missing mentally incapacitated boy or Burke and Hare might never have been caught. Reporters serve a great public good."

Mother would have canonized any reporter with a byline—she worked as a copy editor for a small tabloid to pay the rent and, occasionally, sold a feature story.

"So, Burke and Hare were killing for money. It was a business for them. Murder as a business doesn't sound very interesting. They weren't psycho like Jack the Ripper. He's a household name. A useful bogeyman to scare little kids." I was beginning to get her attention as her eyes narrowed at me.

"I suppose well-meaning parents and *aunts* tell children about monsters like Jack the Ripper so they won't wander down dark alleys or talk to strangers. I *never* tried to frighten you with such lurid stories. What have you been reading?"

Thinking on my feet, as usual, I had to convince Mother that while I was doing a school report on Queen Victoria at the New York Public Library, I'd simply stumbled across Jack the Ripper. "They have these old *Punch* magazines with great cartoons showing inept police wearing blindfolds, looking for Jack."

"Those sound harmless enough. Political cartoons. More interesting I suppose than Blondie and Dagwood. Today, Hitler is the subject—Jack the Ripper would take a back seat to that madman." Then Mother launched into her favorite lecture on "narrowing the topic" because of Victoria's long reign. "Provide detailed information on a very specific subject if you want to write a good paper, Clio."

I had already done that. When it came to serial killers, I was somewhat of an expert. You could ask some of those suspicious librarians at the New York Public Library how much wool I pulled over their eyes to get access to psychiatry journals.

From schizophrenia to major depressive disorders, the symptoms I manufactured for Mother ran the gamut. The slight welling of tears and a few smothered sobs did the rest of the trick. Those librarians hauled out the mother load of psychiatry journals for me to study.

I wanted to know what made monsters like serial killers tick. What I learned fit a pattern—most psychiatrists claimed that killers weren't born that way. They came from alcoholic homes; they were abused as children; they were lonely and isolated; they were bed wetters; they were cruel to animals; and, they had uncontrollable tempers.

Queen Victoria's stodgy life couldn't hold a candle to the report on serial killers that I wrote for my fifth grade teacher in New York. What I couldn't find in psychiatry journals, I made up. Added a bit of color—mostly blood red to engage the reader.

My teacher called Mother for a conference to discuss my natural aptitude for research—or so I believed until I saw the grim expression on Mother's face as she exited my classroom.

"Mutilation in its various forms is not subject matter for a research paper on an English monarch. You were supposed to be writing about Queen Victoria, not Jack the Ripper, and every other pervert you managed to exhume. Really, Clio. You exhaust me. Library privileges are over unless you go with the Abrams or me."

Then, she added in an over-the-top voice so my backstabbing teacher could hear: "Your footnotes and bibliography were exceptionally well done."

No one supervised my library visits after Mother dumped me in Wolfe Flats, where the only librarian just rolled his eyes heavenward when I asked about psychiatry journals. Just as well. I had all the facts about sickos memorized. However, nosing suspects out of the church membership would require a different kind of research.

I looked over at Aunt Harriet, poring over the purple list of church members. Her knowledge of these people might help me sort out a few who fit the bill. Within thirty minutes, we had worked our way down almost half the list when my brain went into high gear. The name of Lewin snaked around two obvious clues. I don't know if he wet his bed, but Whitey most surely peed down his leg. That's why his great-granddaddy put him down a well.

Cruelty was second nature to Whitey when he was a child. My mother and Manboy had tied him to a tree as punishment for chopping off the heads of baby birds. When Whitey came upon me by the old well in his back yard last night, he said that he poked sticks through the chain link fence at his great-grandfather, Gideon Lewin. Whitey fit the profile. Trying to muster the objectivity needed by a good sleuth, I could feel my morning pancake turning to bile as it traveled down my gullet.

I detested that slimy man for two reasons: he had put his mitts on me in my aunts' parlor; and, because he pandered to old ladies in the church, he'd cost me the trust of Manboy, who was determined to think of Whitey as an upright citizen.

Getting caught up in my own cause and effect moment was risky if I torqued the profile of a serial killer to fit the suspects. I needed to rethink the profile. Booze was a major factor in the lives of perverts. Here in Wolfe Flats, no one mentioned alcohol in the same breath with a Methodist. They were all teetotalers; they signed temperance pledges as children, so that was out.

Back to Whitey. Being left to dangle down a well as a five-year-old probably filled the bill for child abuse. As a glad-handing, hymn-singing Methodist, Whitey might not fit into the "isolated and lonely" category. My sudden intake of breath startled me. Whitey Lewin barely spoke above a whisper. George Whittaker sang a duet with Eula and had a monstrous temper. A crafty killer might easily disguise a victim's blood in a pickup bed with a conveniently slaughtered hog.

Remembering Sherlock's warning to Watson about that "one little point which is the basis of deduction," I started wiggling those little file drawers in my brain, looking for snippets of information, for that one little point. The first time I went with Aunt Norma to Lewin's store, Hedy Lewin had said something about the party at Lake Murray when my mother was a senior—it irritated me then and it riled me now.

She implied that if George Whittaker had not interfered, Whitey and my mother might have . . .

Gorge rose in my throat, so I snatched the Methodist Directory out of Aunt Harriet's hands and shoved it back into the cubbyhole of the telephone stand. If my mother had gone noodling with someone in Wolfe Flats, it would have been with a guy that looked like Jeremiah—not Whitey Lewin. I just hoped Jeremiah had managed to pry critical information out of his father.

GETTING INFORMATION OUT of Jeremiah proved to be as slow a process as digging mortar from between the bricks of Robert E. Lee Elementary. "Pa did tell me some things last night, but he kept stopping at the good parts. I will say that Lucinda's fish and hush puppies thawed the ice between us. Pa's not had a good home-cooked meal since Mom left. Not that he deserves one." Jeremiah struck at a loose brick and left it lying.

I picked it up and stuck it back on the wall. "Did you ask about that night at Lake Murray?"

"I did, but I'm not too sure about what Pa said. He sounded like a drunk last night—mumbling his words, and he never touches a drop. Signed the pledge at the church. He'd been working on that stupid tractor of ours all day. He was tired. I did all the feeding and got the milk machines going." Jeremiah sounded tired.

"Any information will help. I've got a theory about Whitey Lewin, but I need to get all the facts before I can tell you." That got his attention, although I wasn't sure just how much I'd share. Jeremiah's father remained high on my list of suspects.

"Let me think. I'll try to get things in order, like you are always telling me—but that isn't how Pa talked last night. Some of the words were almost under his breath. All fragmented. Like Miz Wallace's history lessons," Jeremiah grinned impishly.

Don't edit, I thought to myself. Jeremiah doesn't like to be interrupted. I flashed him a big smile and kept digging out mortar.

"Pa said the MYF sponsored a hayrack ride for seniors at Lake Murray. Not a real hayrack, just an old flatbed truck with bales of hay on it. Your mom, Delia. Well, of course, she wasn't your mom then. She invited Pa. He wasn't then."

Jeremiah was driving me around the bend with his chronology of events—or lack of chronology. "I know. Back then. Before us. Just tell me what happened." I dug mortar furiously to keep from smacking Jeremiah up beside the head.

"You know where that big float is at the Lake Murray beach—a wooden platform hooked onto barrels about 200 feet offshore? The one with the diving board on a big spring with tire treads on it?

I nodded enthusiastically. I'd never been to Lake Murray. At the pace of this story, I'd be gray and toothless by the time I got there.

"As I said, Pa told me your mom invited him to the party, even though it was just for seniors. Knowing your aunts wouldn't like her taking an older guy to the party, your mom went to the Lake with Manboy. Pa said he and some other boys were out on the float when your mom climbed up out of the water." Jeremiah flushed, folding in his lips like a hidden zipper.

"I don't want to say nothing bad about your mom. I'm just saying what Pa said. He said she had on a whitish wool bathing suit. All the other girls had on dark ones. When hers got wet, it sort of exposed her."

"So . . ." I smiled encouragingly, as though an exposed mother was no novelty for me.

"Pa said the boys encouraged her to do flips off the board. He said she was a good diver. When she came up, Whitey Lewin said something really bad, so Manboy head butted Whitey into the lake. It knocked him practically senseless. The guys had to haul him onto the platform to keep him from drowning."

Jeremiah pointed toward the other students heading inside. We hadn't heard the bell. When he started to walk away, I grabbed his arm: "Let's get a tardy. We don't care. We hate Mrs. Wallace's class." *I didn't mind leading Jeremiah astray. I was on to something.*

"Something Whitey said to your mom after that really egged her on. He dared her to swim to the other side of the lake. Pa said it was getting dark. They could see the bonfire on the nearby shore, so he tried to stop her. He said she slipped through his grip like a minnow and struck out with a beautiful crawl across the lake."

That part of the story sounded exactly like my mother. An expert swimmer and taking any dare that came her way.

"Problem was that the boys couldn't see her anymore. Pa said Manboy was frantic. He considered your mom like a sister. He kept calling her name. Not a ripple on top of the lake. He and Pa swam back to shore as fast as they could to get a boat and go looking for her." Jeremiah's voice took on a tone of fear.

The story didn't frighten me. Mother got out of that lake alive. She made it to New York, into a bad marriage, had me, and got out of her marriage. Unless the Nazis had latched on to her, she was somewhere in Europe prying innermost secrets out of our soldiers.

"There she was, sitting on a log by the campfire with a towel around her shoulders roasting a marshmallow. That's when Pa said he had words with her. About her attire. And about her behavior. He pissed her off royally. That's the point where things break down. Except Pa said he and Manboy got into it." Jeremiah shot me a puzzled look.

"Your mom got mad at Pa and ran off into the woods. There's this big rock outcropping that they call Devil's Kitchen. When the WPA worked on Lake Murray, they built a kind of rock circle on it. Like a turret on a castle with stone stairs up to it. It makes a nice place for bird watching. If you're into that kind of thing. The lake attracts different kinds of ducks, but mostly teal and mallards."

Jeremiah's digressions were worse than Aunt Harriet's. Who cared about what the WPA built or where ducks swim? My mother was somewhere out in those woods where something bad was about to happen.

"Pa said he left in his pickup. He had a flat tire just before he got to the gas station at the turnoff to the main highway. That road goes into Ardmore and hooks on around into Wolfe Flats."

"My Mother?" The irritation in my voice caught Jeremiah's attention.

"Pa didn't make much sense after that. He said he heard later that Manboy went looking for your mom and found her on top of Devil's Kitchen with blood all over that white bathing suit. She had a concussion, like she'd fallen or something. Odd, because she was high up on top of the rocks—not below." Jeremiah's forehead wrinkled as though he were trying to process something that didn't tally.

"And?"

"And that's it. Pa said she was in the hospital for a couple of days. No one but her aunts and Lucinda were allowed to see her. I didn't understand this next part." A baffled expression settled on Jeremiah's face.

"Pa said she came to his house a day after she left the hospital. Rode her horse from your aunts' ranch down by the river. He said she had a bandage on her head and bruises on her neck. Pa said she acted really weird. She told him her aunts had betrayed her. That's the word he remembered. *Betrayed.* He said Delia sat on his couch for two days saying that word over and over."

Good word, I thought. I could use that word against Mother for plunking me down in Wolfe Flats.

"Then two guys showed up in a military truck, saying they were from the National Guard." Jeremiah's interruption blindsided me. "Pa said they raked him over the coals. Your mom told them he had nothing to do with her leaving home and got into the truck with them."

Jeremiah reached over and gave my shoulder a half-hearted pat. "Pa clammed up after that. He did say that a few weeks later the whole town was combing the fields and looking in ditches for a missing girl named Eula. That's when your mom left for New York and never came back. Pa didn't say that. I did. I know that much. Manboy told me she went off to study journalism and forgot about her friends."

We'd missed the tardy bell by several minutes. I pretended to have a stitch in my side, and Jeremiah put on a sympathetic front, claiming that he had stayed outside with me to be sure I wasn't having an appendicitis attack.

Mrs. Wallace wasn't as gullible as we hoped. She made us stay after school and write: "A false witness will not go unpunished" one hundred times on the blackboard. Jeremiah says that's from Proverbs. I wouldn't know. I get my quotations from Psalms.

CHAPTER 26

As Jeremiah ripped down the road on his AutoCycle Super DeLuxe Schwinn to face his father's wrath for being late for chores, I wheeled Mother's old Sunbeam right into a rare opportunity.

"Blast it all! When I catch the kid that . . ." Mrs. Wallace's peep-toe pumps were doing their own version of a buck-and-wing tap dance against the side of a very flat tire on her maroon Ford convertible.

"Nice car, Mrs. Wallace. Except for the tire thing. I always carry my bicycle pump and patches. Old tires, you know. Yours don't look that old," I added brightly, hiding my grin as I dropped down to inspect the damage.

"Ellen bought it new. Before you moved here, she . . ."

I waited expectantly for information. Unlike the other two girls who had been missing for years, Mrs. Wallace's niece had disappeared less than a year ago.

"This is the second flat tire I've had this week. Did you see those Simpson boys or Jeremiah hanging around my car?" If anger had a color, it matched the pitch-black pelt of Mrs. Wallace's new bob, cut just below her ears. Considering that Jeremiah and I had just written that "false witness" Bible quote on the blackboard until our fingers were numb, I was done witnessing for the day. Half the boys in our classroom routinely kicked Mrs. Wallace's tires. "Nope. When Jeremiah and I finished our *punishment*, the school grounds were empty."

Smiling blandly up at Mrs. Wallace to show her I felt no ill will toward her, I pointed to the tire valve. "Your valve is lopsided. That can cause a slow leak. Same thing happens on my old Sunbeam here. I can air it up for you."

"You'd do me a big favor, Clio. I promised to help sort for the church rummage sale, and I'm already late. I'm on your Aunt Harriet's committee. She values promptness. I'm not good with mechanical things. Ellen always took care of the car."

After I unstrapped my bicycle pump, I made a considerable show of checking the threads on the valve, buying time now that Mrs. Wallace had dropped her niece's name back into the conversation.

"You must really miss your niece. Sally Tolliver told me about her. I understand she was living with you when she . . ." The frozen expression on Mrs. Wallace's face prompted a different approach. I would go for the warm and fuzzy.

"I know how special the relationship is between nieces and aunts. My aunts and I get along like a house afire." My mouth burned with my own cleverness.

"Ellen wasn't blood kin. She was the daughter of my husband's sister. The sister who gave him influenza before she died—then he did." A slightly annoyed expression settled on her face. "I probably hadn't seen Ellen twice in her life before she applied for the job here. I'm not into mending fences with relatives. She was staying with me until she could find her own place. I have a very small house. Cleaning out the lean-to for a garage took considerable effort." The icicles raining down with every word caused me to get a move on my pumping.

The undercurrent of malice in everything that Mrs. Wallace said sent a chill racing along my spine. Not only did she get her niece's nice Ford convertible, she had her own house back. An aunt without a kind word for her missing niece hopped onto my suspicious people list just as Aunt Norma and Aunt Harriet moved up a notch in my estimation.

"Fat as a mud turtle." I patted the tire and screwed the cap valve in place with a gentle sideways action to create another slow leak. "You should make it to the church. I'd appreciate you letting Aunt Harriet know I helped you with the tire, so I was late getting home."

Two birds with one stone again. I had learned that Mrs. Wallace wasn't grieving for her vanished niece, and airing up her tire caused me to be even later. With luck, no one else needed to know that I was kept after school, writing all that false witness hoopla on the blackboard.

"Truthfully, I would like to give you a lift, Clio, but you have that old rusty bike. I'm quite a good driver.

Mr. Lewin taught me. Came by several times after Ellen . . . well, you know. He said it's bad for a car to sit idle. Helped me get the hang of driving it. So polite and attentive. He came by every day, twice a day sometimes, to find out if I'd heard anything from the sheriff and how to respond to his questions."

My detection cogs whipped into first gear so fast that unbidden words popped out before I could anchor my jaw. "Why didn't Whitey Lewin just ask the sheriff? Curious to me why he'd bother you so often."

"Sheriff McIver isn't known for his tact, Clio. He asked very personal questions. Mr. Lewin was a bastion of support in that troublesome time. He helped me decide what the sheriff *needed* to hear—not those invasive family matters. All the church ladies speak highly of him. Do not call him Whitey within my hearing."

Mrs. Wallace's Victory Red lipstick circled around a tight drawstring mouth as though she didn't want another word to escape. Either that or she had a mouthful of sour grapes.

"Ta ta," I shouted breezily after her disappearing car. When I considered how Sherlock might analyze clues such as "what the sheriff needed to hear," I took on a British persona.

Why would Whitey Lewin be so attentive to Mrs. Wallace after her niece disappeared? What kind of "invasive" questions had the sheriff asked? Manboy had mentioned that Whitey helped elderly shut-in women. Mrs. Wallace might be a widow, but her high-heeled pumps, flashy wiggle dresses, and Elizabeth Arden lipstick suggested she wasn't observing purdah.

TAKING THE LONG way home, I spun past the welcoming open porches of weathered, unpainted houses in the northeast quadrant of Wolfe Flats. Neighbors sat with neighbors, laughing, talking, and trusting each other.

Parking my bike under a mimosa tree, I stood under the delicate canopy of leaves and blossoms to watch the careless camaraderie of children running barefooted across the yards.

Sorting and classifying clues faster than the adding machine at the Wolfe Flats National Bank, I sniffed the honeyed odor of mimosa and tried to recall everything that anyone had said about the trio that had disappeared. Eula sang. Louise created lovely displays for Lewin's Department Store. Ellen played the piano. They all attended the same church. So did Whitey. So did the Mullers, my aunts, and Lucinda. Jeremiah and his father were Methodists.

To check out every male Methodist in the right age range meant casting a very broad net. I thought about Mother's advice about "narrowing the topic." I mulled over the master sleuth Sherlock's counsel to Watson when he spotted his clean boots: "one little point which is the basis of deduction."

Someone in this little burg had very dirty boots. Obviously, the broad sweep—the house-to-house searches of the sheriff and his deputy—netted nothing but resentment among the poorest in Wolfe Flats.

According to Sally, these were the neighborhoods where Sheriff McIver and his deputy concentrated their search when Eula Harrison disappeared—simply because she lived on this side of town. George Whittaker dredged up an alibi for having blood in his pickup from Amos Larson, who lived around here. For no possible reason, the sheriff searched the same houses again when the other girls disappeared.

The injustice of it set my teeth on edge. I mounted Mother's trusty, rusty Sunbeam and rode right up to the front door of what Lucinda called a juke joint and looked longingly at the Nesbitt sign with an orange soda pop on the corrugated metal siding.

I had a nickel and was really thirsty. Right next to that sign was an Atlantic Ale and Beer sign with the oversized head of a dark-skinned man who appeared to have cotton bolls springing out of his skull.

Two men in overalls stared at me from the doorway with absolutely no expression. I sent a friendly wave in their direction and didn't take the least offense when they didn't respond. They probably thought I was scouting out a good site for a burning cross. Sheriff McIver and I shared the same pale skin and chestnut hair. How would they know we didn't share the same views about segregated water fountains?

As I whipped along the road in front of unpainted houses, their facades cheered up by hollyhocks, I remembered a story that Lucinda had told me. In 1924, only eighteen years ago, the Ku Klux Klan held a Big Klan Day in Wolfe Flats. They initiated 500 men and a few women—with the Klan Band from Wichita Falls, Texas, tootling in the background.

Aunt Harriet tried to put a better face on that torrid event by interrupting Lucinda. "Our Good Citizens mass meeting was held a week later with watermelons served and the Park City String Orchestra doing a concert. It was a high-class answer to those Klan cowards. A week after that, our Anti-Klan and Farm Labor Union citizens won at the polls."

I kept my eyes downcast as I peddled past the Booker T. Washington School. The success of Anti-Klan candidates at the polls hadn't solved the separate and not equal conundrum of water fountains or schools in Wolfe Flats.

THE SUN WAS at a lower slant than it should be when summer was just coming into its own. A sinking feeling that I might have loitered too long after school hit me when I eased the back door open, tiptoed down the hall, and stretched an ear toward the crack by the parlor door.

The soft rays of light coming through a variegated panel of stained glass at the top of the west window created a scene that might have come from the paint box of Vermeer.

The needle pinched between Aunt Harriet's thumb and forefinger flashed into the head of a unicorn that hunkered down with its front feet in the lap of a medieval lady.

"You'll stab yourself if you don't slow down, Harriet," Aunt Norma's voice was solicitous.

"I'm determined to finish this tapestry to make a little pillow for Clio. Did you know that Delia went to Paris with her husband on a honeymoon? She told Clio that she spent four hours in the Cluny just looking at the unicorn tapestries. Her husband left in a fit of pique to see some jazz show at the Moulin Rouge."

"Ill-matched from the beginning."

Aunt Norma's assessment grated on my nerves. Arching my back to make a sudden assault on the door and the implied criticism of my mother and father, I stopped to inhale when the next words stopped me short.

"But what a splendid daughter they created. Clio will be as beautiful, if not more so, than Delia. She's sharp as a tack. She can roll out Psalms faster than the speed of light. I am so grateful to God that Delia left her in our keeping."

I shrunk right into myself, the way those little ferns close up when their fronds are touched. Aunt Norma was not only praising me to the high heavens, but she was sending up thanks to the fellow upstairs.

Not two months before, aliens were spotted in their spacecraft over Southern California. They might have made it to Wolfe Flats and invaded Aunt Norma's body. I peeped through the crack in the door again. Her face was as serene as it was after a grueling half hour of Pastor Wyndom's sermons.

A brief spurt of anger warred with something else in my sharp-as-a-tack brain. How could Aunt Norma constantly carp at me, yet say such glowing things behind my back?

"Purty, ain't they?" Lucinda's voice was warm as honey pouring into my ear. "Happier than they been since Delia left."

Watching the way the soft light turned Aunt Harriet's raggedy white curls into a circle of light and the iron-gray braid on Aunt Norma's head into a glowing crown, I was stricken with a tentative fear, the quiet kind that warns of imminent loss—as though something you just realized you had was going to be taken from you.

There were simply no words to express the small slivers of love and belonging and fear that I was feeling as Lucinda drew me down the hall toward the kitchen.

"Yore teacher called from the church to say you might be late because of fixin' her flat tire."

Lucinda fired the next question straight as an arrow. "Exactly what kind of things are keepin' you so preoccupied?"

The lyrics of that blues song by Tampa Red, "so don't you lie to me, don't you lie to me, because it makes me mad," hammered into my head as I tried to ignore Lucinda's cautionary finger.

"I'm just working on my Wolfe Flats mapping project. Stuff like that. You know." I tried for a Shirley

Temple I'm-so-naughty-but-nice dimpled smile and realized that it only worked on a tot.

"Other than digging up the neighbor's dog and trying to find out why nobody in Wolfe Flats seems to worry much about females that go missing? Those kind of things, Lucinda?" I answered nonchalantly, holding my cards close to my chest.

"Fer starters. And why wuz yore eyes all swollen and red after you went to Lester Lewin's birthday party? And why did I find pieces of pink nylon stickin' to the sides of the trash barrel the same day the drapery fell off the wall? After stayin' there for twenty years?" Lucinda's questions rattled me.

"Clio, we didn't hear you come in. It's getting to be dusk. Not a good idea to ride your bike late. Lucinda made chicken and dumplings. Your favorite." Aunt Harriet beamed at me from the doorway.

I beamed back and declared: "Smashing" and scooted into my chair at the dining table. After the telegram from Mother, saying that she would be tucked away safely in the northern part of the United Kingdom, my descriptions had become increasingly English.

Lucinda's questions cheesed me off. She had found pieces of the rayon slip that I had burned and somehow linked those to the broken drapery holder. I didn't dare tell her she was off her trolley. She was on point and knew it.

"Jolly good dinner, Lucinda." I smiled into her skeptical eyes as she ladled more dumplings onto my plate.

"It's been a beastly long day. I'm heading up to read a bit before bedtime."

"Soon as you finish them dumplins. Readin' the King's English tonight? You been talkin' funny lately." Lucinda lowered her head and whispered into my ear: "Whatever you're about, careful you don't make a cock up of it."

CHAPTER 27

As I trotted up to the sanctuary of my bedroom, I stopped on the first landing and looked down at Lucinda carrying plates to the kitchen. She was as formidable as a Sherman tank. She did my laundry, cooked my food, cleaned up my messes, ferreted out my secrets—and now had warned me in capital British fashion not to "make a cock up" of whatever I was doing.

Outsmarting Lucinda was out of the question. Relying on Manboy to help me trap Whitey into confessing something he may or may not have done was no longer feasible. Manboy had declared Whitey to be an "upstanding citizen," whatever that was supposed to mean. Encouraging Jeremiah to act as Watson to my Sherlock might be a possibility, even though his father, with that temper of his, remained a suspect.

ONCE WATSON OPENED his big mouth—or his father did—I knew I was on my own. As we dug away at mortar during morning recess the next day, Jeremiah blurted out: "You might be in trouble with Whitey Lewin, because of what Pa said in the store."

I kept scraping with Jeremiah's knife and listened. It was best not to disrupt Jeremiah when he managed an entire sentence without a digression.

"Lewin's stays open until 8 o'clock on Thursdays. Pa was put out with me for being late yesterday, so I had to tell him we got kept after school. Pa needed a new dress shirt, so we drove back to town after I did chores. I told him the blue was nice but he always takes a white one. Boring." He shot me a grin.

Time to get him back on track. "You said I was in trouble with Whitey. Why?"

"General nosiness, I guess. Pa and Whitey got talking. Pa let something slip." Not a freckle showed through the sudden flush of Jeremiah's cheeks. "Something I said when I was asking him those questions about that night when your mom got hurt at Lake Murray. The questions you told me to ask." Jeremiah's voice soared with imputation.

"Questions such as . . ." I let my voice trail off as though I might be only vaguely interested.

"Like what happened to your mom at Lake Murray at that MYF party."

"Oh no. No. No. I did not ask you about what happened to my mother. I asked you to ask your father about the party. Your father told *you* about my mother getting hit on the head, and *you* told me. You need to get your facts straight." I glared at Jeremiah.

I had been very careful to prime him with general questions about the party—not about Mother—although that had been my objective in getting Jeremiah to quiz his father.

"Well. Whether you did or didn't is up for grabs. You don't need to get pissy with me. Fact is, Pa told Whitey that you have been asking questions about the night your mom got whacked on the head. I told Pa when we drove home that he shouldn't have said a word to Whitey. I thought our talk was confidential. That pushed him out of shape again. Pa takes criticism real hard." Jeremiah folded up his knife and turned away. George Whittaker's son couldn't take criticism either.

WHEN I GOT home from school that day, I went straight up to my bedroom and pulled out my map of Wolfe Flats to mark critical sites: the Methodist Church where Eula Harrison was last seen before heading home from choir practice; Eula's house by the cotton gins; Lewin's Department Store and the drugstore that Louise Lewin passed before disappearing; and, Mrs. Wallace's house, with the city park a block away where Ellen Carson liked to walk in the evenings.

From those sites, I drew lines out toward the Whittaker farm and the old Lewin homestead. No pattern emerged from Wolfe Flats to the Whittaker farm. However, the confluence of lines from key locations to the Lewin property created a spectacle better than the Shenandoah and Potomac converging. I traced that long, straight line following Main Street and another curved one, taking the back road that Aunt Norma had driven when she took me out to see the Lewin house, so that we wouldn't seem to be prying.

"What are you doin' holed up here?" A prying Lucinda popped uninvited into my room. "I done called you three times. Your aunts is doin' their bridge game tonight with Manboy and Claire. I fixed some nice sandwiches for them. Yours is in the kitchen. I'm off to the church. Our Fat Salvage Committee meets tonight." Lucinda lifted a very plump arm in a kind of military salute.

"War effort. I tole you they makes explosives from rendered lard. Ever bit helps. Fat. Paper. Metal. Whatever we can send for our troops. Probably a good idea for you to get on one of them committees, Clio. Give you something useful, something important to do outside of school."

I had something important to do—tracking down three missing girls. Waiting until Lucinda clumped down the stairs, I listened for the front door to close so I could get on with my detecting.

By thumb tacking my handmade map of Wolfe Flats to the wall, I could look for patterns from different vantage points. A straight red line intersected a red loop. What I hadn't noticed before was an odd pattern of alleyways making a tight meridian then angling off— from Mrs. Wallace's house to the park and straight east.

There, at the edge, like a fat, black spider sat the Lewin homestead.

I glanced out my bedroom window. The dusking sky held the promise of light for another hour. By riding slowly along the sidewalks and streets these girls took, I could count the minutes from the place last seen to their planned destination. *That might give me what?* Surely a Sherlock question. It would give me a peek into the window of time that a killer had to seize those girls before they reached safety. I jotted a few more notes in the diary I kept on criminal behaviors of the locals and stuffed it under my mattress.

No better time for sleuthing. My aunts were bent over a bridge table next door. Lucinda was at church figuring out how much fat was needed to make a bomb. I was on the trail of a serial killer, but safely astride my Sunbeam, peddling into the sunset like Hopalong Cassidy on his faithful horse Topper.

My calculations were off. The sun dropped into the void of night just as I headed down the alley that converged with the back road that led to the Lewin property. I had no intention of traveling that road in the dark. I skidded to a stop and reviewed my timetables.

From the church to Eula's house was sixteen minutes; from Mrs. Wallace's house to the park and back took eighteen minutes; from the back door of Lewin's Department Store, around a side street, and past the drugstore took five minutes; at that point, Louise would have headed for the Lewin homestead where she was living with Mrs. Lewin and Whitey.

My best guess put that distance at about twenty minutes of brisk walking. The problem was that houses spotted both sides of the street for half that distance. No one had seen Louise walking once she passed the drugstore. That meant she might have vanished within a five-minute window.

Looking west toward Wolfe Flats, I could see only twinkling lights through windows in the distance. No street or porch lights were on. With the blackout in effect, the entire town resembled a boat with running lights on a great, black sea.

Somewhere in the distance, a coyote howled; a sudden gust of wind smacked my face; long, ghostly fingers of dried grass fluttered as though something invisible paced along the road beside me. Goose bumps exploded on my bare arms.

Sucking in a great, long gasp of air as though it might be my last, I yanked up the front wheel of my Sunbeam and spun it around for a quick takeoff. Determined to be a daredevil like those Army dispatch riders on their Harleys in Aunt Norma's latest *Life* magazine, I popped a giant wheelie. The sound of a tire parting company with its rim stopped me in my tracks.

Fumbling around in the increasing darkness, I turned the bike upside down and poked my fingers into the gap between the rim and tire. Flatter than a flitter. I had a pump but no flashlight. Patching the tire was out of the question, but if it just needed air, my fingers knew the routine.

Huffing and grumbling as I blindly tried to thread the hose to the valve, I was so preoccupied that I missed the sound of a pickup with its headlights off creeping like some kind of stealthy night creature down the road.

The scream of a rusty door opening shot me to my feet in alarm. I froze at the sound of a mocking voice in the still night air.

"Having a little bike problem, Clio? I have a flashlight."

Whitey Lewin aimed a big beam right into my eyes as he glided toward me without making a sound on the gravel road. "I spotted you from the house with my Busch binoculars. German. Expensive. You'd be amazed at what goes on in Wolfe Flats. Cheap at any price."

With one fluid movement, Whitey grabbed my bike, swung it into the back of his pickup and in a soft, trustworthy voice said: "Hop in. I'll run you to your aunts' house. They must be worried sick about you. You take too many chances, Delia."

Hearing my mother's name on his slip of the tongue, I headed for the bar ditch, my legs churning faster than the paddles on Lucinda's Daisy churn.

That's when the octopus grabbed me. I could feel suction cups on all eight tentacles gripping my arms and legs, hauling me backward from the ditch. One tentacle clamped over my mouth, pouring something sweet and cloying down my throat.

Gagging and coughing, I fought against a wave of mucus drowning me from the inside out until I could no longer breathe.

CHAPTER 28

The nighttime sky in rural Oklahoma drowns everything lying under its canopy of brilliant stars. The ebullience of millions of stars against a black velvet sky with no ambient light might have taken my breath away if the stones against my back hadn't already done the job.

"Mother told me that we were meant for each other, Delia. You should have listened when I told you not to struggle. That's why you hit your head. You were the princess in the tower. I climbed up to rescue you from your witchy aunts. I don't think you knew that I had paid you a visit." Whitey snorted like a pig smelling food.

Fighting another wave of nausea, I forced my body to remain rigid while I peeped through swollen eyelids. Fat rolls of logs holding up a massive shingled roof crouched to the left of me; it was the Lewin homestead with every light ablaze to attract Nazi or Jap bombers.

I longed for the sound of a bomber, one loaded with explosives contributed by Lucinda's Fat Salvage Committee. Lucinda would be looking for me immediately when she got back from the committee meeting and found that I was missing. My aunts might already be combing the streets, Aunt Norma behind the wheel of her Pierce Arrow, charging every curb in sight.

Foolish thoughts. Stupid me. No one could imagine that I'd be lying half dead by the old well in the pen where they kept Whitey's great grandfather.

They said he had a mental problem and had to be shipped off to an asylum. Aunt Norma told me albinism ran in Whitey's family. She neglected to mention madness.

A massive spasm clenched the muscles in my left thigh. I pressed my back against the rough stones circling the well, trying desperately not to move, not to alert the man who should have been in the looney bin with his relative.

"Waking up? Aren't you a caution? Raw ether with just a touch of prune juice. Mother takes it weekly. Says it keeps her regular. Too late to ask those girls," he chortled. Whitey swung around from his seat atop the old well bucket and leered at me.

Joviality in the face of evil is an abomination. Moses should have put that up there with his Commandments, so I did it for him. "You know that you are going to the electric chair. Then you're going right to hell. Two hot seats, Whitey." The voice that spoke might have come from me but it sounded unnaturally raspy.

The next voice cut through the summer night with a high, thin melodic note that sounded absolutely angelic. "Lester! What are you doing out there? I heard your pickup leave and then return. I told you that a nice, home-cooked meal was ready an hour ago. You get to the table now. Don't be brooding out there by yourself."

Just as I opened my mouth to shout at Lester's mother that he was not alone and she needed to call Sheriff McIver, a hand clamped over my mouth, stuffing it with a dirty, sweet-smelling rag.

It was my opportunity to move, but I couldn't. The old chain from the bucket was looped around my waist and fastened to a metal ring on the well cover canted to one side of the opening. My bicycle lay next to me, its flat tire useless as a dead snake.

"Coming, Mama. Just out for a little night air. I'll be there in a jiffy."

Effortlessly, Whitey heaved up my bike and shoved it into the chasm. I waited for the splash before it sunk miles below the well water's surface.

The only sound was of metal against stone. Then nothing.

Whitey bent down to unhook the chain, but kept one hand firmly against my mouth. The greasy strands of his hair looked as though a rake had combed them, leaving behind whitish furrows, each equidistant from the next—like a field that someone forgot to plant.

Whitey planted his face right next to mine. The stench of rancid oil and breath that smelled like a dirty rabbit cage might have made me gasp had not my mouth been so full of a dirty ether rag. I simply shriveled up inside until there was nothing left of me for him to touch.

"Lester! This is the last time I'm going to call you! I will come out there if you don't get in here to eat this nice meal I slaved to fix for you."

"Five minutes, Mama. I'm just checking the well cover. It's got some rot. We don't want the cat falling into it."

Two arms snaked around me and pulled me upright. "Unfortunately, a little kitten has to fall into it. You're not Delia. She grew up. Too fast some of the boys around here used to say," Whitey whispered.

Boosting me up to the edge of the well, Whitey breathed into my ear something so vile that I struggled in a helpless attempt to plant a shoe in a place where he'd best remember it. "If Delia hadn't been unconscious, she'd have been grateful. The Lewin name means something in this town. Most girls are just too stupid to know how lucky they might have been."

Being inched over a rough concrete rim to the edge of a bottomless pit should take only seconds. Whitey's murmurs sounded like a funeral dirge. "Delia's nosy daughter will be lost to her forever and ever. Delia's grief will go on and on. Until the end of her days."

Like a canticle in response, something in my head began to drum: "Thy Kingdom come. Thy Kingdom come." I rolled into nothingness; I heard only a clanging sound as spears pierced my body.

THE CHURCH BELLS in Heaven sounded as hollow and tinny as the one hanging askew in the Wolfe

Flat Methodist Church bell tower. I knew exactly how Saint Sebastian felt when he was shot as full of arrows as a sea urchin. Spikes pierced my backside as a loop of metal cradled my head. I might have been lying there for hours, my blood dripping into a void.

Tentatively stretching out one arm, I walked my fingers along a curved metal bar that seemed all too familiar. It was my trusty Sunbeam. I was cradled in space in a hammock made out of a bicycle, my body pinned in place by a wire-spiked wheel.

Cracking open one eye first, then the other, I looked up past slime-covered stones through a gap in the broken well cover at a sliver of a silvery moon. Nothing had ever been more beautiful. It was just as Mr. Abrams had always declared. Geometry shows us the harmony of the world.

Moving my eyes slowly from side to side, I saw that I was in a circle that spiraled down. If it had been geometrically perfect, the sides would be smooth, exact, and flawless. They weren't.

Moving my hand carefully, I touched a stone. It protruded in an irregular fashion. A handhold here. A foothold there. Up above, the moon would be circling the earth on its symmetrical course. I was the axis of symmetry, a body stretched lengthwise on a rusty bicycle that had lodged itself against stones deep in a well.

Thick moss covered the stones. The distance to the well cover appeared to be no more than twelve to fifteen feet. One careless movement would dislodge the bicycle, and I would tumble into the glittering blackness beneath me.

The dirty rag had dropped out of my mouth during the fall. I could scream for help, but only Whitey Lewin would hear me. He'd make some excuse to leave his mother's "nice, home-cooked meal" to drop something down the well to sink me into silence.

If I didn't move, if I managed to stay awake, I might survive for days on my little platform in the well. I shivered uncontrollably. Or, I might die of hypothermia. Someone would probably find something of me. Bodies decompose in water at half the speed of one in air— depending on the kind of water.

This ridiculous plaid skirt of mine would be a dead give-away. Only a consummate liar like Whitey could explain how Mother's rusty Sunbeam got down his well.

Or a two-foot femur with squiggly things growing on its spherical end. The rip-roaring scream that traveled from my aching heart to my flapping epiglottis stopped dead center against my fist.

The bones that I had seen in the Museum of Natural History in New York were impersonal pieces of ossified tissue. This bone was scarier. It must have belonged to Eula or Louise. It seemed a bit weathered to have come from Ellen's corpse. A thought even more horrible struck me. I was hanging above the watery grave of all three girls. I might join them at any moment.

The tears flooding my eyes dripped into icicles on my cheeks. I thought of those big stone slabs that stretched on top of graves, just the right height for passersby to stop, sit a moment, and reflect on mortality. Disrespectful I used to think. I wouldn't dream of perching atop a dead body—even one six feet below.

I thought of those girls savaged by the hands of a madman. They were the reason that I was hanging above their boggy tomb. I wasn't disrespectful. I was dedicated, determined to find out why they vanished.

What other stupid eleven-year-old would go chasing around in a foreign place like Wolfe Flats to find a serial killer by asking who, why, and how? Me. Mother would. Sally Tolliver might if she had been true to her journalistic vocation.

My *former* friend Manboy Muller could have asked more of his lawyerly questions about how young women could disappear so casually. My friend Jeremiah Whittaker should have listened more closely as I hinted that Whitey Lewin wasn't what he appeared to be.

I sighed deeply. The fact is that I'm the kind of person who never wants to share the whole lot. Just like Sherlock when Dr. Watson wanted a clue, a pointer, a little advice, I would clam up the way that brilliant detectives always do.

If I sniffled a bit because I was feeling sorry for myself, I had every right. Not only was I freezing, I was being gored to death by bicycle spokes. If I made any attempt to free myself and climb the walls, the bicycle and I would plummet to the bottom of the well.

At the grimmest moment of my life, I could only think of one thing. Dinner being served by Lucinda as Aunt Norma, Aunt Harriet, and I repeated the Lord's

Prayer softly. Those were the words that had come into my head as I was falling into the well. "Thy Kingdom come." The next words were: "Thy will be done, on earth as it is in Heaven."

I had never given much thought to Heaven, although my Sundays at the Wolfe Flats Methodist Church seemed chock full of heavenly memorabilia. I thought of that soupy song the kids sang: "Happy little pilgrims, going on our way, to a land of beauty, singing all the day."

Then, I remembered the Abrams, our neighbors in New York who looked after me. They had left Poland in the dark of the night just ahead of the Nazi invasion. Hopefulness always outweighed their anger, like those little Methodist kids beaming out at the congregation, singing a half step off key.

People with hope give off a kind of aura that soothes the spirit. The Abrams have that aura. So do my aunts, and Lucinda, and Manboy, and his mother, and Marek Nebojsa and his father.

When he grows up, Jeremiah will probably have that same kind of aura. He was so eager to forgive his father. I would have held on to that grudge longer—maybe even set the post office people on George Whittaker for hiding Jeremiah's letters from his mother.

Perhaps if I forced myself to focus on expectation instead of defeat, I could begin to prepare myself for what was surely a very short stay on this earth.

CHAPTER 29

The small sliver of light coming through the lid on the top of the well shimmered a bit. Maybe when we are dying, any aura we might have been cultivating just breaks away and floats up to join someone else's aura. A living, breathing someone.

"Clio? Can you hear me?" In this darkest of nights, I knew that the eyes filling the small crack in the well cover were bluer than the widest summer sky I could imagine.

The beam of a flashlight replaced the eyes and traced erratically up and down my body. "She's breathing, Jeremiah. Don't move, Clio. We'll figure out something."

The stress of near-death must have improved my hearing. The whispers of Jeremiah and Manboy echoed down to my bier. "We need to break the lock off the cover. Quietly. He's probably armed. Any sudden movement could cause that bicycle to fall. God only knows how far down that well goes and how deep the water is."

"By my calculations, I'm twelve feet from the top and over six feet above the water. What lies below might have been anyone's guess before a femur floated up." I was trying for a clever retort, because I dared not move.

"Thank Heavens! She's conscious. We'll get you out of there, Clio. Jeremiah, grab that iron digging pole by the shed. We can pop the lock off this cover." The crack of wood splintering resounded in the stillness of the night. No one spoke for a minute.

"I'm going down if this old rope will hold. If Whitey comes out, don't hesitate, Jeremiah. Use the pole like a spear on him and then go for help. I left the keys in the pickup. Now, lean over from the other side and shine the flashlight on possible footholds."

Like a trapeze artist over my head, Manboy danced on thin air as he swung along one wall, planting a foot, slipping, and planting it again.

The face leaning over my bicycle bier was Fra Angelico's angel, without the russet, blue and gold wings. The hand that grabbed my arm and lifted me almost effortlessly was stronger than Samson's.

"Can you move your legs, Clio? Do you think you can put your feet onto these outcroppings?" The tremor in Manboy's voice mimicked my useless legs. Paralysis had set in. Maybe the cold. Or, perhaps the spokes had severed my spine.

I dangled from Manboy's hand like one of those Raggedy Ann dolls, big-eyed, empty-headed, and limp.

"No matter. Put your arms around my neck and hold on as tightly as you can. Now. Slide your feet onto the tops of mine. Just like a little girl dancing with her father. I'll waltz us to the top by stepping on each of the stones sticking out. I've got to hold the rope with both hands, so just lean into me."

I clenched two stone-cold hands around Manboy's thick, warm neck and buried my face against his throat. When he said: "I'll waltz us to the top," all I could think of was Aunt Harriet showing me the Hesitation Waltz that she said was popular when she was a girl. Suspend one foot in the air or slowly drag it across the floor as the beat intensifies.

We had it down pat. Pause for three beats, then grope for another foothold. Suspend one foot in the air and drag it up to the next protruding stone. Strauss played in my head as though I were swirling around a ballroom. If I never danced again, this waltz would be memory enough.

I had never been plastered so close to another human being. It was a raw, helpless sensation. Not unpleasant. Mother's hugs had always been swift, almost impersonal. Lucinda's were tight but brisk. Manboy was holding me as though I were breakable but well loved. Something too precious to lose.

Above us, the other trapeze artist had draped the old chain around his waist and was leaning precariously over the edge of the well, stretching his arms toward me like the India-Rubber Man. Two hands locked themselves under my arms and heaved me up, away, and down as though I weighed no more than a feather.

"We shouldn't move Clio more than we have to, Jeremiah. She may have broken bones. She certainly is hypothermic. We need to get out of here before Whitey or Mrs. Lewin hears us. We'll just scoot back through the hole in the chain link fence and drive straight to the hospital in Ardmore."

"No. Straight to Sheriff McIver's office." The hypothermic voice speaking didn't sound at all like mine. It reverberated like Aunt Norma's, whose orders were never to be ignored.

"You've been missing for over five hours, Clio. I have no idea how long you've been down that well. You have puncture wounds from those bike spokes. Your right ankle is big as a balloon, definitely broken or sprained. We'll call your aunts from the hospital. The Sheriff can wait."

The wheels of justice grinding in my head were so persistent that I could barely hear Manboy.

"It was him at Lake Murray. He did it. He told me. Whitey knows I know. He'll split, skedaddle, leave without a trace. The Sheriff has to get him tonight." I tried to control the panic in my voice as Jeremiah nervously eyed the house. Manboy stood with his mouth ajar, not saying a word after I mentioned Lake Murray.

"Sheriff McIver said we were on a wild goose chase. He's not worth a tinker's dam," Jeremiah blurted out. "We showed him your book with all your notes. He said you were nuts."

"My diary? You found my diary? With all my secret codes?" I pivoted on my bad foot toward Jeremiah, slipped to the ground, shuddering with pain, and flopped around like one of Lucinda's headless chickens.

Manboy hoisted me up. "Exactly where Delia used to hide her diary. Way under the mattress so Lucinda wouldn't find it when she changed the sheets." Manboy scooped me up, carried me like a babe in arms over to the chain link fence, and rolled me none too gently through a big jagged gap.

"We're done with Sheriff McIver, Clio. When we read what you'd written, Jeremiah's father, Marek, Mr. Nebojsa, and I all tried to convince the Sheriff that your disappearance might be linked to those other girls. He said his deputy would scout around, but he wasn't going to bother upstanding citizens in the middle of the night over silly drawings." The disgust in Manboy's voice must have reflected the expression on my face.

"I thought your codes could outwit the Germans, Clio. Downright ingenious," Jeremiah said as he opened the passenger door of Manboy's pickup and helped boost me onto the seat, taking care not to touch my bulging ankle.

"I'm not sure that an apple, an open mouth, a window, and a marshmallow qualify as cryptography, Jeremiah," Manboy snapped.

"The teacher Ellen Carson; the singer Eula Harrison; the window decorator Louise Lewin—and the marshmallow, Whitey. I got it immediately," Jeremiah said confidently.

"You wouldn't have if your father hadn't remembered telling you that Delia was roasting a marshmallow while the boys were paddling around Lake Murray looking for her—that was after I head-butted Whitey into the

Lake." Manboy's cryptic response silenced Jeremiah for a minute.

"They were just little sketches to keep me on target, since no one else in this town seems concerned about a serial killer." I glowered at Manboy, trying not to forgive my rescuer for doubting me earlier about Whitey Lewin. "I drew three ghosts at first, but they looked more like the Ku Klux Klan than victims. I can't draw well, but I'm very good at map making—lines, angles, circles, polygons, that sort of thing."

Manboy patted me on my shoulder as he eased into the driver's seat. "You left one map on the wall that we should have deciphered more quickly. It had three circles marked "CS" inside the city limits and one out by what appeared to be Lake Murray."

Manboy shook his head as he turned on the ignition. "Marek and George drove to each of those places in town to search for you. They said they'd go out to the Lake, but none of us made a connection to Delia's . . . uh . . . accident all those years ago." In the dark cab of the pickup, Manboy's head seemed frozen in time, like one of those dark bronze Roman statues with ivory inset for the whites of the eyes.

"Manboy and I went back to your room for one last look," Jeremiah's voice was as chipper as a child at an Easter egg hunt. "We found the map with red lines under the mat on your desk—all the lines led to the Lewin house. So, we drove out here as fast as we could." Sliding carefully next to me, Jeremiah lifted my swollen ankle across his knees. "You'd better kick this jalopy in gear. We need to get out of here before . . ."

At that moment, a strobe light blazed in an upper window of the Lewin house. A sudden flash of fear sent my voice into a piercing falsetto, like one of those eunuch castratos launching into an aria. "Don't turn on the lights. Keep off the road. Drive down the bar ditch as far as you can. Whitey has very powerful binoculars." Feeling all my confidence draining away as I slumped against Manboy, I whispered. "He watches everyone."

As Manboy steered onto the verge, the pickup struggled through a quagmire of thick greenery. "Damned wild spinach. It's clogged the ditch so much that I can't get back on the road." Manboy spun the wheel left and then to the right, trying to get traction to get out of the ditch.

"Not spinach. It's *chenopodium album*. Mother boiled it with a little bacon. Really tasty," Jeremiah piped up. I wanted to smack him for that digression as we flopped around in a pickup skidding from side to side down the ditch. Then, I remembered that he was probably just as frightened as I was and missing his mother, the botanist. I hoped she was safer than we were.

Shifting down into first gear, Manboy stomped on the gas and forced the pickup onto the gravel road, spinning it halfway around before bringing it to a shuddering pause. "We'll take the Lake road just in case Whitey jumps the gun and calls Sheriff McIver about his fence. We need to get across the line into Carter County quickly. You're going to the Ardmore hospital, Clio. I'm calling the feds. That's after I call your Aunt Norma."

Grinding the gear into second, Manboy continued in his take-charge, lawyerly voice. "When she realized that you and your bicycle were missing, Norma called the National Guard four times—presently, the Guard serves the war effort. Norma doesn't accept war as an excuse when the safety of her niece is in question."

Jeremiah shifted my swollen leg and squirmed around to a half-kneeling position, eyeing the back window. "I see headlights, Manboy. Not far back on a kind of side road. Heading this way. Getting brighter!"

The bullet that shattered the rear-view mirror splayed the front window into a craze of crystal fragments. The second bullet ricocheted off the window post like an angry hornet into my arm, exactly where Popeye's muscle pops up.

As blood exploded over Jeremiah and Manboy, I saw Popeye tossing down cans of spinach to feed his muscles before going after the enemy.

Then Jeremiah screamed as the ice-cold moon lit up a truck heading from a northeast angle to skewer us.

At that moment, in the middle of that dark night, the sun came up, duplicating its splendor between two glorious orbs. Then, the lights went out.

CHAPTER 30

After waking up while hanging half-mast down a bottomless well atop my bicycle, any bed was a port in the storm. Even a lumpy hospital mattress felt heavenly. Disinfectant perfumed the air; the stench of decomposing bodies bobbing around in an old well might have been just a bad dream.

The concrete shell weighing down my left ankle and the huge padded sling around my right arm were the stuff of nightmares. The ethereal faces of three women cordoned around my bed were a daydream, one that I never wanted to lose.

"I seen her eyelids flutter. Just like Delia's done afore she finally woke up . . . in this selfsame hospital . . . all them years ago." Lucinda's voice sounded weepy, rung out from crying.

"Please don't bring up that sad time, Lucinda. We have enough to deal with now. It's appalling. Someone we've known all his life. A good Christian boy. I just can't understand how a young man who goes out of his way to help old ladies could do such a thing." Like the antique crumb sweeper she used on the dining room table, Aunt Harriet's soft voice made little whisking noises of disbelief.

Time for Aunt Harriet to face harsh reality.

The truth teller pushed herself up on her good arm for a session of enlightenment: "Serial killers may earn merit badges for good deeds, Aunt Harriet. That's part of their disguise—camouflaging their evil natures by lurking around in churches, oozing charm."

Exhausted by that effort, I dropped my head. "Whitey Lewin just oozed slime. I doubt that you'll find him in the Bible."

"Isaiah 64:6." Aunt Norma's voice thundered in my ear. 'Our acts of righteousness are as filthy rags.'"

She carefully eased her arm under my neck and turned my face against hers. "I'll remember that verse from Isaiah as long as I live. I thought I was doing the right thing when I refused to report a crime against Delia. If I had done what she wanted, none of these terrible things would have happened. The crime might have been solved."

I could bear Aunt Norma's gruffness, her carping, her criticism; I could not cope with her tears. Agatha Christie's gentle detective popped into my head. "Every murderer is somebody's old friend. That's what Poirot says—and he is never wrong, Aunt Norma. You couldn't have known."

"Known what?" A beaming Jeremiah tried to shove a bunch of daisies into my hand as I retracted my good arm, eying the flowers skeptically. "No poison ivy. These came from the flower shop. Ivy vine is just for disagreeable teachers," he cackled.

"Mr. Nebojsa and Mrs. Muller are out in the waiting room. Nurse says no more than four at a time. Pa and Marek had to go with Manboy to see some judge to give statements again."

"Statements about?" I asked with all the sangfroid I could muster. I was flat on my back with no idea how I'd gotten from Manboy's pickup to being tethered to a hospital bed.

"About a burned out pickup with a crispy corpse inside. And an old well full of bones. And you being shot in the arm. Imagine a girl getting shot like that." Jeremiah's voice had risen, taking on an envious tone, as though I had bested him in a shootout.

"Too much excitement. Too much." A nurse who made Lucinda appear almost diminutive in comparison bustled into the room and elbowed Jeremiah away from my bedside, causing him to drop his bouquet of daisies. "She needs rest."

"No, I don't! I need to know what happened last night. We were in the pickup on that gravel road. Lights were coming toward us. Something stung my arm. Then . . ."

"Then, Pa and Marek came down the road toward us at about one hundred miles an hour. Whitey swerved and hit that old Hackberry tree where the road forks toward Lake Murray. He had a propane tank in the back of his pickup. Whoosh!"

Jeremiah's sound track did not amuse Aunt Norma. At the least, he didn't digress as he usually did. He got all the facts into the first paragraph just like a good reporter. I let out sigh of relief. He was coming along nicely.

"My gal is wore out. We need to let her rest." Lucinda pulled her chair next to the bed, plumped up my pillow, forced me to take a sip of water, and whispered. "I'm bringing you chicken and dumplins. Agin the rules. This hospital food is plumb nasty. Green jello. Enough to grow mold on your innards."

WHEN I OPENED my eyes in what seemed only a few minutes later, the room had been cleared of all my visitors. An Amazonian with an arsenal of things for poking and prodding had replaced them. "I'm here to take your vitals. Then flush your system. I'm Nurse Sherman."

"Been to Atlanta lately?" I was trying for a bit of humor, because I didn't like the looks of that red rubber bag with a hose and an evil black nozzle.

She didn't get the joke. Obviously not a student of Civil War history like Aunt Harriet planting Confederate flags all over the Gainesville cemetery on Memorial Day.

Nurse Sherman yanked back the blanket. "I could hear bowel sounds. Need to keep our patients regular. Just roll over, and I'll . . ."

My screech must have alerted the authorities. Sheriff McIver's brick-red face peered around the door just as I yanked the sheet over my posterior. "Clio Clower in here?"

"You are interrupting a procedure! You need to check in at the Nurses' Station. Leave now!" Nurse Sherman waved a clenched fist toward the Wolfe Flats Sheriff. Her face flushed with anger as he swept past her.

I welcomed him with open arms. He had just rescued me from an onslaught against human decency. "He's the Sheriff, Nurse Sherman. He's here to interview me about a serious crime. Several in fact. You can come back later without that thing or I'm out of here. AMA." I fixed a gimlet eye on the nurse until she retreated.

"AMA?" the Sheriff asked.

"Against Medical Advice. I've managed to pick up a bit of their lingo while I've been here. You can't imagine how they sugar coat things that really hurt. 'You might feel a little prick' then you almost pass out from pain. They should tell you the truth. I always do." I smiled benevolently at Sheriff McIver as the skeptical expression on his face settled into disbelief.

"Like the story you concocted about one of our leading citizens? A wild goose chase that led to his terrible death? Did you have a hand in getting a forensic team from Oklahoma City down here? My office will get the bill. Just for sifting through trash in a well that hasn't been used in years. I'm here to get to the bottom of this. I promised Mrs. Lewin. She's in a terrible state about her boy."

Sheriff McIver pulled up a chair, slumped down, and propped a heavy-booted foot dangerously close to my ankle cast. "It's time to tell the truth, little missy. You come from back East stirring up trouble. You even got that lawyer Muller in heat. Not that Germans have a voice around here."

Sneering across at me, he scooted his chair closer to the bed. "You need to retract all this nonsense and tell me how you really got down that well. With your bicycle? I don't believe Lester Lewin would give you the time of day."

I inched my cast towards the edge of the bed. If Sheriff McIver got any closer, I'd simply roll over the side and let the plaster do its work right into his solar plexus.

He papered one of those big I'm-running-for-public-office smiles on his face. "What kind of thinking would cause a smart aleck little girl like you to fabricate a passel of lies?"

"Deductive or inductive. Take your pick. Considering the way you investigated these crimes, I don't think you applied reason at all," I snapped, taking considerable pleasure in the bright crimson of his face.

If I'd been in Wolfe County alone with this pus-gutted Sheriff, I might have curbed my tongue. Right now, he appeared about one heart beat away from a big MI, so I softened my instructional approach.

"I'm happy to share my methods, Sheriff. From the ages of the girls and the fact that they disappeared at about the same time of day, just at dusk, I *deduced* that they were nabbed by the same killer. I *inferred* that they were known to the killer, allowing him to get close to them. From that observation, I made a connection among the girls—the Wolfe Flats Methodist Church."

If a mouth could actually drop to half-mast, Sheriff McIver's settled there. I didn't much care for the gurgling sounds erupting from it. Or the hand that gripped my arm just below a very tender flesh wound.

"Ow! That's where he shot me!"

"That's where you cut yourself crawling through the fence on the Lewin property. Breaking and entering. Getting a puncture wound and claiming you was shot. Mrs. Lewin don't believe a thing you said. She told me you hung around Lester at his birthday party something shameful. She said your mother Delia was a terrible flirt." Sheriff McIver gave a fierce twist to my arm right atop my fat bandage.

All the stars in the Milky Way whirled like a cyclone in front of my eyes as I fought against nausea and an impulse to go out like a light.

When I spotted Manboy in the doorway, baring his teeth like an outraged wolf, I had to stay awake for the action.

The sound of a splintering chair dropping a 280-pound sheriff on his butt was music to my ears. So was Manboy's broadside: "Not your jurisdiction, Sheriff; you are intimidating the victim; and, you are interrogating a child. Shall I continue?" Manboy moved to the other side of my bed.

"Your bandage is leaking, Clio. Did he touch that arm?"

With the most mournful face I could muster, I nodded, holding my arm aloft hoping that the small spot of blood might spread. The Sheriff had added injury to insult.

"Throw the book at him, Manboy. He said mean things about Mother too."

"Assault and battery on a helpless child in her hospital bed will be more than enough to end his career, Clio." Manboy stood defensively by my bed as Sheriff McIver grunted and heaved himself to his feet.

"No one will believe a Nazi spy lawyer like you, Muller. They say you're in cahoots with German prisoners of war over at Gainesville," Sheriff McIver blurted out contemptuously.

A sickening moment of distress hit me. Someone had intimidated the Mullers by throwing paint remover on their house, sending hate notes, and then painting black swastikas on it. If no one would believe Manboy, who grew up in Wolfe Flats, why would they believe an outsider like me?

Just as though he'd read my mind, Sheriff McIver jumped right down my throat: "No one will believe a hysterical girl like this one either," the Sheriff sputtered as he kicked the splintered chair away, rearing himself a good two feet above Manboy with a raised fist.

"I believe both of them. Mr. Muller and Clio. I was right outside the door the entire time." Nurse Sherman's rebuke was as precise as a scalpel. "Two of our aides are coming down the hall. I suggest sheriff-whatever-your-name-is that you take your hat, your badge, and your disgusting self out of my patient's room."

During the commotion that followed, I just hunkered down in bed and watched. Two very determined male aides clamped like barnacles onto Sheriff McIver while Manboy cited a litany of sins. Nurse Sherman threw in a few barbs of her own about "patient safety" and "helpless little girl."

I had become so fond of Nurse Sherman during the brief fracas that I would have submitted to any of her machinations with that snaky tube. If that sort of thing amused her. It didn't.

A few minutes later, Nurse Sherman pushed a wheelchair through the doorway and announced: "You are free to leave with Mr. Muller, Clio. Your aunt called the doctor; he said that your vitals are good. You can recuperate at home. Your local doctor can check your bullet wound tomorrow. The cast comes off in four weeks. You'll stay on crutches in the meantime."

CHAPTER 31

Like a wounded Greek warrior recovering from the battle of Thermopylae, I languished on Aunt Norma's best couch under a feather duvet for two days with no one stopping by but Doctor Lontry, who clucked like an anxious hen as I protested my boredom.

"When Jeremiah got that piece of metal in his eye, you only made him stay in bed for one night. Are you treating me differently because I'm just a girl?"

"I thought you were Sherlock reincarnated, Clio. I'd never accuse you of being *just* a girl. You found a killer who has haunted this town for fifteen years. Tracked him down. Took the law into your own hands." He winked at me. "Thinking of running for sheriff?"

"Nope. I've been considering the Special Intelligence Service. Going after espionage agents appeals to me now. I could have told you that Whitey Lewin painted the swastikas on the Muller house. Black paint under his right thumbnail. I saw it when he shoved that ether rag in my mouth."

My response sounded a bit cheeky for someone confined to a couch, so I mouthed off again. "Right now, I'm bored out of my skull."

"Tonic. That's what you need." He whipped out a small pad and scribbled something on it. I shuddered, thinking of what Aunt Harriet's Sal Hepatica had already done to my insides.

"Orange soda pop three times a day and peppermint candy. Cures almost anything but boredom. A festive occasion will take care of that. Don't you have a birthday coming up?" Doctor Lontry nudged me and left without waiting for my answer.

In two days, I'd be twelve. Almost into my teens. Mother might forget to buy milk and bread, but she never forgot my birthday. Mrs. Abrams always baked me a cake, saving sugar just for the occasion. I stared bleakly at the back of Doctor Lontry as he left the room. Mother was probably ducking into foxholes without a free moment to remember my birthday, even if she wanted to. I struck a pose, holding my wounded arm aloft, hoping someone might notice.

In Sherlock's *Adventure of the Cardboard Box*, Dr. Watson said that he was in a "brown study." When I asked Mother what that meant, she told me that it dates way back to somewhere in the Fourteenth Century. "It means dark and melancholy. No one uses that phrase anymore. My editor told me it was obsolete," Mother said.

Well, her editor didn't grow up in Wolfe Flats. He didn't pay it a short visit and get shot and end up with a broken foot. A brown study was exactly my state of being. It lasted for two days.

"GOOD MORNING, CLIO. You've slept until almost noon." Aunt Harriet beamed down at me and pulled aside the lacy curtains of the downstairs guest room that had become my makeshift bedroom while I was unsteady on crutches. "Lucinda and I are going to help you upstairs for a good soak in the tub. You can stay in your own bedroom today to catch up on the schoolwork that Mrs. Wallace dropped by."

I glowered at Aunt Harriet and sent a few daggers toward Lucinda as she hoisted me up. Not even so much as a weaselly birthday wish from either of them. What else could I expect? I'd been nothing but trouble from the minute that Mother chucked me away on their doorstep. No one wanted to celebrate me being on this planet.

All three of us were exhausted trying to winch me up into that monstrous claw-footed tub with my cast anchored high and dry. To get even for all the trouble I'd caused, Lucinda dumped a bucket of water on my head and scrubbed my scalp as though I'd picked up an army of itch mites.

What should have been a special day went to pot when I opened the fat envelope from Mrs. Wallace. Page after page of word problems fluttered to the floor. A list of essay topics smacked me broadside: What I Will Do on my Summer Vacation; Walking Is Good Exercise; and, Teachers Who Influenced my Life.

Good grief! Was the woman mad? I intended to rest on my laurels all summer long for having nabbed a serial killer. I didn't intend to walk if I could ride my bike. And, what was obviously a bid for compliments, the last topic really rankled. Mrs. Wallace couldn't influence a goat.

My face fell. I wouldn't be riding my bike for exercise. Whitey Lewin put the kibosh on my Sunbeam when he tossed it down his well—then me on top of it. It was wartime. Factories made tanks and airplanes, not bicycles for civilians. I'd be putting leather to the pavement, not zipping along on my trusty bicycle.

Opening *Jane Eyre*, I searched for the section where her evil aunt and the servant throw her into the bedchamber where her uncle died. I could identify with Jane in that part of the novel. No one wanted her around, especially her hateful aunt, so they locked her in a haunted room until she screamed and fainted.

I could hear the buzz of activity downstairs, but clearly no one wanted me down there. I could hop around upstairs with my crutches, but I was leery of trying the stairs alone. I played the sick card to get a good supply of orange soda pops delivered upstairs by Lucinda.

"You wearin' me out, Clio. These stairs is tarsome. I got other things to do." Lucinda patted me dismissively. "I'll hep you downstairs after a while."

When I woke from another long nap, I counted the front door opening and closing a dozen times. It must be one of those Methodist committee meetings Aunt Norma loves to host. Tea and soggy cucumber sandwiches.

It took forever for today to be over. Shadows stretched before a sun anchored to late afternoon. Heat rose up from wide walnut planks in the floor, bringing musty scents of the past. This dark room with its ponderous velvet drapes weighed me down with thoughts of my Clower ancestors.

I pulled the bedspread over my head and pretended that I was in the Blitz with Mother, waiting for the blast from a German Stuka, and longing for the sound of Mother wishing me a happy birthday.

"What are you doing hiding under the covers, Clio? Your Aunt Norma says I can help you downstairs. She told me you're still wobbly on your crutches." Jeremiah plopped down on the bed and frowned. "You want me to get your brush? Your hair is all poofy."

"The tousled look is in," I said snidely. "It's called a Victory Roll. I spent an hour sticking bobby pins in it. Nothing else to do up here. No one comes to see me anymore," I added peevishly, sliding off the bed and grabbing my crutches.

Then it struck me. Behind that well-controlled expression lay a load of mischief. "What are you doing here this time of day? It's past five o'clock. You are usually doing chores. Won't your father be upset?"

"Nope. He dropped me off so I could . . . um . . . visit. Yep. Visit with you. Haven't seen you since you were in the hospital. It was time I paid you a visit." Jeremiah was wound up like a top. In a tight spot, lying was second nature to me. Jeremiah was right up there with George Washington and his hatchet when it came to telling a lie.

By the time I had hobbled to the first landing, with Jeremiah insisting that he go first "to catch you if you fall," I looked down into a foyer that was transformed.

Small rings of construction paper looped over every doorway. Streamers of crepe paper fluttered like a Fifth Avenue parade before anyone had to save all the paper for the war effort.

"Happy birthday to you!" The assembled voices rang out in song as Aunt Harriet pounded on her Chickering in the parlor.

Marek Nebojsa and his father beamed up at me while a waspish Mrs. Wallace appeared to be sharing the good will under duress. Next to her was Sally Tolliver holding aloft a small package. Manboy and his mother Claire stood next to Aunt Norma.

"Out of the way! Out of the way!" Lucinda bellowed as she swept down the hall bearing a two-layer chocolate cake covered with twelve blazing candles.

"They's saving wax for emergency candles, but I found this old Emkay box with a dozen birthday candles down at Lewin's," Lucinda blurted out.

As a hush fell on the room, Lucinda looked a bit crestfallen as though she'd just realized her faux pas.

Then, she marched straight up to me and with a voice that resonated to the rafters announced: "With every candle I lit, I sent up a little prayer of thanks for Clio who made this town safer for other girls."

What followed wasn't exactly a roar of applause, sort of a tentative clapping of hands, as though the horror of Whitey Lewin could dampen the most festive of occasions.

Then, the piercing whistle of Jeremiah was followed by his shout to break the hush: "Let's hear it for the Yankee girl!" Then, a thousand hugs and kisses fell upon me.

The gifts were incredible. Lucinda had transformed a red-checkered, linen tablecloth into two pairs of shorts with clever little bibs and elastic around the legs. I could push them way up high on my legs as soon as Aunt Norma turned her back.

The photograph album that Sally Tolliver put together almost broke my heart. There were pictures of Mother when she was just my age and all through high school. Mother in a tree. Mother on the Sunbeam. Mother as prom queen.

The leather-bound set of Sherlock Holmes that Aunt Claire and Manboy gave me was a bit worn. That made the books special. Well-loved books are a priceless treasure.

"What's this, Jeremiah? I held up a smoothly polished curved stick about a yard long. Along the top edge my name had been burned into the wood.

"Your own noodling stick, Cleo. For going after catfish. Not many girls will have one of those."

Probably not, but I flashed such a look of gratitude that Jeremiah flushed up to the roots of his cinnamon hair.

The velvet box that Aunt Norma and Aunt Harriet handed me held a family heirloom—the pearl necklace and bracelet that their father had given them when they graduated from high school. "You can only wear them on special occasions, church and the like until you are older. But they are yours."

"Time to get it, Marek." Mr. Nebojsa's Slavic whisper sailed above the general conversation as he moved close to me. "Your mother sent a telegram before all this happened asking your aunts to buy you something special for your birthday. They couldn't find one for sale. So Marek and I just took what was left and made this."

The shape and size and tires looked exactly like my mother's old Sunbeam that had taken its last voyage into a deep well. The handlebars gleamed as though lit from within by a new moon. The raggedy seat had been replaced by sleek padded red leather. The greasy, rusty chain had been restored by slightly oiled, bright, silvery links. The bicycle's fenders were a burnished copper color with little flying victory "Vs" on the front and the back.

I gasped. For once in my twelve years, I couldn't say a word. The parlor had been transformed into what Mother called a "wonderful melting pot." She meant the streets of New York. But here was the same diversity in Wolfe Flats.

The two Czech refugees holding up my bicycle grinned proudly at me, Marek's burned face a reminder of the horror of war. Like co-conspirators, Jeremiah and Manboy elbowed each other aside to get a closer look. They must have fished the bike out of the well while I was in the hospital.

Marek and Jeremiah settled me on Aunt Norma's Victorian settee as I watched all my friends and relatives mingling, in that effortless way of friends.

Sally Tolliver hung on Marek's arm. Mrs. Wallace tweaked her sour little mouth into what she imagined was a pleasant smile as Aunt Harriet bent her ear about getting Latin reinstated in the curriculum after a fifty-year hiatus. Mr. Nebojsa and Manboy carried on a heated discussion about the not-so-secret rendezvous of Mr. Churchill and President Roosevelt. Jeremiah polished off my birthday cake with the eagerness of a boy too long deprived of butter fudge icing.

Under the twinkling lights of the chandelier, Aunt Norma, Aunt Harriet and Lucinda stood like the Three Graces of Greek mythology: Lucinda is the Grace of Good Cheer; giggling Aunt Harriet would have to be the Grace of Mirth.

Aunt Norma moved quietly through the group, refilling glasses, seeing to the comfort of all her guests, and I knew that she was absolutely the Grace of Splendor, stately, majestic, and almost, always right.

This small group of new friends and old relatives, this band of souls, seemed infinitely precious to me at that moment. Sad things had brought us together. Mother had chosen a war over me; Jeremiah's mother had left him behind; crimes against those poor girls dropped into a cold, dark well could never be righted. For a moment, as I looked around the room weighing the value of this group, my breath stopped. The value was incalculable. I came uninvited into their lives. They had taken on the burden of me; they were rejoicing as though that obligation were a gift.

"Do you want to say something, Clio?" Aunt Norma's soft voice encouraged me, but all I could think of was that bouncy wartime song of Billy Cotton and his band.

So, I opened my mouth and out it came: "We must all stick together, all stick together and the clouds will soon roll by."

From the other side of the room, Aunt Harriet's wavering soprano picked up the next stanza: "We must all stick together, birds of a feather, and the clouds will soon roll by."

The pandemonium of our voices reached the rafters, moved over states, and sailed across the North Atlantic Ocean where Mother might be listening.

The End

ACKNOWLEDGMENTS

I am grateful to the friends, colleagues, and relatives who have read *Clio at War* and suggested improvements, especially the Bandon Writers Group.

Many thanks to Debbie O'Byrne for her superb cover designs.

About the Author

Peggy Gardner began her career as a journalist, taught English Literature, managed medical education, clinics and research for a major hospital, and has traveled extensively with her husband, daughter, and son. She currently resides in Oregon for the incomparable splendor of its coast.

www.ingramcontent.com/pod-product-compliance
Lightning Source LLC
Chambersburg PA
CBHW061545170626
46811CB00001B/89